Echoes in the Wind

by

Debra Jupe

Echoes in the Wind

Cover Art by *Rae Monet, Inc. Design*

The Wild Rose Press, Inc.
PO Box 708
Adams Basin, NY 14410-0708
Visit us at www.thewildrosepress.com

Publishing History
First Crimson Rose Edition, 2013
Print ISBN 978-1-61217-979-7
Digital ISBN 978-1-61217-980-3

Published in the United States of America

Darla could not lose control here. She needed to say something and leave. But the strange pattern on the fabric of her rescuer's shirt grabbed her attention.

She tipped her head slightly and frowned. She stared harder, blinking several times. What th… A loud gasp escaped as she slapped a palm over her mouth. This night kept getting better. She lowered her hand and gaped at the pink tinge sprayed across the Raging Impulse lead guitarist's chest.

"That's not good." He wiggled a finger over the scattered glass, apparently unperturbed she'd ruined his shirt. "What were you drinking? I'll get you another."

Darla stared, speechless. The inflections of his strong accent made him difficult to understand yet the mere sound of his voice caused her heart to almost stop. It was rich, deep, laced with enough of a rasp to carry a trace of seductiveness. The kind of voice that could convince a woman to do practically anything.

"What were you drinking?" he asked again. A long moment passed. Those disturbing cobalt eyes continued to study her. "Are you okay?"

Darla gulped. She was fine except her mind experienced a complete meltdown. Her heart beat in triple time, she couldn't catch her breath, and she appeared to have lost the ability to speak.

"Wine," she blurted. "White Zinfandel." Surprised she'd almost found her wits, she paused and made an awkward gesture over the fresh stain on his shirt. "I don't know what happened. Um, I got…you were there, it…" Her arm dropped, and she released a heavy sigh. "The glass slipped out of my hand."

A slight curve formed across his lips as a wicked twinkle entered his eyes. "I noticed."

Dedication

This book is dedicated to the most giving person on earth, my mom, Mildred for her unyielding support and her strong belief that if I dreamt it, I could do it. Thanks mom, for giving me the courage to spread my wings and soar.

Chapter 1

"I can't believe I let you talk me into this." Darla Hennessy twisted an errant curl around her finger as she watched the craziness surrounding her. "This was a bad idea and yet you convinced me, no wait, you dragged me here kicking and screaming. I'd much rather stayed at home to catch up on my self-pity wallowing."

"You needed an evening out. It'll do you good to socialize with people." Her best friend, Stephanie, stood beside her, enthralled by the wildness. "A night on the town is much better than you sitting at home sobbing."

"This party is not better, Steph."

"It's not so awful." Stephanie defended but stopped. Her eyeballs almost popped from their sockets as a man strolled past them wearing only a metallic G-string and a huge boa constrictor draped around his neck.

"You're right on one account, though." Her friend laughed. "This isn't the type of crowd we normally hang out with."

Reptile guy turned around and walked back to Darla. He nodded downward where the boa's large head hovered over a glittery slip of material that barely covered an oversized bulge, and then looked at her with a wide smile.

She rotated to Stephanie who giggled. "I think he

wants to show you his snake."

"Did I mention this was a bad idea?"

"Will you stop complaining? Seriously," Stephanie replied in a defensive tone. "This madness wasn't my intention. I just hoped to meet some singers or musicians."

They made a quick move from the man to a nearby floor-to-ceiling window and gazed through the glass. Beyond the home's eve, the ocean washed across the shoreline as the waves flowed in slow motion and harmonized perfectly with the setting sun.

Darla didn't answer but continued to observe the evening tide force its spray over the shore. Under normal circumstances she preferred the beach's solitude to interacting with a bunch of people she'd never met. Tonight she most certainly wanted to be alone. It took everything in her to resist the urge to run outside and disappear.

"Maybe we could find a place to sit."

Darla sighed. "I'd rather do something productive."

"How bout we mingle?"

"How bout we don't?" Darla's voice rose. "I was leaning more toward leaving since I didn't want to be here in the first place."

Stephanie had learned about this party during a trip to her hair salon. She'd eavesdropped on a woman as she discussed the shindig with her hairdresser. When Steph discovered the location was only a few houses from where Darla lived, she managed to catch Darla in a weak moment and persuaded her to crash.

Less than an hour ago they'd entered a stranger's home. A strong stench of tobacco and sweet perfume hung heavy in the air while loud chatter drowned out the background music. The invitees included everyone from the beautiful to downright oddballs. All were crammed into the sparsely furnished space. Thus far, they'd wandered within the crowd thrusting through throngs of guests only talking to each other.

"Come on, Dar. The guy who owns this place is a concert promoter. I came to intermingle with some rock stars."

"I thought we're here to get my mind off my ex."

Stephanie lifted a shoulder. "That too. But I've seen quite a few musicians just roaming around."

"And are there any who make you scream and want to hurdle the furniture to get to them?"

"There's a group of guys standing over in the corner." She nodded to where several men stood on a raised area in an odd angle of the room. At least a dozen women circled them. "I wouldn't mind hooking up with one of them. They were once a lot more than stars. Back in the day those men were mega huge. Superstars."

Darla's gaze followed to where her friend indicated. "I don't remember them."

"Yes, you do. Ah, what's the band's name?" She paused. "Ahm, that's it. Raging Impulse."

"Oh wow." Darla leaned forward with narrowed eyes. "They sure look different." She straightened. "I recall they had lots of hair and were very popular with the younger girls." She laughed. "Appears they've gotten haircuts and graduated to almost women."

"Seems so."

Darla glanced at her friend with a hint of a smile. "Don't tell me you had a thing for one of them."

"My crushing days on cute boy band guys were

long gone during their time, though I'll confess to a slight interest in the bass player. I went as far as to go to their concerts. Stood on my chair and screamed along with the teenagers. I even tried to sneak backstage to meet them."

Darla's brow furrowed. "That's more than a slight interest. Is the entire band here?"

"I think so." Stephanie lifted to her tippy toes and raised her chin. "Well, I see four of the five members. And a couple of other guys." She lowered to the balls of feet.

"They've changed a lot," Darla said. "I mean, they're men now."

"Yes, they are." A smile played at Stephanie's lips as she threaded her fingers through a silver chain around her neck. "And they're definitely better as men." She shot Darla a full grin before she returned her attention to the band.

Darla lifted her shoulders in a careless shrug and turned away from them. "I suppose they aren't bad if you're fond of manufactured appearances." A tidal wave of anxiety slammed against her insides. The mechanics whirling in Stephanie's brain were almost visible.

Stephanie grabbed her arm, spun her around, and scowled. "So what if they're manufactured? Live a little, Darla. We're here to meet people, not make a lifelong commitment."

"I have no interest in either. Besides you're the musician freak. I could care less about meeting any teenage has beens."

"You know this break up has sure brought out the negativity in you." Stephanie's mouth flattened into a straight line. "I'm only trying to support you and help take your mind off your troubles."

Darla gulped hard and then made a face. Guilt tasted like bad cheese. She should ease off her friend. If it hadn't been for Stephanie's alliance, she probably wouldn't have emotionally survived these past few weeks.

"I'm aware, and I appreciate the effort. Except I think I'd been better off left to myself to work through this."

"I'm all for a good cry to help clear the soul, and there will be plenty of time to reel in your sorrows." Stephanie's tone exuded sympathy which irritated Darla almost as much as her usual persistent one. "Later. Tonight is rough. I wouldn't be any kind of friend if I let you do this by yourself."

Darla didn't want anyone's pity. "Maybe being home alone and crying is what I needed to do. You know, purge the pain." She slanted a look in Stephanie's direction with raised eyebrows. "And did you really use the word reel?"

"Staying by yourself and bawling your eyes out would allow your no account ex to win. You don't want that."

"This isn't a race, Stephanie. There's no victory for anyone."

"Race," Stephanie repeated. "Competition has nothing to do with what I'm talking about. The point is he didn't give a rat's gluteus over you or your years together when he dumped you and hooked up with that, that cash cow. Now he's with his new rich bitch while you're alone mourning the loss of the relationship and him." She stepped in front of Darla and looked at her with a perceptive frown. "Mourning the loss." Her brows lifted. "Seriously? Hard as this is, you need to shake this off. He doesn't deserve such a depressing tribute. You've suffered in silence the past eight weeks. By now you should be jumping up and down because you found out where his priorities lie. Be glad you're rid of him and move on."

After her breakup with her longtime boyfriend, Darla did her best to swallow her pain whole and dry, willing the years to evaporate from her memory. Until today. Today her tears were unstoppable. If Stephanie hadn't dragged her out tonight, she'd be lying in bed, eating chocolate ice cream and watching old movies while she floundered in her own devastation.

"I wish moving on was that easy."

"It's simple, Dar." Stephanie raised a hand and snapped her fingers. "Make up your mind to be done and be done. Seriously, the guy's not worth crying over. Save those tears for someone who matters."

"Yeah, okay."

"Don't be so sarcastic. Things are crazy tonight, and we should do something insane too." She grinned mischievously. "We ought to go talk to those boy band guys."

Darla awarded her friend a glare that conveyed she doubted her sanity, but apprehension fully set in. The idea petrified her.

Those guys, even among the hoard of barely dressed, barely out of their teens women surrounding them, would notice beautiful, tall, blond Stephanie in a heartbeat. With Darla's confidence level plummeting lower than ever, plus the additional parade of gorgeous females here tonight, she wasn't up for meeting anyone even if she'd wanted to. "This party is beyond adventurous enough for me. And I don't get the idea of how interacting with a bunch of ancient rocker wannabes would make me feel better even under normal circumstances."

Darla glanced at the guys again. Big mistake. She caught one of the member's eyes. Her heart bounced. In the brief instant she knew he'd spotted her too. Beautiful eyes, bluer than the ocean, returned her stare. She started to smile, then stifled the reaction when his attention diverted from her to zero in on a pretty thing that sashayed by and gave him a "come hither" glimpse.

She jerked her gaze away. Who was she kidding? With her emotions immersed in her relationship failure, she couldn't endure even the smallest of slights. And seriously, she'd never be able to compete with "little miss wiggle her ass" who was currently enticing him.

"Suit yourself." Stephanie spun away and took a step toward the group. "I'm going to take a shot."

A sharp pop echoed through the crowd, followed by the tinkling of glass. The noisy room instantly hushed.

Stephanie twisted back to Darla. "What was that?"

Darla's pulse leaped. "It sounded like a gunshot."

Pop. The lights flashed twice, then the entire house became dark. Screams erupted at the same moment flocks of people stormed the home's exits.

Darla and Stephanie were caught up in the middle of the stampede. Within seconds, the mob drove them outside and onto the sandy beach. The crowd milled over the grounds, most kept a wary eye on the darkened house.

A jolt of adrenaline vibrated through Darla as she

stared into the night. An imaginary red 'S' appeared on her chest, and she shed all fear, prepared to take on whoever got in her way. For a brief moment. Then sanity overtook her, and the idea of rushing home and burrowing under the covers with ice cream made much more sense. She so wanted to go home.

"What do you think is happening?"

"I have no idea." Darla heaved a loud sigh. "But we're going to be on the news, for sure." She glared at Stephanie. "Did I mention this was a bad idea?"

Chapter 2

The lights from inside the home flickered and then turned on. A pale, thin man dressed in studded, black leather pants and a dark mesh tank top climbed upon a connecting deck's rail and screeched. The huge group returned his shriek.

"Not real, people." He raised his arm and held up a revolver. "Not real ammunition." He laughed. "Did I scare everybody?"

"Wax bullets," Darla murmured in an annoyed tone.

He howled an eerie laugh and swung the arm holding the weapon at the house. "Back inside, peeps. Party's starting to rock."

The mob cackled and shouted as they advanced toward the residence's entrances.

"Whatever. Just a prank." Stephanie snatched Darla's hand and tugged. "Everyone's going back in. Let's join them."

Darla jerked away and stared at Stephanie. "You're joking? Now would be the perfect time to leave."

"What's the problem? No one was hurt." Stephanie waved at the boy band members who were already heading to the doorway. "Please. I want to meet that guy."

Darla shook her head. Tightness constricted her chest. She had no desire to return. She wanted to flee, burrow in her bed, and consume the entire gallon of ice cream waiting for her in the freezer.

Stephanie looked at her. "You can have a glass of

wine while I try to talk to him. If I'm successful, then go ahead and walk home. If this doesn't work out, then we'll both leave."

"Fine." Darla fell into step with her friend. "Let's get this over with."

The party remained a popular place despite the ruckus. Apparently fake gunshots were the norm with this group. People pressed into the inner area and many others lingered outdoors, socializing on an oversized deck while some strolled across the beach. Indoors, a huge crowd gathered around the bar.

"Okay. I'm going to meet the bass player. Why don't you come with me and try to hook up with one of the other ones? The lead guitarist is a real hottie."

Darla glanced at the bar. Forget men. This night screamed for alcohol. "Meet them if you want. I'm getting a glass of wine and after that I'm outta here." She marched away before giving Stephanie a chance to reply.

Darla took her place to stand in the long line to get her drink. While she waited, she witnessed a confident Stephanie advance to where the men congregated among their harem. The musician Stephanie had her eye on, Darla remembered his name was Blaine, detected her friend the moment she walked into his viewing range. Steph sauntered over to him wearing a huge smile. He disengaged from the cluster of women and almost ran to meet her. He offered her his arm, and together they disappeared into the crowd.

Darla shook her head. She wished she possessed a teaspoon full of Stephanie's poise. With her friend's evening decided, she was free to leave without a worry. She glanced around. Though the craziness here did provide a multitude of entertainment—until she caught a near naked couple behind an oversized sofa doing things one didn't do in a room full of people.

Thankfully it was her turn. She stepped to the bar and tried to avoid the embarrassing scene, but her movement put the pair in dead center of her viewing range.

"I hope they're drunk," said a deep voice behind her.

"Huh?" Darla slid her drink off the surface.

She spun around, smashing into the man next in line. A small "oomph" escaped her when they hit. The collision knocked the glass from her hand and hurled it through space. She blindly lunged to catch it, stumbling forward. Her arms flailed in a desperate act to save herself from trailing the goblet. She grasped at air in search for something, anything, to latch onto.

A hand grabbed the front of her shirt. She stopped in mid-fall, clutching onto a sturdy forearm. He drew her to him to keep her from dropping further. The action put Darla in a secure embrace, against an extremely firm, warm-bodied male. Time stopped.

He lifted her to her feet and stepped back a proper distance. She blew out a stream of air while her heart pounded in high-speed from her near crash and burn. Prepared to give a mountain of gratitude to her rescuer she looked up, her gaze linking with a pair of thickly lashed cornflower blue eyes. Eyes bluer than the ocean.

The words "thank you" never made it from her brain to her mouth. Only a soft "whoa" slipped past her lips.

Time stopped again. She tried to swallow. Except a lump formed and now lodged in her throat and blocked the passageways. Her palms dampened. A fiery itch stung around the edges of her shirt collar. Her internal radar soared into high gear. She broke the eye contact. Darla could not lose control here. She needed to say something and leave. But the strange pattern on the fabric of her rescuer's shirt grabbed her attention.

She tipped her head slightly and frowned. She stared harder, blinking several times. What th… A loud gasp escaped as she slapped a palm over her mouth. This night kept getting better. Darla lowered her hand

and gaped at the pink tinge sprayed across the Raging Impulse lead guitarist's chest.

"That's not good." He pointed and wiggled a finger over the scattered glass, apparently unperturbed she'd ruined his shirt. "What were you drinking? I'll get you another."

Darla stared, speechless. The inflections of his strong accent made him difficult to understand yet the mere sound of his voice caused her heart to almost stop. It was rich, deep, laced with enough of a rasp to carry a trace of seductiveness. The kind of voice that could convince a woman to do practically anything.

"What were you drinking?" he asked again. A long moment passed. Those disturbing cobalt eyes continued to study her. "Are you okay?"

Darla gulped. She was fine except her mind experienced a complete meltdown. Her heart beat in triple time, and she couldn't catch her breath. And she appeared to have lost the ability to speak. But yeah, she was okay.

"Wine," she blurted. "White Zinfandel." Surprised she'd almost found her wits, she paused and made an awkward gesture over the fresh stain on his shirt. "I don't know what happened. Um, I got…you were there, it…" Her arm dropped, and she released a heavy sigh. "The glass slipped out of my hand."

A slight curve formed across his lips as a wicked twinkle entered his eyes. "I noticed."

He moved to the bar, leaving her to fume over her inelegance. Could she be any smoother? She barely spit out a word, forget about completing a sentence. She came off better mute. Twisting a curl around her finger, she remained in place staring at him.

Like a magnet to steel his gaze connected with hers. A rush of inner heat pulsated and scorched her entire body. The warmth stretched to the outer edges and spread a crimson flush over her skin. Her tongue crossed over her parched lips as she tore her eyes away.

Stupid hormones. They didn't just betray her. They'd stepped outside her to do a happy dance.

She supposed she should give herself a break. The man sizzled hot. Was his thick brogue Scottish or Irish?

Darla stopped. She needed to get some control over these out of control sensations before she sank to below zero on her shame-o-meter. To divert her attention from him, she stooped to pick up the larger shards of glass scattered across the floor. She still needed something to mop up the liquid. Maybe the guy would let her use his shirt again.

Darla waved an arm to get his attention, then elevated her voice above the chatter. "Please ask the bartender for a towel or something so I can wipe up the spill."

Much better. She, an educated, self-sufficient woman contained her emotions. She didn't have meltdowns over former teen idols. A white dishtowel spiraled and dangled in front of her face. She snatched the cloth.

He squatted next to her and held out a dustpan with a nod toward the scoop. "Put the glass in here."

With a whiskbroom, he swept up the remaining broken pieces while Darla dabbed up the wine. Once clean, he took the wet towel from her and walked back to the bar. Within minutes he returned with her new glass along with a drink for him.

"Thank you." She grasped the goblet and looked up at him. Her mouth went dry. Too busy admiring his other delectable qualities she'd missed how he towered over her. Though not a giant by any means, the way he carried himself made him seem even taller than he actually was. "And thanks for catching me. I'm, I'm sorry about your shirt."

Could she not spit out a simple sentence? Okay, so the wet material clung to his chest outlining a pair of broad shoulders and a very muscular torso. She had to get a grip on this situation.

"Shirts wash." He flashed a smile, which made him go from good-looking to oooo-la-la. "Teach me to wear a light color, eh?"

Teach her to not focus her attention on naked people and look where she's going. Darla ought to walk, correction, run away from this man. Except her feet had somehow super-glued themselves to the floor.

"My name's Eric Boyd."

Eric. He said his name was Eric. Now she should respond. Maybe try to speak intelligibly. "I'm Darla. Darla Hennessy."

"Darla," Eric repeated. "Pretty."

He didn't offer a hand for her to shake, prompting a mixture of relief and disappointment. Then again after their initial encounter he must find her clumsy and graceless and not worth the effort. His all-knowing gaze peering from under his somehow perfect yet shaggy hair sparked an aura of perceptive danger.

"It was nice meeting you," she rushed, "but I need to find my friend. Again, I feel terrible I ruined your shirt." She stepped backward.

"Can I ask you something before you go?" His overpowering presence stopped her.

"I suppose." Darla shrugged. She hoped to appear indifferent, although she knew she failed.

He took a step closer, then leaned in. His mouth hovered close to hers, his voice low. "Why are you here?"

"Excuse me?" Darla shifted away and stared him down.

"I was wondering what made you show up tonight. I saw you earlier." A curve lifted the corner of his mouth. He stepped back farther and gave her a lazy once-over. "This doesn't seem the type of crowd someone like you would want to mix with."

She glanced around. The two of them appeared to be in a circle of amplified madness.

"Someone like me?" Darla shot him a tight smile

and ignored his obvious ogling. "I don't know why you say that, everyone is niccce…"

Eric grabbed her upper arm to drag her from where she stood. A loud thump landed behind them. She stumbled against him, clutching her wineglass. The liquid sloshed although didn't spill this time. Once she was steady, he freed her. Darla spun around and released a whispered squeak. A large, unconscious man lay sprawled in the space she'd occupied moments before. A breakout of an argument followed. Fists began to fly among shouts and curses.

Eric slid his palm down her arm and grasped her hand to hold in a protective grip. He slightly tugged. "We'd better move."

He maneuvered her away from the chaos. Her entire body constricted from the implied intimacy. She maintained enough of her faculties to be aware of his hard fingers and the light gentleness of his palm loosely covering hers.

Oblivious to the mayhem around them, she followed his lead willingly with no idea or concern where he led her. His abrupt release jolted her back to reality. She blinked several times. He'd guided her outdoors onto a massive attached deck.

With a rueful smile, Darla took a giant step away from him. She had to. Before she lost control and hurled her body into him. This guy practically had her libido exploding. But was her reaction to him even genuine? With the end of her relationship not emotionally set in, how could she want someone else, someone she didn't know, this quick?

More yells hailed from within chased by bumps and crashes.

"Do you think we should call the police?"

Eric peered inside. "If somebody hasn't by now, they will soon." The shatters of something breaking indicated the commotion escalated. His attention returned to Darla. "Maybe we oughta get you out of here."

"I was thinking the same thing." A mixture of relief and letdown charged through her. She sat her full goblet down on a nearby table. "A pleasure meeting you, Eric."

She spun away and hurried toward the house. She almost made it the door before she stopped. The unruliness indoors sounded worse than before. Some of the guests were leaving. A dining room chair flew out a nearby window. Darla let out a short scream and whirled back to Eric. He'd leaned a hip against the deck rail with a cigarette clenched between his lips. His drink sat on the banister while he concentrated on the lighter underneath, clicking twice before a blue flame appeared. He inhaled deeply as the flare licked the tip.

He removed the cigarette, exhaled, lifting his eyes to Darla. "Why are you going inside?"

"I need to find my friend. We're together. I can't leave her."

He sucked in a long drag, blew out a hazy stream, and shook his head. "It's not safe."

"But I have to go back for Stephanie." Darla took another step toward the door. "What if she's caught up in that? She might get hurt."

A small table soared through the same window. Quickly, she jumped to the side to avoid the flying wood. The fixture smashed into tiny pieces on the ground next to her.

Eric nodded at the mess. "So could you." He took another puff. "She was talking to my friend, right?"

"You mean the shorter guy? Yes, she was with him."

"Blaine Stewart. He's a good man. He'll make sure she's okay." He shoved off the rail. "You need to leave b'fore this gets any worse." He motioned to the street in front of the home. "Is your car over here?"

"No. I walked. I live a few houses down, so I'll go back the same way." She stepped to the stairwell which led down to the beach.

"Let me finish my smoke, and I'll come with you."

Darla spun around and shot up a palm. "Oh no, that's not necessary."

"Don't get excited." Eric grinned and gestured down the shore. "My home is that way too." He picked up his drink. "Neither of us needs to get caught up in this shit." He lifted her wineglass and held it out to her. "Don't forget this."

Darla extended a hand for the glass. Their fingers grazed. She resisted the urge to tremble and wished for the courage not to care what he got caught in. She wanted to tell him she'd rather walk alone, which wasn't true, although she needed it to be.

"Do you think it's okay if we take our drinks?"

"Can't see anyone will notice. Let's move away from the line of fire."

He nudged her from the party's tense atmosphere and to the side of the home, closer to the water. She relaxed against the banister, enjoying the secluded darker area. A salty fragrance filled the air as echoes of the breakers floated through the winds and a soft hum of waves synchronized with the final stages of dusk. Eric leaned on the rail next to her, his gaze fixated on her.

Darla took a tiny sip of her wine, hoping he didn't notice her hand shake. "Are these parties always this wild?"

"Sometimes they're worse. That usually brings in the rag mags. One of the reasons I want to get out of here. I'd prefer not to make the front page of the tabloids."

"What a treat."

He chuckled. "Been in news enough. Believe me, there's no pleasure."

A chilly blast of wind lifted sand particles from the beach and stung her skin. Nevertheless, the coolness was refreshing. Darla's nerves began to settle. Perhaps her new composure originated from the security of the darkness, the wine, or because of the nearby ocean's gentle hush.

Not that any of those factors overshadowed the vibrant presence of the man next to her. His nearness kept her senses on high alert. Yet, she was glad her nerves were no longer in knots, and a tiny part of her could enjoy the excitement of spending the evening with the gorgeous Eric Boyd.

"I guess you have experienced some sensationalist journalism attacks. You were in a band, right?"

"I was. Fame came sudden. Didn't handle it well. I paid the price. I've done much better since we broke up. But there was a time my name seemed to be in the headlines every day. Vicious."

"Lots of lies, huh?"

"Not exactly." The dim reflection of light revealed a small curve of his mouth. "They're vicious about the truth."

"Their type of reporting is so spiteful and malicious. I can't imagine anyone respectable condoning that kind of work, much less publishing it."

"Yeah," he said quietly. "But they do." He tossed the smoldering butt over the edge, then found his shirt pocket again and removed the cigarette package and his lighter. He shook out another, placed the filter between his lips, and lit up. "I know it's not my business but why were you at this party tonight?"

"Long story."

She clamped her mouth shut, refusing to go there. Not this evening and not with him. The darkness prevented her from seeing his eyes although she sensed his gaze on her. He wouldn't give her a pass on this.

He picked up his glass and took a long drink. "It's early, and I've got time.

"To be honest, I'm beat. I didn't sleep much last night. I want to finish my wine, head home, take a hot bath, and go to bed."

Eric grinned. "I like the sound of that," he said in a low and easy voice.

Darla's knees buckled. She clutched the stem of her glass, almost tumbling to the ground. Was he flirting with her? She should flirt back. She wanted to, except her tongue retied itself.

She coughed before finding her vocal cords again. "I'm making this short because I am tired. I was with a guy for several years. We were getting serious, but his affluent family convinced him, and by convinced I mean they held his trust fund over his head, to dump me and get engaged to someone within their social circle. That was two months ago. They're getting married this evening."

"At least it explains why you were a stray tonight."

"Right." She took a ragged breath of air, loving the fact her new prospective object of affection clearly believed she didn't belong in his world despite her crappy circumstances. "My friend Stephanie heard about this party earlier today. She suggested we come here to meet some different people, so we're checking things out."

Neither spoke. The silence amplified by a sudden wind gust. Foggy clouds trailed a cold current of air, rolling overhead to blanket the night sky. A faint boom rumbled in the distance.

Darla hugged her middle with her free arm and eyed the rotating swirls above. "Looks like we might have some bad weather blowing in."

"You probably should try another kind of party to meet people."

"Sure, wait, what?" Her interest returned to Eric. "Why should I find a different type of party? You didn't seem to be having any problems."

"Yeah, but that's the kind of crowd I hang with."

Two women wearing micro bikinis strolled past them. Each flashed a sexy grin at Eric before they giggled and hurried downstairs toward the beach.

"Naked females are the kind of crowd you hang with?"

Eric laughed. "I go a little wild when I get out. I've been a bit repressed over the years."

Darla rocked back on her feet. "You sure don't act suppressed to me."

"My former manager was something of a dictator. A long story in itself but we, my band mates and me, were prisoners of our success for many years. Now the guy's no longer a part of our lives. We've gone kinda crazy from the freedom."

"I did read once you guys were squeaky clean types." Darla grinned and pointed to his glass. "You only drink milk, right?"

He laughed again. "There might've been a few lies printed about us." Thunder rolled, closer. Eric looked up. "You called it. We are in for some nasty weather. We should get going." He tossed his cigarette over the side. "Ready?"

Darla headed toward the stairs, her hand slid along the rail.

Eric shadowed her close behind. "What do you do for a living?"

"I teach geology at a local college while I work on my PhD."

"Ah, smart girl."

They were almost to the bottom when the lights from inside the house flickered like before. A thunderous blast boomed and shook the staircase where they stood. The discharge was reminiscent of the fake gunshot earlier. Then the place became dark again.

"What th—" Eric twisted around.

Darla flinched and cranked her neck too.

Flashes of lighters and cell phone lights made the area murky. A rush of guests exited one more time. Screams followed by a large amount of swearing echoed above running footsteps. Darla and Eric dodged and ducked to evade getting trampled by the charging masses as the mob fought to make their escape. People then disappeared in every direction.

Darla raised her voice over the noise "Looks like the party is over." She looked around. "I wonder what happened now."

A faint resonance of sirens screamed in the distance. Those pesky anxieties returned as tiny chills peppered her neck.

Eric mounted two steps then glanced back at her. "I don't think we want to hang around to find out." He climbed down and touched her arm lightly. "Let's go."

Shrieks continued to rise from the darkness. "Stop him," a voice yelled.

"Don't let him get away," someone else cried.

Heavy strides pounded across the wooden planks. Darla spun halfway around. A shadowed blur smacked into her and shoved her onto the staircase support. The shaded figure hit the ground and sprinted underneath the deck.

"Hey," Eric shouted. "Watch where you're going, fucker." His hand slid across her back and drew her against him. He gently straightened her and stroked her arm. "You okay?"

Darla caught her breath and nodded. "He startled me but I'm fine."

Groups of partiers dashed from the darkness. A rev of an engine echoed, as the headlight of a motorcycle whizzed from beneath. The cluster of people scattered as the bike penetrated the circle, drove up the beach's incline, and disappeared into the night.

Eric turned to a bystander and tapped him on the shoulder. "What happened in there?"

"The gunshot was genuine this time." The man pointed at the elevated dust made by the departed bike. "He had a gun. And he didn't miss. He just killed someone."

Chapter 3

Emergency lights pulsated streaks of red across the shoreline where police vehicles lined parallel along the curb surrounding the neighborhood. An ambulance had parked in the driveway, its doors wide open. Waiting.

"This is taking forever," Eric groaned. "I wish they'd hurry." Arms folded across his chest, he leaned against the deck's banister and watched the crime scene personnel cautiously shift about collecting evidence then taping off the area.

"Murder investigations take a while." Darla sat on the bottom step rolling the empty wineglass between her palms. She glanced toward the home crawling with detectives before she returned to Eric. "I'm sure this case is going to be difficult to solve with so many people involved, especially when a bunch of them disappeared before the police arrived."

"Still no reason to keep us this long," he mumbled.

This was the most Eric had spoken since the authorities arrived. Once he seemed reassured of her safety after tussling with the motorcycle guy, things between them settled into an uneasy silence. Darla had long given up on getting him to talk. The whole night altered from something wonderful into a huge horrific, nightmare.

She didn't blame him for his impatience. For the

past several hours the two of them remained parked at the foot of the house. A photographer snapped photographs outside and presumably inside, while uniformed police officers milled through the crowd taking information from the guests. The party goers who'd stayed drifted about speaking in hushed tones. Everyone appeared on edge.

Eric studied the veiled sky. "At least the rain's stalled." He heaved his body away from the railing to sit on the step next to her. Lightning flickered, jumping from cloud to cloud as booms rattled above. The strong breeze carried the distinct smell of rain. The storm had been a slow mover, though the grumbled churns progressed.

"Not for long, I'm afraid."

"Yeah, they need to speed up the interviewing. We don't wanna end up as lightning conductors. The idea of being fried into something extra crispy doesn't thrill me."

"They'll let us leave as soon as they get our statements." Exhausted, Darla didn't want to appear disrespectful toward the dead either, but she wished the authorities would hasten the process too. She wanted to rush home to check the locks on the doors and windows, just in case. "Though, I'd rather the police hang around since a killer is on the loose in our neighborhood."

"The guy is long gone. The person killed was marked. Probably a drug deal turned bad."

"What makes you think so? Has something like this happened before?"

He lifted a shoulder. "Speculation. An assassin waltzes in and shoots someone with hundreds of people around, and no one can identify him. Gotta be a hit and done by a pro. Could be over money or maybe a defunct affair."

"I'm withholding my opinion until we get an official word from the authorities."

Eric stared at the sky again. "You do that."

Seconds ticked by converting into minutes. Strong winds thrust the surf near the deck propelling an icy mist to lightly blanket them. The added damp annoyance didn't motivate Eric to move, therefore Darla stayed put too.

"Does this happen a lot? Do all of your parties result in homicides or is tonight a onetime occurrence I got lucky enough to experience?"

"I've been going to these things for years. Seen overdoses, a couple of suicide attempts, and one heart attack, but never a murder. Nothing surprises me, though." A corner of Eric's mouth lifted. "Welcome to my world."

"What about the victim? Do you think you may know him?"

"I suppose there's a possibility, but I doubt it." He retrieved his smokes. "I'm only acquainted with a handful of people here. I've never met most of them, and that includes the guy who threw this disaster."

"Eric?" came a masculine voice from behind.

Eric looked up from lighting his cigarette. "Shane." He rose from the step and climbed over Darla to meet the person approaching them. "I wondered what happened to everyone."

A sturdy, light-haired man stopped at the side of the stairwell in front of them.

"Blaine got a date. Finn and his asshole brother

declared the party too tame, and they went to find something more exciting. Drake talked about cutting out. S'pose he wanted to get home to his bride." The man glanced around, shoving his hands into his pockets. "Hell of a situation. Do you know who it was? Who was killed?"

The new arrival turned and glimpsed at Darla, giving her a brief nod.

"Nope." Eric pointed at her. "That's Darla." He swung his lit cigarette toward the guy. "This is my manager, Shane McIntyre. He's with Blaine and me."

A quick but peculiar look passed across Shane's face before his expression altered into a smile. He extended a hand. "You're not a regular at these bashes, are you?"

"My first time." She stood and brushed her palm down her skirt before she took his offered hand.

A policeman strolled to the threesome and told Eric they were set to question him.

"Good. I'm past ready," Eric mumbled, then said louder, "Stay with her, Shane. She's a bit nervous after all of this." His eyes shifted to her. "I'll be back."

Shane flashed another puzzling expression. Darla's cheeks burned. Her throat tightened as she swallowed a trace of anger. This guy must hold the same opinion as Eric on her appearance here tonight. Even though the belief was true, she'd grown tired of the insinuations that she didn't fit in.

"Not a great impression of our bunch, huh?"

Darla released a bitter chuckle. "It's been an interesting experience."

He cast a glance over his shoulder to where Eric stood. "You've known Eric long?"

"We met tonight." She stepped from the deck and onto the sand, moving around the tall, wooden handrail to get a better view of the man who'd captivated her attention the entire evening. "You're his manager."

"Right," he replied blandly.

"You seem familiar. We've met before, haven't we?"

"I don't think so. I was inside earlier. You may've seen me at the party."

Darla nodded. "In Raging Impulse's group along with their many lady friends. I bet I'm making the connection from that." She clutched the glass between her hands. "Eric mentioned a former manager who controlled and repressed the band. I'm assuming you're not the person he's referring to?"

Shane's stare was blank before her question apparently registered. "No. I only work with Eric and Blaine. Our professional association is fairly new, although I've known them for several years. I took the job a few months ago. I usually stay in Scotland, but I travel to the states often. I have a son in the UK, so my visits are never long."

"Are you a musician also?"

"I dabble, but no, I don't actually play." He twisted to her and scrutinized her with a raised brow. "Tonight's been a real shock for everyone. I suppose this incident has been pretty upsetting for you."

"More than you can imagine. I was shaken after the murder first happened, but we've been waiting a long time to be interviewed, and I'm so tired now that I'm almost numb." Her internal shudder whispered a severe contradiction, but she discounted the shock. "I'm sure it'll hit me again after a good night sleep, if I can sleep."

"Did you see anything?"

She shook her head "Not really. It was dark before the blast. The supposed killer did run past me and shoved me into the stair rail when he was making his getaway."

"Wow, that's pretty unnerving."

"I didn't realize who he was, so it wasn't as disturbing at the time."

"Did you get a look at the guy?"

"Just a person dressed in dark clothes, and I think he wore a helmet. I couldn't see his face."

"What happened after he pushed you?"

"He took off on a motorcycle. It was hidden under there." Darla motioned in the direction of the deck's underbelly where officers were inspecting the area. "I wish I was more educated about bikes so I could tell the police the make and model. But that knowledge is beyond me." She paused. "You weren't here when the shooting happened?"

"I was outside too. In front of the house." Shane almost smiled. "And I did witness the motorcycle drive away. I told the detectives when they interviewed me. I didn't realize he had anything to do with the murder either. I couldn't identify any specifics, so I doubt if I helped. Too many people here. I don't believe they'll ever solve this."

Darla eyes drifted toward Eric. Head bent to study the officer's notes, he lifted his chin, flicked his gaze over her at the same moment she looked at him. He winked. Her stomach tightened, and her heart jumped as she suppressed a smile.

"Hope you're not entertaining more than a single

night with him." Shane's voice held a hint of warning.

Darla jerked around and stared at him defiantly. "Excuse me?"

Shane inclined his head in Eric's direction and grinned. "Woman come and go in his life and usually don't hang round for more than a few hours. You're out of luck if you are planning anything other than a one nighter. He doesn't do sentiments, feelings, or all the crap that goes along with emotional ties."

She clutched the wineglass's stem, pointing the glass's bulb at him. "I realize I'm not worldly enough to be here. I chose to wear clothes over just underwear, my skin's not inked or pierced, and I don't use ten pounds of make-up. You don't have to spell things out for me. I get it, okay? Eric Boyd isn't interested in me."

"Hold the hostility." Shane glanced at Eric, who'd finished with the officer and was strolling toward them. "He's interested, all right." He turned back to her. "That's what I'm telling you. It'll be only for one night."

Darla's insides froze. Eric wanted her. Of course he did. Why else would he keep hanging around her? Because he actually liked her or he desired to know her better. The idea was crazy. And she was attracted to him too. Could she do it? Could she sleep with a guy she'd just met and walk away after. And be okay?

Eric looked at Darla. "The detective wants to talk to you now."

She didn't speak. She spun and marched to where the investigator waited. Skyrockets exploded in her chest, though not because of the upcoming interview, but from what Shane had told her. And more so from what she considered doing.

Her meeting took very little time. The policeman wrote down her information and gave her a card with instructions to call if she remembered anything else. Interrogation completed, she glanced at Eric who gazed at her as he continued to speak with his manager. She took this as a sign. She was going to do this. She returned to Eric. They both said their goodbyes to Shane and started down the beach. Neither spoke for a good minute.

"You and Shane seemed to be getting along."

"He was enlightening," Darla replied in a clipped tone. "Why do you have a manager? I thought your group broke up."

"We did. But that doesn't mean we're out of the music industry."

"Most of the band was at the party. Was that intentional?"

"Shane, Blaine, and I planned to meet up with Impulse's keyboardist, Drake Mahoney. He's retired from the business, and we don't get with him often. It was only by chance we ran into Finn O'Conner and his brother, Richard, who played in our band."

"I guess you had a pleasant reunion."

"And you'd guess wrong." He slowed his step. "Where do you live?"

Darla pointed as they advanced toward her residence. "My house is over there."

Eric whistled low. "Nice. I've admired that one for a while."

"All of the homes are well kept in this vicinity."

The dwellings in her area were older and constructed in many shapes and sizes. Darla's certainly wasn't a larger one, although it was well maintained to uphold its elegance. Built in the 1920's, the house's charm remained preserved by the owners, who'd kept the structure true to the period with the addition of modern conveniences and integrated them into the era. Though out of her price range, she loved living in the area since her breakup. If it weren't for her boss's friends, who owned the place and needed someone to housesit most of the year, she'd never be able to afford such a luxury.

"Yeah, but some are better than others." He indicated farther down the beach. "Blaine and I share the one with the smaller deck. We've been there for about six months. It's decent although I've had to do loads of maintenance, and the flat still needs lots of work. But I like to do repairs in my down time, which is why I moved there." He turned to her as they stopped in front of her property. "You must not get out much or I'd have seen you around."

"I've only lived here for eight weeks."

Eric took a step closer and leaned in with a grin, his voice a raspy whisper. "Then you haven't been properly welcomed to the neighborhood."

She looked him in the eyes and swallowed. A murmur of Shane's words flashed through her mind. This was it. The moment. Do or die, sink or swim, and all the other clichés as to what choice she would make for the rest of the night. She wished she was more like Stephanie and could enjoy the experience for however brief and then move on.

Eric placed a finger under her chin, lifted her face, and tilted his body further toward her. His mouth lingered above hers, so close his warm breath grazed against her skin.

"Eric," came a cry from the blackness.

"Shit." Eric dropped his arm and twisted in the direction of the voice.

The two stared into the darkness. Shane's running silhouette appeared from of the gloom. He sprinted to where they waited. "Did you hear?"

Shane stopped, out of breath, though Darla got the sense his panting wasn't from his quick sprint. He bent at the waist, resting his hands on his knees. "I found out who was—" He gasped for air then puffed. "Murdered."

"What?"

"Killed. At the party. It's—" He gulped and inhaled again. "It's Drake." He panted and swept the sweat off his brow. "Drake Mahoney was the person shot. He's dead."

Chapter 4

"Tonight was sure unusual."

Eric nodded as he and Shane trekked across the shoreline toward his house. He'd lost someone he considered more of a brother than a friend, and in a violent way. *Unusual* hardly described the night, but he didn't argue.

"The party was rougher than normal, and this..." Shane trailed, his voice choked.

Eric sighed. "I know."

He fumbled for his cigarettes, glad he'd refrained from smoking the entire pack while he waited for the police to complete their investigation. He shook the package until the thin rolls appeared. With a stick gripped between his lips, he found his lighter and flipped the clicker. The spark swayed under the smoke until it lit, then he inhaled and blew.

"You're sure Drake was the victim? Did someone identify the body? They're certain the weird guy in black was the killer?"

"Apparently most of the victim's face was shot off. Hit from the back, behind the ear as he was coming out of the john. And from what I'm getting, witnesses claimed the motorcyclist was holding a gun when he left."

Eric's stomach lurched "Coward. How did they

determine the dead person was Drake?"

Shane shrugged. "Rumor mill says he had a picture ID on him, and someone recognized his clothing. I haven't heard about anyone actually witnessing the crime, though."

The whole idea was too upsetting to comprehend. Right now Eric couldn't register this awful thing that happened to his former band mate. "I don't wanna to discuss this anymore."

"Understood. Let's change the subject." Shane hesitated. "I'm wondering about this girl. Darla."

"What about her?" Eric did his best to make his voice sound casual as he tossed his smoldering butt into the sand.

"You tell me."

"I pegged her for a crasher the moment I laid eyes on her. Hell, her whole demeanor shrieked outsider. I wondered what possessed her to intrude in a situation where she clearly didn't belong, so I went to find out."

"Why did it matter?"

Good question. One that'd bothered him the entire evening. He'd gotten bored early and wanted something to liven up his night. Enter Darla. Compelled to discover her story, he found a way to meet her, thus his being behind her at the bar wasn't a coincidence. The plan, find a bit of entertainment and move on.

What he didn't intend, was for her fall literally into his arms. Nor did he mean to like her so close to him. Not in the usual way he enjoyed being near women. This was different, unidentifiable. These odd feelings kept messing with his head despite the disturbing circumstances.

"It doesn't matter."

Shane snorted. "I'm calling you on this one. Do you realize in all the years we've been friends this is the first time you've ever introduced me to a woman you were entertaining?"

Eric didn't respond.

"You actually told me to look out for her when you left to talk to the cops." Shane chuckled. "You wanted to protect her, to be her freaking hero. And you almost insisted on walking her home. This isn't the nineteen fifties, so what's up?"

"You're overthinking the situation. There's nothing special about this girl, especially compared to the women I've met. She kinda pretty, but unsophisticated." He touched his pocket, then changed his mind. "I like her hair, though." Images of thick, wavy ringlets, almost black, raced through his head. Curls swirled over her shoulders and shimmered in the light, resembling a halo.

"You meet pretty, hell, *beautiful* women every day, all with great hair. Tall, leggy, large chested females."

"True. This one's working on her PhD. And I'm not attracted to the smart types. She's got an intelligent mind, but she's average everywhere else. Medium height, normal build, style of dress, all average. Even her story rings typical. Dumped, brokenhearted, whatever—common." He should've forgotten her name by now, yet her dark eyes seemed imprinted in his consciousness. "I don't wanna talk about her either."

"I bet you don't."

"Believe what you want, I'd have dumped her hours ago except for the—Drake—you understand."

"I do." Shane turned to him and smiled. "But if you're not interested...she's pretty cute, maybe I'll have a go at her."

"She's not your type either." Eric rushed up the stairs to his back porch.

"If you say so." Shane veered away. "I'm heading home unless you need me to hang around."

"I'm fine."

Large cold drops pelted the minute Eric mounted the first step leading into his house. Once inside, he balanced against the wall, shifting his weight as he toed off his muddy boots. He glimpsed out the window to view the storm before he edged across the darkness using the lightning flashes to guide him until he reached his room. Inside he fumbled for a lamp's switch. Light on, he kicked off his damp jeans, yanked the shirt over his head, then searched the floor for the towel he'd dropped from an earlier shower. Once he'd dried, he snatched a pair of sweats draped over a chair and slipped them on. He glided to his bed and rifled through the covers. Locating his pillow, he fell onto the mattress and stuffed it behind him. He lay quiet, staring at the ceiling fan whirling in slow motion.

Drake. His good friend was dead. Murdered. He still couldn't understand. He'd lost others before. Family, friends, people he'd cared about. All tragic but nothing compared to this senseless heartbreak. Unable to cope, he refused to contemplate the horrible occurrence now. He'd hash and rehash the whole thing with his friends later and be forced to read the story in the media. God, the media. They'd carry on over this incident for years. Drake would never be at peace.

He needed to refocus his mind or he'd go insane over the loss. Stretching for a legal pad sitting on the nightstand next to him, Eric held the tablet under the lamps dim glow and studied the scribbles on the front page. This song had given him hell. He and Blaine had hammered out the music though neither of them could come up with decent lyrics. Staring at the pad, an impulse swept over him and urged him to play. He stood up. A swift search through several drawers produced a pen. He swiped up the paper and his guitar, then perched on the edge of the mattress. He strummed the instrument. For a brief moment, the haunting melody drove away the pain from his loss and coincided with happier thoughts.

Of Darla.

Words formed. He grabbed the pen to write them down, matching each word with a chord. Before he realized, the first verse, then the second were complete. He carried on, building the chorus. Words flowed from his heart to his fingertips as he put them to the music. Excited, he played again. This time he sang softly as each note bounded into his soul.

A tap at his door interrupted him. He glanced to where beams of light shined from underneath. Blaine must be home.

"C'me in," he mumbled. He continued to scrawl notes on the edge of his tablet.

Blaine poked his head inside. "Hey."

Eric stole a glimpse at his partner, nodded, and went back to his writing.

His friend entered the bedroom. "You're 'bout finished."

Eric looked up and frowned.

"The song."

"Yep. Needs a few tweaks here and there. It'll be ready soon, though." He paused to make another notation, laid the pen down to give Blaine his full attention. "The storm seemed to inspire me."

"Sounds like a hit." Blaine's head bobbed. "We need to include some more ballads."

An uneasy silence filled the room. Eric set his guitar aside. He slid from the bed's edge and relocated to the top of the mattress, leaning against the headboard.

Eric stared at Blaine. "You heard, right?"

Blaine's face paled. "I'm sick about the news." He paced to the window to stare into the night. "Drake's the nicest guy in the world. Who'd do this to him?"

Eric shrugged, still wanting to stay away from the subject but realized the uselessness to keep putting the topic off. "The shooting doesn't seem random, yet it's hard to believe Drake did something so bad someone would do this to him."

Blaine threw a quick glance over his shoulder. "Maybe we didn't know Drake as well as we thought we did."

Eric lifted his brows with a "you've got be kidding" expression.

Blaine rotated away. "I can't come up with any other reason."

"I can."

Blaine turned around and leaned against the window frame, arms folded over his chest. "I know what you're thinking, but that's not possible." He uneasily cleared his throat. "He's in jail."

"This sounds as if the shooting was done by a professional. Like a hired gun. He managed to get in and out of a house full of people and blow Drake's head off without anyone able to recognize him. Someone knew what they were doing."

"The idea is crazy."

"I don't think so," Eric argued. "He's associated with some shady people. How hard would it be for him to hook up with someone in jail and pay them or one of their associates to murder Drake?"

Blaine hesitated. "I hope you're wrong."

"Give me another reason why anyone would want to kill him."

"I can't. If I'd had any idea how sick he was, I'd have walked away from the money and fame and stayed in Aberdeen forever." He paused. "It's got to be something else, Eric. Something we're unaware of must have happened in Drake's life. We've been concerned over the demons he was dealing with for a long time."

Eric's chin dropped. "Drake had a drinking problem. Although since he'd quit the business and got married, he had it under control."

"That's what he told us, but is it the truth?"

Eric's head shot up. "I choose to believe so."

"For his family's sake, we'll say you're right."

"I am. Dugan Holt was a first class crook among other things. I dunno why you think he'd be above getting rid of anyone he viewed as an enemy. Don't underestimate the man, Blaine. That would be a huge mistake."

"I don't take Dugan's past deeds lightly." Blaine's tone turned grim. "As a matter of fact, I always thought he'd come after us some day. But I figured he'd hurt us in other ways. Ways where we'd suffer in life. I never believed he'd outright kill one of us."

"In a normal mind, your type of revenge makes sense. But we ruined him. Destroyed his reputation and we sent him to jail. He's not going to forgive us without a major retribution."

"Still, killing one of us?" Blaine balled a fist and drove it into his palm. "I've been afraid everything will crash down on us at any moment since the day we called the police on him." He glanced at Eric, his expression irritated. "I'm still unsure about the way we handled things."

Eric grunted. "This wasn't a situation where we needed to stop and talk or discuss our feelings. Our circumstances had already exploded."

Blaine's eyes narrowed to focus on Eric. "Yeah, and you didn't help out in that incident either."

"I did what needed to be done." Eric straightened his back. "No one else wanted to take a stand and things were out of control."

Blaine spoke carefully as if he were choosing his next words. "You realize your method wasn't the best way. What happened after was the catapult for Raging Impulse's destruction."

"You're saying our band's demise was my fault?" Eric rolled off the bed and surged to his feet, fists clenched.

"Of course not. Everyone knows your first love is music." Blaine shot Eric a dark glare. "But I am saying there were more appropriate ways to work through our issues."

"Finn wanted out. He'd done nothing except talk of leaving for the last year and because he wished to leave, he behaved like a fuckin' ass. More so than usual." Eric fell backward into the mattress and landed on his back. He lay quiet for several seconds, inhaled deep, then sat up. "I just gave him the way. And the authorities needed to know about what else I discovered." Eric's eyes turned into slits, his vocal cords shook. "If you want to place blame for Raging Impulse's collapse and demise—put the responsibility on the person who caused the shit. Our former manager, Dugan Holt. We were stupid since we didn't bother to find out what he was when we hired the guy. And we ignored his misdeeds until things got out of hand because the money and fame was too good to give up."

"Yeah. And here you're suggesting he may have something to do with Drake's murder. I don't mind telling you, the thought scares the hell out of me. Dugan sitting in jail has never given me a bit of relief."

"Me either. The guy holds a grudge. Anyone he determines as an enemy is a target. He views us as enemies, and I'm terrified Drake just paid the ultimate price."

"I hate to believe Dugan's that cold, although I'm not going to say you're wrong." Blaine shifted to the border of the bed and picked up Eric's song pad for a closer inspection. He studied the ballad. "This is good. Reads like you felt something for someone."

Eric shrugged carelessly. "It's just a song." His stare dropped to the floor. "Doesn't mean anything. The words fit the music, that's all."

He squirmed, unable to erase the image of Darla out of his head. He wished he'd never written those lyrics and fought every instinct to lean forward and snatch the tablet out of his friend's fist.

Blaine looked up with a half grin. "There must be some lady who affected you more than you're willing to admit. You appeared to be moved by a pair of haunting, dark eyes." He tossed the pad in Eric's direction. "You should read what you wrote." Blaine walked toward the doorway. "Saw Finn at the bar. Made a real pest of himself. I know you don't want to, but he wants us to stop by tonight to look at this big discovery he's made."

Eric glanced at the clock. Past midnight. Too late to go anywhere. Even if he had the desire. "He's still harping on the big deal he couldn't shut up about at the party? I don't think so."

"I know it's late but if we want him to quit bugging us, we ought to go and get it over with." Blaine clutched the doorknob. "Think about it."

Eric gritted his teeth. He had no desire to speak with Finn ever again and just the mention of Holt made his insides jittery.

Before he became Raging Impulse's manager, the band knew of Dugan Holt during his stint as a music teacher, mysteriously dismissed from the university some of the members attended. Although the group didn't officially meet him until he approached the guys after hearing them play at a dingy backstreet pub one evening.

He thought they possessed potential and made them an offer. He wanted to help them get to the next level. While he'd never managed a band, he convinced them he would make them bigger than the Beatles. Dugan's inexperience didn't concern any of them. Nor did they question his past.

The men, young and naïve, only wanted to play their music, produce hit records, and become immortalized as rock and roll deities. They needed someone to help get them there. They happily accepted Dugan's proposition. A decision each member had come to regret.

Eric rolled off the bed and strolled to the window. He stared into the foggy darkness. The rain had passed. He turned away to dress. After he put on fresh socks and shoes, he swiped up a jacket, then stepped into the next room.

Blaine was on his phone. He swung Eric a worried glimpse as he paced the floor. Eric slipped an arm through the sleeve of his coat and struggled to get it in place while he waited for Blaine to finish the call. His gut coiled from the sight of the lines in Blaine's forehead deepening.

"I guess you're right. He managed to slip out of jail and now he's gone missing," Blaine told him in a strained voice after he disconnected. "Dugan. He's escaped. The news is all over the UK. Things have started. He's disappeared because he's coming after us."

Eric drew a sharp mouthful of air as his insides plummeted. "He's already gotten one of us. We need to get ready."

Chapter 5

Darla bolted upright and rubbed her eyes. Angry slashes burst through the windows while noisy roars rattled the house. A loud pop dimmed the lights. She held her breath and turned a gaze to the ceiling. The thunder faded, and the power returned to normal. Relieved, she swung her feet to the floor, spun off the sofa where she'd been dozing and stumbled across the room to switch off the lamps. Storms made her nervous, but tonight fatigue overruled fear.

On her way to her bedroom, she passed her open laptop perched on the edge of her coffee table. She took a step back and tapped the mouse pad. She lifted the nearby wineglass and traced the rim with a finger as a tiny smile played on her lips

Another roll blasted followed by a loud pounding. She flinched and released a small scream. The roar diminished, although the hammering continued coming from the front of her house. Someone was at the door. She set the glass down, lowered the computer's lid, and then cautiously stepped to the entryway to put an eye to the peephole.

She threw the door open. A drenched Stephanie stepped inside.

"Towels." Darla hurried away. "And I'll bring dry clothes," she said over her shoulder.

She returned moments later carrying the promised goods and handed them to Stephanie. "The pants are too short but the shirt should fit."

Stephanie took the things from her. She unfolded a towel and patted her face. "Anything will work at this point." She whirled around, spraying water droplets over the hardwood, rushing toward the spare room. "Back in a few."

Darla waved a hand. "Take your time. I'll go make you some hot tea."

Darla lighted her way to the kitchen. Within minutes, her friend reappeared dressed, her hair slicked back, and the towel draped around her neck. She leaned against the doorway and dried the damp strands between the cloth's edges.

"What a night."

Darla glanced up as she stuck a cup under the faucet.

"I wonder how your ex's wedding is surviving the storm. Rumor is the social function of the year was to be a huge outdoor extravaganza. Hope they had a plan B in place."

"Don't know, don't care," Darla replied airily as she shoved a mug of water into the microwave and punched in the minutes. She turned to Stephanie. "You know what happened at our party, right?"

"I heard."

The thunder growled, prompting the lights to flicker again. Darla winced and looked across the room at her friend. The microwave dinged.

"And you're aware who the victim is?" Darla picked up a teabag and retrieved the steaming cup. She handed it to Stephanie, then brushed past her.

Steph followed her close behind, traveling into the living room as each woman claimed a side of the sofa.

"Unfortunately, yes. I got the word about Drake Mahoney's murder when I was out with Blaine." She put the mug to her lips and took a sip. "I'm sorry for Drake, but the news was just the perfect end to the worst date ever."

"Stephanie. A man is dead. Murdered." Another crash shook the house. "And you're concerned over a bad evening with a guy you picked up? Did it occur to you we were at a party where a killing happened, and we could have been in danger?"

"I doubt if we faced any real risk." She placed the teacup on the table in front of her. "We're nobodies. No one would want to do anything to us."

"You maybe." Darla scowled at her. "The killer ran past me. He rammed me out of the way when he was leaving."

Stephanie gasped as her palms fluttered across her cheeks. "Did he hurt you?"

"I'm fine. I didn't find out he was the murderer until later on. Still, the thought of being near someone who did something so horrendous is scary."

Stephanie nodded and dropped her hands. "I'm sure. Did you have to speak with the police about this?"

"After waiting for what seemed like hours."

"Sorry. But you told me you were going to get a glass of wine and leave. How did you end up staying longer?"

Darla straightened. "My nerves are giving me the munchies. I have double chocolate chip ice cream. You want some?"

"Ooh calories, yeah, bring 'em on. Let's make this

a true party. Our style, anyway. Get the bag of cookies I spotted earlier today too."

Darla jumped from the couch and raced into the kitchen. She retrieved some bowls, ice cream, and then dipped. After putting the carton away, she grabbed their frozen treats and hurried back to Stephanie with a dish in each hand and the cookies clenched between her teeth. She handed Stephanie her dessert and opened her jaw to drop the sack onto the coffee table. Seated, she spooned the extravagance and glided the sweet blend into her mouth.

"Not to change the subject, but what happened with your guy from Raging Impulse? Why was the date such a bomb?"

Stephanie opened the package to remove several cookies. She twisted one apart and ate the icing from the middle. She nonchalantly raised a shoulder. "The beginning wasn't awful. In fact, most of the evening was good for the time we were together. We left the party to go have a drink at the little bar across the highway from this subdivision. I didn't realize Blaine lived close to you. We exchanged phone numbers, so we'll see."

"You swapped numbers? That's it. No wonder the date was a disaster."

Stephanie took half of a cookie, scooped up some ice cream, and shoved the concoction into her mouth. "Yeah. There were..." Her expression displayed a trace of frustration. "Complications."

"Do you even like him?"

"I do," she admitted. "I love the Scottish accent or brogue, whatever you call it. I kind of get the idea there are some problems connected with his former band, possibly a few unresolved issues. The lead singer, Finn O'Conner, was at the bar too. With his brother." She shook her head. "The guy is messed up. I was so disappointed because during my younger days I thought he was sooo cute. His brain is fried, I'm guessing from past drug use. I'm not sure he wasn't wasted tonight. His brother." Stephanie rolled her eyes "Talk about a first class jerk. He showed up later on. I didn't realize he'd been a backup in their band. He kept mouthing off, like he hates everybody in the group for whatever it was they did to him. Finn wouldn't leave us alone either. He insisted he needed to talk to Blaine right away and Blaine should phone the other members and meet with him. Blaine kept telling him they'd get together another time. The two of them were such huge pests, and then Blaine got the news about Drake and everything was over. I told him to call me later and walked here. I wish I'd taken my car so I wouldn't have ended up soaked. End to a perfect night."

"I read Finn had substance abuse problems. Eric told me the band had been repressed because their tyrant manager treated them like prisoners for years. He implied they'd all been a little crazy since the break-up. I'd imagine some of Finn's difficulties stem from that."

Stephanie's eyebrows rose. "Eric?"

Darla stiffened.

"Darla." Stephanie leaned closer. "Eric? As in Eric Boyd, the lead guitarist from Raging Impulse?"

She looked down and stirred her ice cream. "Yes."

"I was unaware you were acquainted with Eric Boyd. You flat refused to meet any of those guys at the party. What happened to change your mind?"

Darla snapped her head up. "Nothing changed

anything. Eric Boyd and I don't know each other. I may have spilled my wine on him after I got a drink. We talked for a few minutes, things began to get out of hand, and we started to leave. Then the murder happened, so we were stuck together. Waiting forever. After we spoke with police, he walked me home." She shrugged. "That's all."

"Oh." Stephanie scraped the bottom of her bowl. "Sounds innocent enough. Except he told you about the group being suppressed by their nutty manager, and he made sure you got home okay. Kind of personal. A lot more information than Blaine gave me."

"Your circumstances were different."

Darla placed her empty dish on the coffee table and tucked her legs underneath her bottom.

Awkwardness swept over her that she didn't understand. The talk about Eric with her best friend made her uncomfortable. Normally they discussed everything. This should be no different, yet she wanted to keep her meeting with Eric to herself. Plus, she was uneasy admitting her eagerness for a casual hookup.

"Wait." Stephanie frowned and studied Darla. A slow smile spread across her face. "You *may* have spilled your wine on him?"

"Okay, we met when I spattered my drink all over him and I ruined his shirt." She gave a self-conscious chuckle. "I made a lasting impression, I'm sure." She continued to fill Stephanie in on most of the details.

"That's so not you. You're proper and always in control." Stephanie relaxed into the sofa. "What's Eric like? Did you have fun, at least until the tragedy happened?"

"It wasn't a big deal. We didn't form any real bond

or anything."

"Would making a connection with him be so bad?"

"I just got out of a relationship." She grasped for her favorite curl to wind around a finger. She wanted ensure her friend she indeed hadn't developed feelings for a man she'd only spent a few hours with. Plus she needed to be convinced.

"It's perfectly normal for you to have an interest in someone else even if you just split from your boyfriend."

"The guy broke my heart, remember? I'm only allowing myself to deal now. I'm having a hard time getting past the fact I've spent the last four years with the wrong person and not feeling like a total fool."

"We're all a work in progress. Let the experience with your ex help you learn something about yourself." Stephanie surveyed Darla. "Soooo, did you like Eric?"

"I guess he was all right." She pressed a hand to her forehead to fight the visions of those mind-blowing blue eyes. She needed to resort to throwing things at Stephanie to get her to quit talking about the guy so she'd stop thinking about him. Like that would happen anytime soon.

"There wasn't a lot for us to discuss. He's a musician. I'm a geologist. We don't have much in common."

"Oh, I don't know." Stephanie laughed. "You study rocks, he plays rock."

Darla chuckled too. "I hardly call that common ground."

"Yeah, though you have to agree. He's one fine-looking man."

"I think he's gorgeous. But he and I live in a

completely different universe. I tried to intertwine dissimilar lifestyles before. Things didn't work out so well. I'm not going there again."

Stephanie gave her a knowing glance. She set her bowl aside and leaned forward to open the laptop sitting nearby. Eric's picture instantly appeared on the screen.

Fan-friggin-tastic. Busted. Any logical explanation of why she'd been viewing Eric Boyd's photograph online other than the real reason failed her. In the end, she wouldn't be able to fool Stephanie anyway. She may as well come clean.

Darla's shoulders casually lifted then lowered. "I was curious."

"As you should be." Stephanie glanced at the photo before shifting back to Darla. "The two of you have a very opposites-attract kind of thing. That's huge. I bet some major sparks flew when you met."

"Yes on the opposite, no to attraction. There weren't any fireworks between us. Okay, well maybe a few. He seemed to like me a little. And I admit I thought about following in your footsteps and just going for it, but the murder destroyed the mood."

"Yes," Stephanie shouted. "To be continued later?"

"Doubtful. The idea has passed," she lied.

"If you say so." Stephanie stretched her legs and propped them onto the table, crossing her ankles. She lifted the computer to her lap. "Since the Raging Impulse website is open, I think I'll do some research on Blaine."

"Be my guest." Darla picked up the bowls and carried them into the kitchen. She flipped on the faucet and ran the dishes full of hot water, then returned to the living area to reclaim her spot on the sofa. A comfortable silence settled between the women. Darla's head drifted back as her eyes closed. Slowly, she gave into her weariness and drifted into a restful doze.

"Hey, did you read this article on their manager?"

Darla's head jerked up. "What?" She blinked several times, de-fuzzing her mind.

"Raging Impulse's manager."

"Shane?"

"Who?"

"Shane Macinsomething. I met him tonight too."

"I'm talking about their former manager. The bad guy." Stephanie gazed at Darla. "It says he was arrested and has been in jail for a while, and he recently escaped."

"No, I didn't read anything like that, but I wasn't searching for information about him." She shifted closer to Stephanie and looked over her shoulder. "What does the story say?"

"The beginning talks about how he broke out of prison, but that's not the interesting part." Stephanie leaned into the screen to read aloud.

"Pop artist's managers are often viewed as more infamous than the singers they represent. Dugan Holt joined the group of managerial disgrace many years ago. Holt, best known for the guidance of chart-busting protégés, Raging Impulse, raised them to staggering heights, but his career remains marred by a series of scandals, ending with a prison sentence for a number of illegal transgressions.

"He helped the band rise to fame from their obscure start, often playing at a now defunct club called Nutscrub. The members consisted of five Aberdeen University students: keyboardist Drake Maloney, second cousin Mitchell Young, who played drums, lead guitarist Eric Boyd, bass guitarist Blaine Stewart, and their singer, Max Sharp.

"Through musical contacts, Holt secured more gigs for the ensemble. As their reputation grew, he assumed the role of manager. Not happy with the singer, his first act as their leader was to replace Sharp with Finn O'Conner, an up-and-coming crooner from Ireland.

"Throughout their years together, they became a huge success. But the constant touring with little social life, plus the youngsters evolving into men caused many stress fractures to appear. Members got tired of the endless road trips and resented the purging of their private lives.

"Raging Impulse did not find their final years kind. Fans grew up, musical directions changed, but Holt refused to allow the band to evolve. Disagreements and hostilities surfaced even more. The turmoil between members remained constant throughout their time together, fueled by Holt as his way to maintain his hold over the men to focus away from possible shady dealings.

"The end occurred over two years ago, when an onstage clash, centered on O'Conner, who'd become increasingly difficult to work with, walked off and quit. The same night, a band member made the discovery of pornographic paraphilia on Holt's computer. During the porn investigation, the authorities also discovered a large amount of cannabis in his possession. Those findings led to Holt's arrest.

"After he was charged and booked, the remaining participants stood up and fired him, something they claimed they'd wanted to do for many years. The band tried to carry on but found no success. Their time was over."

Stephanie lifted her head from the article. "Nice guy."

"Seriously." Darla bent farther over her PC. "Turn the computer so I can see his picture."

Stephanie angled the laptop toward Darla. "Why? He's a creep and certainly nothing to look at."

"I'm curious. It occurred to me when you were reading, that this guy may hold some kind of resentment over the band. Drake might have been the one who fired him."

"You're thinking Dugan Holt escaped from prison in Scotland and managed to sneak into the U.S., and he killed Drake over a personal vendetta?"

"Stranger things have happened."

"Did you get a good look at the guy?"

"No." Darla fell back against the sofa. "He was dressed in dark clothing, and his head was covered with a motorcycle helmet."

"If you couldn't distinguish the guy's face, how is viewing this photo going to help?"

"The police asked me about height or build, but I can't recall anything specific. Maybe an image might jar something from my memory." Darla shook her head as she viewed the picture. "This guy appears heavier. The man that rammed into me was definitely muscular, though I guess that could change."

"Right. Anyone can lose weight and firm up." Stephanie's voice sounded cautious. "What happened after he ran into you?"

"He hurried underneath the deck, hopped on a motorcycle, and sped away."

"Were you able to spot anything unusual about the bike?"

"Just the color, which was black. I believe it was one those racing types where the rider has to hunch over. His helmet was a star-trooper meets oversized ant-man. Sinister looking."

"It may have been custom made."

"I'm not familiar enough to even make a guess. The only thing I know for sure is the scary life-sized action figure shoved me as he escaped."

Stephanie's eyes widened as she gasped loudly. A hand flew to her chest.

"Besides the obvious, what's wrong?"

"You're not going to believe this. When Blaine and I were walking to the bar, I swore that ant-trooper passed us on a dark motorcycle. He disappeared into a garage before I got a better look."

"In this area?"

"Yeah. I can't remember exactly where it's located, but the home was for sure in this neighborhood."

Darla stared at Stephanie. "So you're saying the killer lives nearby."

"That's exactly what I'm saying."

Chapter 6

Eric tugged his jacket closer to guard against the ocean's sharp breeze. He moved relatively normal for someone who'd taken huge sucker-punch. It'd been stupid of him to choose this route when the street seemed a lot more sensible. And it would have saved him from muddying up another pair of shoes.

Except being close to the water made him feel better. So instead of cutting through and heading home by way of asphalt, he continued his hike down the beach. A surge of fury tightened in his chest and once again he resisted the urge to smash something, an impulse he'd fought since he'd left Finn's. After many deep pants, he swallowed hard and relaxed his rage.

He touched his shirt pocket. Shit. He'd run out of cigarettes hours ago. This newest dilemma seemed to invoke a short-term memory loss, and he'd forgotten he chain-smoked an entire pack at Finn's. He was surprised he could breathe after inhaling so much nicotine. His lungs must love him right now.

Eric stopped. He plowed his fingers through his hair and stared into the blackness. A blast of cold air smacked him in the face, knocking him backward. Nothing new. Every time he took what he perceived as a step forward, something always shoved him back. Not a couple of steps either, but flat on his ass. This past year he'd finally gotten things under control, or so he thought. Now he understood. Any power he believed he may've had over his destiny was nothing short of laughable.

At least everything made sense. If understanding was a consolation.

He turned to the homes across the beach. Unlike earlier, they were dark now, sitting eerily quiet. A murky gray fog hovered around the bottoms. Kinda like he felt. Jamming his fists into his pockets, he bowed against the strong wind and moved forward. Several lengths down the shoreline, he drew up to pause again. Darla Hennessey's house sat about a hundred yards away. He shook his head and wished for memory loss concerning this girl.

Yet, she'd stayed in the back of his mind. Even after Drake's death, and during his meeting with Finn, he couldn't erase the image of her. He didn't have the energy to analyze these unwanted feelings either. He wanted to smother them for good.

He almost laughed out loud. It'd probably help if he quit acting like some lovesick teenager, and not stalked her home in the middle of the night. Maybe he should cut through to the street now. Go around the block and miss her house altogether. He was an idiot. At this hour smart girls like her were snug in their beds sound asleep. Usually alone.

Eric took a step then froze. Did he spot a movement on her deck? He remained motionless and watched. Nothing happened. Exhaustion and frustration must produce hallucinations. He gave the house a final glance, and took another stride.

A shift in shadows once more caught his attention.

He stopped again and focused through the hazy vapors. An outline of someone stood on her deck, but he didn't know if the person was Darla. It might be, so why go by there if he didn't want to meet up with her again? He made a sharp turn to cut in between two houses, prepared to finish his journey on the road. No more taking gambles in his life. He was done.

****

Darla slid open the door and stepped outside. In an instant, her bare feet were wet from the rain's residue streaming across the deck. She treaded carefully upon the wooden planks until she reached the edge and leaned over the rail to stare into the mist, listening to the rumble of waves.

A frosty breeze followed the storm, triggering her body to shiver. Darla didn't like the cold, but tonight the nippiness held a certain allure. She inhaled deeply to swallow a bite of bitter air. Eyes closed, she wished she'd fall asleep and stay asleep for a week. Too many things weighed on her mind. The murder, the possibility of a killer living near—her ex.

The guy was the love of her life. He'd made promises, promises that turned into lies. The harsh reality proved to be clear. As of tonight, he was a married man. Then there was Eric. What were the odds she'd meet him on the evening of her former boyfriend's wedding? If nothing else, their encounter was a pleasant diversion from the disappointment she'd suffered. She needed to keep their meeting in a "distraction" perspective, although she didn't want to.

A sudden heavy gust blew right through her. The thin pajama bottoms and tank top offered no protection against the chill. Her feet had already converted into blocks of ice. Enough invigoration. She turned to go inside.

"Darla?"

Darla whipped around and peered over the edge of the rail.

"That's your name, right?" Shane climbed the steps to her deck.

Darla clenched her fists. Shane was a good-looking guy, but his association with Eric Boyd was what expanded her heart. And Eric wasn't with Shane.

"Why are you out this late?"

Shane chuckled. "I manage musicians. I never sleep." He climbed to the top of the deck and stopped near her. "Hey, I think I know where you might've seen me. You're a walker, aren't you? You walk the beaches path?"

"Every morning."

"Me too. Actually I'm a runner. Sometimes I crash at Eric's place and I like to go for an early jog. I bet we've seen each other then." He placed his hands on his hips. "Speaking of Eric, you two didn't hook up?"

Darla glanced from side to side before she returned to Shane. "You don't see him here, do you?"

"Ah, touchy, aren't we?" He held Darla's stare. "It's surprising he didn't find his way back to you. That's all."

Darla dropped her gaze and leaned against the rail, arms crossed over her middle. "He seemed pretty torn up about the loss of a friend."

"He is. But if his sight is set on you, the death of someone close isn't going to stop him."

Her eyes ripped back to Shane. "That's an awful thing to say."

Shane's mouth lifted into an almost serene smile. "I'm aware I'm making him sound coldhearted, and he's not really. You have to understand the world he lives in is completely different from ours. His crowd bends the rules beyond the realms of acceptability sometimes, at least in the way normal people view things."

"I suppose, but I still don't get it."

"Me either." Shane shook his head. "You seem like a nice girl. Maybe it'd be in your best interest to steer clear of the guy."

"I don't believe that's going to be a problem." Darla pushed off the banister, running her hands up and down her bare arms.

"Cold?"

She nodded. "The storm made it feel like winter is here again."

He shook out of his jacket and draped it across Darla's shoulders. She almost refused the offer, wanting to remove the coat, and hand it back to him. But his body heat generated from the inside of the material was too enticing. Shane slid his palms over her covered arms, then drew the lapels together.

"Regardless of how you perceive the situation with Eric, he'll be around." Shane's tone almost held a hint of warning as he dropped his hands.

"He won't. We're too different."

Shane chuckled and nodded toward the beach. "Are you?"

Darla followed his direction to capture a blue stare piercing into her. She sucked in a gulp of air with a groan. "Oh no." Her palms cupped her warming cheeks as she returned Eric's unreadable look.

Shane bent closer to her and spoke low enough so that only she could hear. "What'd I tell you?"

Darla ignored him and continued to watch Eric. What were the odds two men would show up at the same time? In the middle of the night, no less. The love gods must hate her.

"Thought you'd gone home." Eric spoke to Shane, though his eyes remained on Darla.

"Too upset to sleep. I needed to walk, and the shore was inviting."

"I hear you. I'm functioning on caffeine and nicotine overload. The need to get close to nature is necessary so I don't explode." Eric paused. "Where are you off to or—?" He sent a sharp nod toward Darla.

"I planned on staying at your place, but I think I'll go back to my hotel." Shane glanced at Darla before he stepped down from the staircase. "I'll be headin' that way now." He released a soft chuckle. "You two have a wonderful evening."

He vanished into the darkness leaving Eric to scowl at her.

Eric finally broke eye contact followed by a solid shake of his head. "Sorry for the interruption." His voice sounded colder than the icy wind.

A tiny tremor zipped through her veins, then she mentally reminded herself any involvement with the guy would mean swimming into rough waters. "No interruption. I'm just like you guys. I couldn't sleep and stepped outside for some fresh air. Shane walked by, the same as you."

"Right. You needed air." His jaw tightened as he eyed her up and down. "Nice jacket, by the way." Eric turned away. Pools of eerie streetlights silhouetted his frame. He gazed into the ocean's darkness, hands thrust into his pockets. He remained stoic, surveying the angry breakers. Waves rushed over the blackened sands and stopped at the tips of his shoes.

Darla stared at him, shocked by the edge in his voice. Did he really think something was going on between her and Shane? And—was he jealous? She might be out of practice, but he acted as if he resented his manager spending time with her. The idea, especially with Shane's blasé attitude was preposterous.

Darla's lips twisted as she gazed at him almost innocently. "Does my wearing Shane's coat bother you?"

****

Hell yes, it bothered him. But not as much as Shane touching her. He didn't understand why either. Frustration oozed from every point of Eric's brain. Fury had overcome him when he'd spied what appeared to be an intimate conversation between his buddy and Darla. After everything he'd learned tonight, plus the loss of someone he loved as a brother, these unwanted—what?—feelings for this woman didn't make sense.

He'd performed in front of royalty, government officials, and hundreds of thousands of people without sweating a drop. He was known for having ice water flow through his veins. His middle name was control. Yet, here he was. Darla Hennessy somehow had him fighting out of control emotions.

"None of my concern." His voiced hitched a little. "You might want to rethink getting involved with Shane McIntyre, though. He's not the best choice for smart girl types."

Darla laughed.

"Did I say something funny?"

"Kind of." She carefully stepped down the decks stairs, walked across the wet sand, and stopped next to him.

"Laugh all you want. Ignore my warning." He lifted a shoulder. "Your call."

"Warn me, huh?" She was clearly still amused. "He pretty much gave me the same advice about you."

It was Eric's turn to laugh. Only it wasn't a humorous one. "I bet he did." He kicked at a shell with more force than he intended. "The guy's a player. You should be careful around him."

"You're suggesting he wants to play me?"

A gust of wind lifted her curly locks. She shook the wild mane from her eyes, knocking the jacket to the ground, and revealing a lightly colored top. There was just enough light from the street behind to reveal a faint outline of her pert nipples through the thin material. The superb sight sent a low burning jolt inside his belly, and propelled all thoughts of Shane into obscurity.

"He insinuated you weren't to be trusted either."

His gaze remained on her breasts as his mouth curved. "I'm not."

The dim glow caught her surprised expression. She fidgeted, seemingly struggling for words. "I suppose I'm grateful for your honesty."

"It has nothing to do with honesty. I just don't play games."

Again, she appeared to strain to reply. "So what should I do with this information?" She bent to pick up the coat, swung it over her shoulders, and drew the edges together.

"Dunno." He shrugged as he turned away. "Do whatever you want."

****

Darla let out a lengthy breath. She wasn't sure how to proceed. Maybe the smart move would be for her to bid him good night, walk inside, and go to bed. She jerked the lapels tighter.

He bent to catch her gaze. "Jacket keeping you warm?"

"It helps. But I'm still a little chilly."

His lips turned into a slow easy smile that was somehow lethal and dreamy at the same time. His accent thickened. "Anything I can do to heat you up?"

"You're going to offer me another jacket?" Darla managed to maintain his level of intonation.

He took a step closer, leaned forward, and rumbled in a deep, low chuckle. "I know of a few other ways to warm you." His voice filled with a raspy passion she found startling, alluring. He glided his arm around her waist and dragged her into him, fitting their bodies together. Shane's jacket slipped from her shoulders again, but she was no longer cold. Eric held her tight, letting her know she couldn't escape even if she'd wanted to.

In a split second Darla found her insides quivered from need. Her hands automatically floated over his chest until her fingers linked behind his neck. She drew his head down. Their gazes connected.

A corner of his lip lifted, his eyes glittered with a knowing tease. Then his mouth closed over hers. Her mind froze. His lips were firm as he kissed her hard and hungry. His tongue filled the inside of her mouth, stroking, teasing, tasting her with a fierce exploration, carrying her away in his desire. His grip tensed around her to draw her in closer. There would be no barriers with this man. He wouldn't allow it.

Internal heat roared faster than the storm earlier, searing into every single one of her pores. She craved more. The musky scent of his skin, his mouth, the tobacco taste, the way he held her. She wanted all of him.

Abruptly, he broke the kiss and took a step backward. Darla looked at him, blinking in confusion. Disarmed—naked. Her mind whirled in a jumbled uncertainty. She lifted a hand and touched her burning lips.

His gaze skated across the darkness, and then he returned to her with a wicked smile.

He bent to pick up the coat and brushed away the sand. His eyes twinkled as he wrapped the jacket around her. "Don't know about you, but I'm a bit overheated after that."

With a step backward, he flicked his gaze to her one last time before he turned to disappear into the night. "Sleep tight, luv."

Chapter 7

His world was going to hell. Eric let the door slam behind him as he entered the house. He kicked off his muddy shoes and wrangled out of his jacket, dropping it to the floor, then he walked straight to the bathroom. After a harried search through cabinets and drawers, he found a plastic bottle of antacids. He held the frosted container up to the light fixture. Fuck. Almost empty. The interiors of his gut exploded like a million pound wrecking ball swung inside. He needed something for relief.

Maybe he could drive to the all-night convenience store located several blocks over and pick up some meds along with a pack of cigarettes. He was in dire need of a smoke. Except he was too tired to go anywhere. With a flip of a thumb, he popped the lid, filled his hand with the bottle's contents, then he shoved the pills into his mouth. He dropped the empty tablet jar back into the drawer, leaned against the bathroom sink, and shook his head.

This evening started out a good one before turning to shit in a hurry. Drake's death, Dugan's disappearance, Finn's revelation, Darla.

Darla. What the hell was he thinking? He'd kissed her. His life took another major plunge, one to where he may never recover. Instead of working on rectifying the situation, his attention stayed on her. If he'd taken the street route as he intended, the kiss wouldn't have happened.

He had to loop back to check out the person on her deck and satisfy his curiosity. Well, he found satisfaction all right. If he hadn't kept enough of his sanity to break away after the one kiss, he'd have lost all his senses and taken her on the beach.

And what was she doing letting Shane touch her that way? Eric already had the answer. Shane was a total ass when dealing with women. The two of them together perturbed the hell out of him. Then he wondered why he cared.

He struggled to swallow. The meds morphed into the equivalent of a mouthful of compressed chalk swollen between his jaws. He gulped several times. The mass caught in his throat. Too big to force down.

He fell to his knees and leaned over the toilet. After taking a deep breath through his nose, he tried to exhale in an attempt to dislodge the oversized glob, but he gagged instead. With the edge of his palm placed under his diaphragm, he gave his gut several hard thrusts. The blockage finally broke free. He spit the grit into the commode, and then dissolved into a choking fit.

"You okay?"

Eric looked up.

Blaine stood in his bathroom doorway. His expression appeared wary as he studied Eric. "Sounds like you're dying in here."

Eric swallowed, hacking a "Yeah, I'm fine," and sat back onto the floor.

Blaine leaned against the frame and crossed his arms over his chest. "You're doing better than me, mate."

"I meant I'm not dying from the overload of antacids I tried to inhale." He reached to a rack above his head, ripped the towel away from the bracket, and swiped it over his mouth. "If you're asking me if I'm okay from the ass-kicking we've just discovered from our visit with Finn, then no, I'm no good at all." He wadded the towel into a ball and flung it across the room. "Please tell me Finn is playing one of his sick jokes."

Blaine gave a shrug followed by a heavy sigh. "I wish."

"I don't understand how we were so stupid."

"Don't know either." Blaine rubbed the back of his neck and stared at Eric. He appeared to be in a dazed fog. "But we were."

"You say it almost too easy."

"To be truthful, this news has stunned me. Once Finn accused us of taking his money, my gut told me something was up. Only I didn't think things would be this bad. The realization hit me probably 'bout the same time you figured the problem out too. I couldn't breathe. My chest got tight. I was scared I'd pass out." Blaine's skin flushed from the memory. "Sorry I left you on your own, but I needed out of there. The tension filled Finn's house the moment we stepped inside. Seemed to get worse the longer we stayed. I'm surprised you hung around as long as you did."

Blaine was right. The pressure was high when they arrived. Finn expected them to not only apologize for their behavior toward him during their final performance, which they did, but he also wanted the two to write him a check to return funds he was sure the band had stolen from him throughout his span with the group.

Which they had not. After calming Finn down, they convinced him they hadn't taken his money. To help him out, the men spent several hours assessing the shape of his accounts, and then they examined his income. They realized Finn was correct. The compensations he should have been paid for his time as lead singer of Raging Impulse wasn't there.

"I tried to quiet Finn a bit, although Richard being 'round didn't help the situation. I hate that guy." Eric shook his head. "He despises me too."

"I think he dislikes all of us, including his own brother." Blaine nodded. "Finn's an ass, whereas Richard is scum. I can't believe we kept him around for as long as we did."

"If he wasn't such a spineless perv, I'd suspect him of working for Dugan."

"You mean as his hit man?" Blaine bit his bottom lip. "Yeah, I could believe that."

"But I don't think Richard's our problem. We have to deal with the fact Finn is now our ally. I'm not sure that's a good thing. Anyway, after I left him, I took the long way home by walking the beach. I wanted to clear my head. Maybe come up with some ideas on how to fight this."

Eric did his best to put away his reflections of Darla Hennessy. The mention of his trip home brought on a rush of memories of her. He needed to get this woman out of his head. There were too many other issues to deal with right now. He rose from the bathroom floor and walked into his room. Blaine trailed close behind.

"I don't understand," Eric seethed. "We are the highest selling teen band of all time. Twelve number one records plus seven top-selling albums. We were on the road almost every day for eight years. Our concerts sold out, including standing room only. The T-shirt and merchandising sales alone should've made us enough money to retire on and live comfortably for the rest of our lives. We also were to be paid residuals for our song writing, not to mention compensation for the music we published. What the fuck happened to it?"

"Good question. There should be some major royalty checks from our record company too."

Neither spoke for a full minute.

"Seems unreal we're broke. All those years, now we've got nothing to show for the work we've done." Eric tracked to his closet. He opened a small trunk and rummaged through. He lugged out a thick folder, then carried it to his bed. Sitting on the side, he sifted through the pages in the file. "I checked in my bank account this morning, I had plenty of cash."

"Same here." Blaine picked up a binder he'd evidently left on Eric's dresser when he'd come in earlier. He settled on the opposite side of the mess of paperwork. "I went over my contracts after I got home."

He held open a marked place in the notebook and pointed to an area for Eric to examine. "I found the exact clause in every one of them. It's in small print, like we discovered in Finn's. I bet you'll find the same in yours."

Eric glanced over at the passage Blaine indicated. "Yeah, I'm thinking that too." He returned to his papers, taking several minutes to research before he nodded with a frown. "Here it is." He tapped the paper with a forefinger. "Same as yours, same as Finn's." He shifted on the bed and stared at Blaine. "Dugan maintained power of attorney over all of our assets. We unknowingly signed every penny over to him." His grimace deepened as he released a massive sigh. "This means he went into our investment and bank accounts at will. I'm guessing he cleaned each one of us out before he closed them down. Now he's disappeared with nearly all of our cash."

"You said he'd be coming after us. What better way to get to us than take our holdings. He left enough in our principal account to last for a time while we were none the wiser. Now he can hide anywhere in the world and live off our millions."

"And use our money to hire someone to get rid of us. How's that for poetic justice?"

Blaine's mouth twisted. "Bastard."

"That he is. But we already knew that, didn't we? Yet we trusted him to act in the band's best interest. We were fools." Eric gathered his documents and straightened them before he put them back into the binder. "I'm sure we'll get a better idea how this all happened by looking up this stuff online. We may find out if he took everything at once or a little at a time. Except, he probably pass-coded those accounts so I don't know if we will be able to get in."

"More than likely he's shut 'em down, but we should check anyway."

Eric glanced at Blaine. "Did you call Mitchell?"

"I did talk to Mitchell. He's pretty upset about Drake, and this news makes things even worse. He's gonna investigate on his end and let us know what he finds tomorrow. Though he figures he'll get the same results."

Eric slammed the folder shut. "Shit. I can't believe we were so damn gullible. We should've watched our money closer."

"Look, I know we're troubled over this, but still we can't go kicking ourselves over something that's already done. It's not an excuse, except we were young when we hooked up with Dugan. We come from meager backgrounds. None of us knew much about investment management, because we didn't have any money to worry over. Like you said, we always assumed Dugan took care of our finances."

"Oh, he took care of them all right."

"He did. Once we got a taste of having cash all the time, we never thought we'd need to bother ourselves over money." Blaine rolled off the bed. "Why would we? We were a huge success. Dugan always made sure we had enough in our pockets. We assumed there'd be plenty."

"True." Eric motioned to the folder. "Except us being naïve about investments isn't a good excuse. We could've become smarter. It was clear early on what Dugan was. We looked the other way on a lot of things. Our minds were on making it big and he was doing that for us, so who cared about his outside activities. My parents were against me getting into the music business, but I told them I planned on following my ambition regardless. My dad suggested a lawyer review every document before I signed anything. In the beginning, I couldn't afford one. After I had the money, I didn't want to bother. We were too busy. So I lied. I said I handled things as a way to blow him off. He's gonna have a say after I give him this news."

"My family advised the same thing," Blaine agreed. "They'll be disappointed in me too."

"Damn, I wish we had listened. When Dugan was still our manager, we may have had some options. Now I'm not so sure." Eric lifted his shoulders. "We're just aware."

"I'm holding out we're wrong. Maybe Finn's confused about what he spent."

Eric gave him a doubtful look. "As long as you're not holdin' your breath." He nodded toward the file in front of him. "From the way those papers read, we're fucked."

Blaine began to pace. "Yeah. I guess Finn going through cash like water is a good thing, or it might have been months, even years before we made this discovery."

"We can go over this stuff more thoroughly tomorrow. See what we find. I'm hoping there's a legal loophole which will give us a way to recover our losses without having to hire a shitload of attorneys we can't afford." He ran a hand through his hair. "Although I'm betting these contracts are airtight. More than likely we will need to go to court, and we stand a chance of losing. We'd end up spending the money we have left on lawyer fees and get nothing."

"You're forgetting something else." Blaine stopped wandering. "Eric." He directed a worried glance toward the closed binder lying on the bed. "We've funded this new band with our own money. We've footed the bill for everything. Studio time, producing, marketing, you name it, the costs has been on us. We're only in the beginning stages, so we're hardly in a place where we're gonna be earning our investment back anytime soon. If all the money we have is in that one account, we'll need to keep every penny to live on. We're going to have to put this venture on hold."

Eric scowled as he considered what Blaine told him. Each word made perfect sense in his head, yet his gut yelled no. He wouldn't surrender his goal easily. One he so desired to reach. "We'll find other ways to raise funds."

"How? We tried to regroup after Finn quit and we canned Dugan. No one would touch us, although I'm sure the exposure of Dugan's activities may have something to do with that. We were a teen band. We're like poison in the legitimate rock world. The negativity and rejection disillusioned Drake and Mitchell so much they retired from the business to do other things. We're lucky Shane is around to manage us, though I dunno how long we'll be able to afford to keep him."

"There has to be a way. We've worked too damn hard, Blaine. Money aside, you and I are literally crawling out of the depths of teen idol hell, and are working into the ranges of respectability. I don't want to throw that away or let this dream die."

"Yeah, but we've been quiet about our newer happenings. People are starting to hear our later stuff, especially in the UK, although no one has an idea it's us. We must maintain our anonymity for continued success, at least for the time being. Any rumblings from our camp will kill us professionally. Your idea to keep our presences out of the new band was great and helped us acquire many new fans. But even if our songs are good now, we can't risk being discovered, and asking someone to bank us could bring us down. The music world may be massive, but it's a small one too. People talk. Word surely will get out and sink us again. Our time and money would be wasted."

"We've got to work at something, for something. I'm not gonna quit, Blaine. I'm going to find Dugan Holt. He has our money and I'm getting every cent back."

"I hope you do," Blaine said as he left the room. "I hope you find him before he finishes off any more of us."

Eric stared at the door. His mind whirled over the chaos from the last few hours. He slipped off the bed to put his folder back in his closet, and then stomped into the bathroom. He stretched inside the tub and twisted the knob. Water spurted from the showerhead. He quickly undressed, leaving his clothes in a heap beside the sink before he stepped into the bathtub and yanked the curtain. After a long, cool shower, he swiped up the towel he'd thrown earlier, dried, and dropped it back onto the floor.

Naked and exhausted, he walked into his room, then fell onto his bed. With his mind in a constant churn, sleep wasn't going to come. For the first time in a while, he wished for a dose of the barbiturates Dugan use to give him regularly. The pills didn't necessarily let him rest as much as they numbed him. Right now he needed not to feel.

Because of his past addictions, he refused to take the risk. Strong sleep medications, even the over-the-counter kind would never pass across his lips again. Not only did his physical strength depend on him staying clean, but also his psychological concentration needed him to keep his head clear. There was one other thing that helped him relax.

Sex.

Once more he fought the mental picture of Darla. He rejected going back to that place. He pulled a sheet over him, closed his tired eyes, and willed his attention in the direction of sleep. Neither his mind nor body obliged. Reflections of her materialized, then transformed into sexual fantasies. He became restless, excited with urges impossible to overlook. He wanted to see her, touch her, and to kiss her. He wanted her.

He tossed the covers away and rolled off the bed. He had to get this woman out of his system. A quick glance at the clock told him daybreak would be approaching soon. Too late to go to her or too early depending on how she'd view things. Besides, he didn't mentally want to be with her. The rest of him was the problem, overruling his stupid head. An idea arose.

He might be able to find another resolution. A substitute would do the trick, yes, a stand-in. His body wouldn't know the difference. He was lucky enough to be acquainted with several ladies he could call on for this sort of occasion. They'd come to him even at this hour, no questions. These women would give him the physical relief he needed and politely leave after. A good romp with someone else may get Darla out of his thoughts. Help form a detachment from her.

He took several long strides across the room to find his phone. His foot tapped an object on the floor. The thing skidded over the aged hardwood and stopped against his dresser. He frowned as he walked to where the entity lay. His song writing tablet.

He bent to pick it up and reread the words of a sweet, innocent girl with haunting dark eyes.

Forcefully, he flung the pad through the air. It hit the window and dropped to the floor with a loud plop. The early stages of dawn filtered through the exposed glass. The light molded an odd but beautiful radiance over the pad, as if this were a sign. The words he'd written were his promises to her, penned for her from the depths of his heart.

He commanded himself not to be so farfetched and fell onto his bed, sick of his over-analysis of a woman he most positively didn't plan to see again. Palms pressed against his eye sockets, he realized no physical replacement would suffice tonight. So for now, he'd forget the idea of calling someone else. He grabbed the covers bringing them to his neck and closed his eyes. He tossed and turned for a short time, then fatigue overcame him.

A soft noise made him jerk his head up. Did he dream the knock or was someone tapping on his bedroom door?

The rap occurred again. "Eric?" Blaine called quietly.

Eric fell back against the pillows as he answered a tired, "Come in."

Blaine rushed inside and stood motionless in the middle of the room almost as if he was lost. Eric rose to his elbows not needing to ask if something else happened. Even in the dim light, his partner's skin appeared pallid. Visibly shaken to the point of looking ill.

A dark premonition overcame Eric. This bombshell Blaine was about to drop would have a permanent effect over the rest of their lives and they'd never be the same.

Chapter 8

"Stephanie." Darla hurried inside barely shutting the back door before she remembered a killer may be lurking within the neighborhood. Backtracking, she rushed to the door and twisted the lock. After she was sure everything was secure, she sped through the house, stopping long enough to toss Shane's jacket across the sofa, and then onto the spare bedroom to where her friend slept.

Stephanie had decided to stay the night instead of driving home in the middle of the thunderstorm, and she was surely asleep by now. But it was necessary to rouse her to update her on this newest event while fresh in Darla's mind. Besides, Stephanie would yank every strand of hair out of her head if she waited until morning to deliver this news. Plus, she needed to talk about it.

She knocked on the door and opened it, surprised to find the light on and Stephanie leaning against a stack of pillows studying her phone. She tore her eyes away from the device as Darla entered the room. "You're still up? You went to bed a long time ago."

Darla nodded. "I couldn't sleep, so I stepped outdoors to get some air."

She eyed Darla and frowned. "Do you think it's such a good idea to be outside alone at night after what happened several houses away, just a few hours ago? Especially when we believe the guy may live close by."

"I'm aware. But as you stated earlier, we're nobodies within that circle. I doubt the assassin possesses a guest list nor would he care who was there." She strayed closer to the bed. "After I gave the situation some thought, I tend to agree with Eric. Drake was a target and someone hired the killer to do the job. I'm not familiar with the profession, but from stories I've read a trained assassin's goal is to go unnoticed. Blend in, so no one can identify them. Why wouldn't he behave like a normal person and live in our neighborhood? Though this guy wore a space suit, which hardly fits the obscure description."

"True. But even in costume, he managed to cover his tracks well. He was capable of killing someone and slip in and out of a house full of people without anyone able to describe him. Perhaps he's an introverted exhibitionist kind of killer."

"Whatever he is, he got the job done."

Stephanie's cell beeped. She looked down at the screen and smiled.

Darla's brows dipped as she watched her friend. "You're still on your phone at this time of night? Or morning. Are you addicted to the thing?"

She chuckled, and glanced at Darla. "No. I've been talking to Blaine. Texting actually. Or we were. He had to take a phone call a while ago. Now I'm rereading our conversations."

Darla clenched her jaw while Stephanie clicked away on the miniature keyboard. Envy welled in her chest. She wished Eric had been interested enough to ask for her number. It'd be nice to be texting sweet nothings instead of enduring his carefree triviality.

Stephanie sat back and motioned at the small screen. "We were talking about getting together tomorrow." She giggled again. "Go out to dinner and do something after."

"How wonderful, Steph. I'm glad the number exchange is a success."

Darla lay across the end of the bed and played with a loose thread on the comforter. She shifted to her butt, unable to get comfortable.

Stephanie's gaze returned to phone. "We both love Polynesian food. Can you believe that?"

"You're like the same person."

Steph leaned forward and made a soft "hmmm" noise.

"That sounds promising. What's the discussion you're reviewing now? Names of your children?"

"No. Actually, I'm online checking Raging Impulse's website. The person who keeps the page maintained does regular updates."

"Any more news about Drake's death or their fugitive manager?"

"Nothing on either, other than what we already know. Although the author does give a rundown of all of the members, past and present. I didn't realize they'd been together for so many years." She held out the cell. "You want a peek? The site has some interesting info on Eric's background."

"I'm sure it does, but I'll check it out tomorrow. Maybe. I think I need to get past wanting to know anything about him."

Darla rolled her shoulders and skimmed her tongue across her lips. She needed to reveal to her friend about

Eric and their kiss. Several times she'd tried to say the words, except they caught in her throat. She couldn't understand why informing Stephanie was difficult. This entire situation knocked her to the ground and she didn't know what to do with these feelings. She craved her friend's dose of commonsense and rationality so she could move on.

"Something else happened. Here tonight."

Stephanie's attention refocused to Darla. She gave her a worried stare. "You're making me nervous."

"Yeah, I've shaken me up a little too." She paused. "It's like I've always thought of myself as a together person and—I don't know."

"Tell me everything." Stephanie gave Darla a meaningful look. "Whatever it is, I'll support you. I may rip your hair out for doing something stupid, but I'll be there for you in the end."

Darla gasped and shook her head violently. "I didn't do anything bad."

"Then what?"

"Eric Boyd. He showed up. Here."

Stephanie's eyes widened. "Eric stopped by to see you? When?"

"More like passing the house."

The memory of Eric's kiss scorched her lips. She reached for an errant curl to wind the lock though her fingers as she dealt with another upsurge of sensations she had no clue how to deal with. A stitch of dread escalated over the mere idea of explaining the situation.

She giggled nervously. "He walked by when I was outside."

Stephanie blinked several times and stared. "So he passed your place. Why is that weird? He lives a few houses down."

"He stopped."

"Well, you did just meet. It's only polite. Are you tense around him?"

Darla expelled a long flow of air. "Yeah, I'm jittery whenever he's near. And I think he's aware of what he does to me."

"Okay, so what'd he do to make you feel that way?"

"He seemed a bit agitated." Darla's tone elevated.

"Start from the beginning. Tell me the whole story."

Darla inhaled and explained the entire event, but stopped before the kiss.

"He sounds upset, but that would make sense. He's gone through a lot tonight." She hesitated for a moment. "Did he think you have something going on with this Shane person? Romantically?"

Darla took the edge of the comforter, drew it over her legs, and uneasily smoothed the cover across her lap with both hands. "I wondered that too."

"Maybe he was jealous." Stephanie sounded mystified. "Are you sure nothing went on between the two of you?"

"Shane and me?"

"No dummy. You and Eric."

"I think I'd know if something happened with us."

Stephanie gave her a doubtful look.

"Okay, in some situations I wouldn't, but this time I do." She stopped glanced downward before she raised her eyes and gazed at Stephanie. "He kissed me." Heat prickled across her skin just from saying the words out loud.

Stephanie's face brightened as she sat up straighter.

"Eric Boyd kissed you?"

Darla nodded.

She pointed a finger at Darla. "You tell me everything, and you tell me now."

"This is so unfair," Stephanie cried when Darla finished her story. "You got to kiss Eric."

"Not in a romantic way or from some deep feelings he has for me. This stemmed from something else, Steph."

"So you're saying the kiss wasn't any good?"

Darla opened her mouth to protest, but her vocal cords stiffened. She sighed, almost defeated. "No. Truthfully, even unexplainably, he was amazing. I can't stop thinking about it."

Stephanie waved a hand in front of her. "There you go. You wanted to leave the party the minute I suggested you meet the guy. You almost ran out of the house. Then you dump your wine on him and he walks you home. He comes back in the middle of the night and gives you a wonderful kiss."

"His behavior was probably rooted from some strange—phenomenon. Possibly the storm or the violent death of a friend caused him to act irrationally. Or maybe the incident stemmed from pointless male competition with Shane. Who knows?"

Stephanie barked a laugh, although it held no humor. She blinked hard at Darla. "I had a drink with Blaine and his former band mate made such an ass of himself, we barely exchanged names much less anything else. I walked here by myself, through a frickin' thunderstorm. I didn't even get a handshake out of the deal and you're complaining about a wonderful kiss?"

"Stephanie. You and Blaine are texting and are planning an evening. I'm sure you'll get a lot more than a mocking kiss. Come on. Eric kissed me because he was only trying to establish territory. The whole thing could have been much better." Darla released a huff.

"Like you said, he's from a different world, but that isn't a factor."

"Now what are you talking about?"

"Karma. Fate, chance whatever. I don't believe in coincidences, Darla. You fought meeting Eric Boyd, yet somehow it happened." Her voice quieted. "The guy entered your life for a reason."

"Now you sound like my mother with her beliefs in crazy hocus-pocus stuff."

"Think what you want, but your interactions with Mr. Eric Boyd are far from over."

Darla made a face as she shook her head. "I guarantee we're done."

An unexpected tingle surged over her spine. She didn't understand if the sensation was a foreshadow of Stephanie's prediction or a rush of disappointment of never seeing Eric again.

"When we met earlier, Shane told me of Eric's interest, but he also warned me that Eric was only a one night kind of guy. He won't hang around for an encore where women are concerned."

"Okaaay." Stephanie's fingers clicked at her cell. "Take things at face value. You've been warned. Still, that doesn't mean he can't change or won't change. And even if what Shane says is true, then be glad you got a real kiss from a hunky star. How many women get to do that in their lifetime?"

Darla yawned. "I suppose." She pushed the covers

back, scooted off the bed, and straightened the edge. "I don't want to think about him anymore. I am so tired," she grumbled. "I bet I won't rest though, thanks to Mr. Boyd." She glanced at Stephanie and almost smiled. "I believe I'm beginning to dislike men."

Stephanie laughed. "Sometimes I do too. I think I'm writing off sleeping tonight and catching my z's after the sun comes up."

"You do whatever." Darla moved to leave. "I'm going to bed and try to sleep."

She'd barely left the room when Stephanie whispered a breathy, "Oh my."

A sudden shock of fear swept through her. She cracked the door and peeked inside. From across the way, she met Stephanie's gaze.

"This is so awful."

Darla inhaled deep, clutching the jam. "Did they find the manager? Is he behind Drake's death?"

Stephanie shook her head. "I just received a text from Blaine. Another of Raging Impulse's members was shot."

Her heart clenched, her immediate thoughts leaped to Eric. What if something happened to him? She couldn't accept the idea of him being gone.

"Mitchell Young was discovered with a bullet wound in his head," Stephanie whispered, her expression terrified. "The good news is, though, he's still alive."

A mental relief rushed through Darla, and then almost immediately guilt swallowed her. She shouldn't focus her worries on Eric. Instead, she should be remorseful for their family. First Drake was dead and now Mitchell was injured.

"Does he say what happened?

Stephanie lifted her phone to read. "Sorry, I won't be able to continue our conversation tonight. Just got the worst news as if anything else could be more awful than what's already occurred tonight. Mitchell Young, Raging Impulse's drummer, was found shot behind the ear at his house. The doctors haven't released a lot of information except he is still alive, though barely. Gotta go. I'll call you tomorrow." Stephanie dropped her arm to her lap. "This is too strange. But I believe there's something to what you were saying earlier. These occurrences have to be the work of an expert gunman, though I wonder why anyone would do this."

"I don't understand either." Darla turned her gaze to her friend. "But I do have one fear."

"Which is?"

"The band is being targeted. Someone is trying to eliminate the entire group. Maybe we need to stay away from them."

Chapter 9

Eric grazed the tips his fingers over his forehead as he studied the computer screen. Brows drawn together, he looked away from the monitor to scan the mounds of legal documents strewn across the dining table. He selected a particular page to study, his eyes seesawing between the paper and the display.

"Find anything?"

He jerked his chin as Blaine entered the room. He gave his head a solid shake and flipped the sheet onto a pile, prompting pieces to scatter then float to the floor.

"My mind is numb from going through all this shit." He rubbed a hand over his face. "These contracts are worded in a confusing way. I can't make out what most of this crap means."

Blaine picked up a stack of documents and after a glimpse, made a face. "I just got off the phone with our record company. They're going to be emailing us our royalty information and some documents for us to sign to have any money we're entitled to from past albums deposited into a new account."

"That's good, I guess." Eric paused. "But I think we need to break down and hire a lawyer."

Blaine turned back to Eric. "I hoped we could avoid doing that, but I guess it makes sense. We should keep everything nice and legal if we hope to get any of our money. I looked over my budget. I can make living expenses for a good while, but as far as funding this new band…" He shrugged.

"Yeah, I suppose we're back to square one. Unless Shane wants to work pro bono, we may turn him loose till things get better." Eric stretched in his chair. "His salary will have to go toward attorney's fees. And I'm thinking we ought to consider hiring a private investigator too."

Blaine dropped the paper. "Why would we want to do that?"

Eric fished into his pocket to remove his cigarette pack. "We need to track down Dugan." He opened the top and studied the container before he spoke again. "The police will do what they can, but I can't see their finding him a priority. In their eyes, the guy's a two-bit druggie who likes to look at bad pictures. I don't believe they suspect him in Drake's death, even though I told them they needed to try and find him when they questioned me. The authorities are aware Dugan is associated with some less than desirable people who are connected enough to hide him, especially since he has access to our money and can pay them well." He lifted one shoulder. "They're not gonna put forth a lot of effort. Besides, I doubt if the police have the adequate resources to do much more than what's already been done."

"You're probably right." Blaine nodded. "What you're suggesting is a good idea. I think that Finn will be on board. An attorney might provide us the name of a private eye."

"Hey, brothers."

Both men turned as Shane entered their home

through the back door.

"I wanted to stop by and give you guys good news for once."

"We certainly could use some."

"I heard about Mitchell's accident. It's blaring from everywhere. Hope he'll be okay. Really tough right after Drake dying." Shane lumbered to the table and stopped. He stuffed his hands deep into his pockets and studied the stacks of paperwork. "What's going on?"

"Long story." Eric shifted in his chair. "Tell us the good news."

"Right. I'm sure you remember I made a trip to the UK a couple of weeks ago. During my visit, I distributed your new tune to a few of the local radio stations and convinced them to play it. I didn't want to tell you anything in case the experiment was a bust, but..." Shane smiled wide. "They're going nuts for you guys over there. I just got word. "Eyes and Lies" is the top requested song for this week. You're back."

"Fantastic." Blaine whirled a fist in the air. "This is great news."

The men high fived and knuckle bumped. Despite all the sadness, Eric couldn't help but grin, if only for a few minutes. They'd been hoping for a break like this. "No one knows we're the artists, do they?"

Shane shook his head. "Not yet. We'll let them in on things when the time is right. But we're getting close. You need to consider returning to the UK for an extended stay. The wave is starting over there, that's where you should be. We can begin by booking some of the smaller clubs and work our way up. I'm supposed to return to Scotland in a couple of days. I still got a child support issue with the ex. She's hauling my ass back into court. I'm going to try and hang out with my kid, if she'll let me. While I'm there, I also plan calling in a few favors with some more dj's I'm acquainted with. I want your music on the air. Once we get things moving across the ocean, we can hit the stations in the US, and then you can come back here if you choose."

"That's great Shane, except we have a problem." Blaine motioned over to the heaps of paper on the table.

Shane placed his palms over his ears. "No. I don't want to hear about any problems."

"But we've got one. And it's a biggie."

He dropped his hands. "Go."

"We've discovered Dugan embezzled all our money. We're basically broke and we can't continue funding our plan."

"No shit." Shane gave them a disbelieving stare. "We must find a way. We're on the verge of becoming something big. I feel it."

"I'm with Shane," Eric agreed. "We're too close to stop. Still, I can't see how we'll be able to continue without money."

Shane held his palms in front of him. "Minor setback. We can deal with this. Don't make any kind of decision yet. Let me brainstorm, call some contacts, and see what I come up with."

"But we can't pay you," Blaine repeated vehemently.

"Worry about that later." Shane headed for the door. "I'll talk to you guys when I get back."

"Man, that's the best news we've gotten in a long while." Eric extended his arms over his head. "And I'd like to revel in this joy for a bit, but we need to focus on our many complications starting with locating a good attorney."

"Finn probably knows someone. He's been in enough trouble. Which by the way, he's already called me twice. Richard once. They've tried to phone you too. I wish you'd turn your fuckin' cell on. You always keep it off."

Eric gave him a crafty grin. "We'll talk to Finn at our meeting tonight. We should check on Mitchell too. Damn, this is got to be tough on their family." He paused. "This is too damn hard, but we've got to form a plan quickly. One of us ought to contact Drake's wife on our behalf. I'm assuming she'll inherit Drake's portion. If we gain anything, she'll have a say in what we do." Eric didn't want to get further into a deeper conversation about his friend's passing or Mitchell's situation, yet it was disrespectful to glide over the incidents to only discuss the financial aspects. "I'm wondering when would be the right time for us to approach the relatives."

"They're probably messed up pretty bad after this. Drake and his wife waited a long while to marry and Mitchell—man, this is hard for me to talk about too."

"I'm not doing great myself." Eric removed a cigarette out of the box and rolled it between his fingers. "I've known Drake since my first year of college. I met Mitchell not long after. We played together for, what, three years before we became famous. I considered them both more like my brothers than friends."

"I'm the same way." Blaine looked past Eric through the bay window located behind him. He stared out at the ocean for several seconds. "What time are we supposed to get together with Finn?"

"He wants us at there by eight. He says he's got a party to go to, and it starts around midnight. Also, he's meeting friends for drinks at ten, so we need to be finished by then." Eric gave a cynical smile. "Hell of a way of grieving a friend's death. I hope that asshole brother of his is already gone. You think we oughta take the car over to his place or is walking okay with you?"

Eric preferred to go on foot. Finn's neighborhood was several blocks away and not in the best area, but the distance wasn't too far. He'd rather be outdoors. Plus, he needed a shit-load of fresh air before and after he "enjoyed" Finn's company again. They may have formed an uneasy truce because of their mutual predicament. But they were hardly friends.

"What are we doing?" Eric paused. "Car or walk?"

"I'll meet you at Finn's."

Eric's brows dipped.

Blaine kept his voice calm. "I'm not going with you to Finn's house. I phoned Stephanie this morning. We're getting together for dinner tonight."

"You made a date?" Eric's eyes narrowed. "How can you even think about a woman after everything that's happened these past few hours? You knew we had a meeting, and you're well aware what's at stake."

"I am. But I need a break from this crazy shit. I'm about to go insane. If anything else happens to us, I will. I like Stephanie. Because of this crap going down, I don't think I'll get more than an evening or two to take her out, plus I'm afraid if I'm with her too much, I'll put her in danger. I'm spending what little time I have with her. Maybe I'll feel normal for a few minutes."

Eric chuckled sardonically. "Normal. Do you even know what that is?"

"Don't worry. It's only dinner. We'll make this an early night. I'll be at Finn's by eight."

Eric fumed as he shoved away from the table and sprang to his feet. "I need a smoke."

He withdrew his disposable lighter from his pants pocket and was clicking as he stepped outdoors. He held the cigarette between his lips, then lifted the fire to the end. After taking several drags, he sat down on the top step to rest on the small weathered porch as he regarded the azure sea.

Today was a gorgeous spring day. The sun shone bright, a light breeze carried a sultry heat making the morning almost hot. Gulls dived gracefully to skim the tops of the swells in efforts of catching their next meal. Usually, the tranquil sights gave him a sense of peace, but today even the water's hypnotic lull didn't do anything for him.

While recent events weighed heavy on his mind, he was unexplainably pissed at Blaine. Eric understood his motives. Yet—he was jealous. Probably because he'd never gotten the chance to rid himself of his need for Darla Hennessy.

The news of Mitchell's injury only put his urges farther on the backburner, though his want for her had by no means disappeared. This made him wonder what kind of person he was. Thinking about a woman instead of focusing on his friend's dire predicament. But hard as he tried, he couldn't control his brain. The idea of finding a replacement to take care of his physical necessities was still appealing. Then he'd be able to concentrate on his grief and search for their lost fortune.

Maybe he'd join Finn tonight. Find someone at his party. If not, he had other options. One thing for sure. He wouldn't be looking for *her*. He stared down the way at her empty deck, resisting the impulse to leap from the step, run down the beach, knock on her door, and kiss her again. He ground his cigarette into the dirt of a nearby flower pot whose plant had seen better days. Nope, he was done with her. He stood up to go back inside.

"I'm sorry about your friend," said a soft southern drawl from the side of the deck. "Any news on his condition?"

Eric flinched before he glanced down. "What are you doing here? You're—"

Darla held up a palm. "I've walked this route every morning since I moved by the water."

He took in her sweat pants and tank top as he scanned the mass of curls she'd unsuccessfully attempted to tie back, flowing in the wind. The sight of her all messy and pretty stirred a tingle of excitement in his lower gut that whirled into a sphere of pleasure, instantly blowing up like a balloon. It took every scrap of willpower not to jump over the side of the rail and wrap her in his arms.

"I've never noticed you walking this way." Eric was careful to keep his tone even, uninterested as he tried to reel in his elation over her appearance.

"So because you haven't seen me means I'm not on this trail daily?" She gave him a smug grin. "Seriously. Are you normally awake at this hour?"

Eric swiped a quick glance at his watch. It was

early in the morning. Damn, she had him. A tremor of disappointment vibrated in his chest. A part of him wanted her to be passing his house because of him.

His licked his lips and answered a quiet, "No."

"I suppose now is about bedtime for you. I'll let you get some sleep." She lifted a hand, giving a small wave before she moved down the shoreline. "Again, I hope the best for your friend."

He paused a second before he yelled, "Wait."

She came to an abrupt halt and spun to face him. She stayed. So now what? To give himself a moment, he bound down the stairs, then rushed to where she stood.

"Last night." He motioned toward the area where they'd shared their kiss. "Here. On the beach."

"This morning," she corrected. "You're referring to what occurred here this morning."

He shot her an irritated glare. Ms. Smarty was almost annoying today. But he guessed he had it coming.

"Right." Eric thrust his hands into his pockets. "I want you to understand, I was upset from many things and I lost control. I didn't mean to kiss you, it just— happened. Sorry."

"Oh, okay, I get it." Darla's mouth twisted into an ironic smile. "You must have caught me on an off night too. The evening was crazy or it might've been the full moon."

"Was there a moon?"

She shrugged carelessly. "Also, I want to make sure you're aware in normal circumstances when someone invades my space uninvited, I tend to put a knee to the groin area."

"I'm glad last night wasn't normal circumstances," he muttered.

"No matter. There's not a need for us to concern ourselves over what happened. It was just a kiss, right? We don't know each other, but if you're worried, let me assure you I'm not one of those women who stalk guys over something so trivial. In fact, I'm leaving town for a while." She twirled around to walk home. "So, no worries."

She was going away. He watched her hair bounce with each confident step as she strolled away. His eyes dropped to view the natural swing in her cute, round butt. He swallowed. Because of his money situation he might not be able to stay in his house. He may never see her again.

"Where are you going?" he shouted above the wind. "On your trip."

"Texas. To visit my family," she called over her shoulder.

"You're from Texas?"

"Born and raised." She gave another small wave as she walked. "Have a nice life, Eric Boyd."

"Hey, you know what?"

She spun to face him, slowly striding backwards.

"Regardless of the circumstances, the kiss was a pretty damn good one."

Darla smiled. "It wasn't awful." She laughed and turned to continue down the beach until she was home. She jogged up the steps and gave him a quick glance before she disappeared inside.

Eric stared. What the hell just happened? He'd lost control. Not physically, not yet, but somewhere in the span of these last five minutes, she'd managed to gain the mental command between them. And he explained to her why he kissed her?

He was in trouble with this one. Big trouble.

****

Eric pressed on the bell again this time with extra force. The trill's vibration pulsated down his arm as the buzzer disrupted the night's stillness. He released the button and waited. Hands jammed into his pockets, he whirled around to survey his surroundings.

Dusk arrived quickly. The only light fell from a solitary streetlamp covered in grime, glowing through near-naked tree branches. The shaded beam cast lengthy shadows across the front of Finn's clapboard home giving Eric a bit of the creeps.

He rotated and shook off an edge of wariness. This house with the paint peeling and weed infested flowerbeds had to be the result of Finn depleting his finances. He'd likely been forced him to move into this dilapidated residence. Something Eric hoped would never happen to him.

Although now he didn't give a fuck where Finn lived. Irritated, he rang the bell one more time, and one more time he got the same results. Typical Finn. He'd stood Eric up. Finn probably headed over to the party early. Yeah, not a big surprise over his former friend's irresponsibility, but where the hell was Blaine? He'd promised he cut his date with Sandy, no, Stephanie, short.

Eric checked his wristwatch. Fifteen minutes late. He'd give him a little longer. Then Blaine could expect calls in five minute intervals until he showed up. He dug into his pocket, removed his cigarette package, and shook one out. He grabbed the tip with his mouth and lit the point. He blew out a puff of smoke and stared at the front entrance.

Finn was notorious for pulling all-nighters and sleeping until early evening. Could he still be asleep? Possibly, he didn't hear the bell. Maybe a different method would work. With a balled fist, Eric reared back and punched the door, prepared to keep pounding until Finn answered or the thing fell off the axes. The door swung open after the first strike. With the cigarette clenched between his lips, Eric peered inside. It was pitch black. Just like he figured. The son of a bitch already left.

He doused his smoke and called out, "Finn?"

He pushed the door open wider and sucked in a lungful of air as the hinges gave an eerie groan. Timidly, he took a step into the entryway. The air inside smelled stale. Lifeless. He walked in farther before he stopped to get his bearings. This place wasn't familiar at all. He had no idea which way to move.

The surface beneath him appeared slick, almost as if a filmy vapor slithered across the floor. He staggered to stay balanced. The only sound was the light reverberation of his sneakers against the tiles. He did his best to ignore the strange quiet and concentrated on walking without busting his ass.

Another problem. He couldn't see shit. Gliding a hand over the wall, he searched for a switch until he collided into something solid, probably some sort of partition. He gave up on finding a light and plowed into his pocket for his lighter. He flicked several times before producing a flame. He swung the flare from side to side. The beam displayed shadows of scattered containers and furniture. Outlines danced over the bare walls.

Jitters leaped deep inside his gut, the hair on the back of his neck stood at attention. He should leave. Phone Finn. Find out where the hell he'd disappeared to and give him a piece of his mind for putting him through this crap. But he continued forward as if an unseen energy drew him further in.

"Finn?"

He wandered down a short hall, shining the small blaze in front of him. He made out a triangle of rooms at the end. These should be the bedrooms. He turned into the first room and stood in the doorway. It resembled a cave's interior. He held the glow inside. A heavy, dark drape covered the lone window to block any light that may try to filter in. A shaded plank filled the area. Must be a bed. An uneven bulge lay on top.

A pile of laundry or a person? Whatever laid there didn't move. His blood ran cold. He longed for laundry. Eric paced farther inward and immediately took a step back. An unfamiliar, rank odor saturated the room.

"Is that you, Finn?" He inhaled to hold his breath before he stepped inside and treaded carefully to the bed. He stretched to touch the stationary mound then snapped his hand back. Something most definitely was off. He walked toward the headboard and lowered the spark of fire.

"Shit." He stumbled against the wall and smothered the flame. Eric took several deep inhalations through his mouth before he flicked the lighter on again to make sure shadows weren't playing tricks on him. He held the light in front of him.

A dark stain sprayed over the pillow. Hair appeared matted and half the face looked to be missing. Eric quenched the flame, turned away, and swallowed hard to keep his dinner down. He shoved a hand into his back pocket yanking out his cellphone.

He'd worked to press the on button when a muffled whine made him glance up. He sensed the explosion a split second before he it penetrated his skin. A solid jolt tore into his arm. Odors of burned flesh covered the room. Eric collapsed to the floor and landed with a jarring thud. The impact sent him rolling until he crashed into something hard. A rough groan ripped from his throat.

His upper arm seared as if a sharp, scorching object had pierced him. He gritted his teeth and covered the wound with his hand. Warm, sticky, wetness squashed around his fingers. Okay. He may have been shot, but he was alive. He had to keep his wits about him. Decide what his next move should be. He needed to call someone for help. With a ragged wheeze, he struggled to a sitting position. He stretched his good hand and patted the floor, searching for his phone.

As he leaned forward, his head struck a long, cold, piece of metal. Then his world went dark.

Chapter 10

Eric lay crouched against a frozen, hard surface drifting in and out of consciousness. He shivered uncontrollably and tried to move, except his body refused to obey his mental commands. He crunched his limbs closer for warmth. A sudden spasm triggered a violent quiver and seemingly held him airborne, before he collapsed into the floor.

"Eric?" There was a pause. "Eric."

Someone kept calling him. The realization he wasn't alone left him with some comfort. Whoever spoke to him sounded familiar, and instinctively he realized this person didn't mean him any harm. But why was he in such pain? Did someone intentionally hurt him? Was that the reason he ached from head to toe?

The voice spoke his name again. The vibration echoed as if the person stood inside a faraway tunnel. A part of him wanted help while the other half wished to be alone. His injuries combined with the powerlessness to do anything kept him in an obscured numbness. Darkness plagued his mind as the gloom threatened to take over.

"C'mon, Eric."

He didn't respond. His awareness floated upward and hovered into a content shade of gray. His company should go away. He wanted them to. The pain subsided and he was good here. Safe. If this is what death was like, he'd surrender without a fight. A hand clasped his arm and gave him a vigorous shake. He inhaled a quick gasp, stiffened, surfacing from his secured trance. Sharp, white-hot pain rushed through him. A hiss of air leaked between his teeth as if someone bludgeoned him with a hammer held over an open flame.

"Easy. Take it easy."

The torment gradually lessened, his frame slackened. Somewhere deep within he'd returned to the real world for good and now he was forced to deal with the torture his body doled.

"Can you open your eyes?"

Eric licked his parched lips and worked to pry his lids up. He blinked, but the bright light singed his corneas. The shifting glare pierced his eyeballs. He snapped his eyelids shut.

"Almost. Try again."

Though he was unable to hold his eyes open long, he couldn't tolerate lying on the inflexible ground another second. The hardness against his aching body became unbearable. He forced his body upward.

"Wait." Someone gripped him by his shoulders. "I'm all for you getting up, but don't do this by yourself. Let me help you."

His rescuer steered him onto his butt and guided him to lean against something hard, like a wall. Every movement invoked a loud moan. While Eric was dizzy, he preferred this position to lying down. Problem was his head was too heavy and his neck wasn't strong enough to keep him upright. He leaned back. His lashes fluttered until his lids finally lifted. He jerked a hand to his forehead, shielding his eyes from the brightness.

"Talk to me. Eric, say something."

He inhaled. His lungs filled with oxygen and his chest constricted. He couldn't release the air. He dropped his hand and broke into a violent cough. The aches throughout his body screamed foul. He managed to regain some control and hacked a "What the fuck happened?"

"I was hoping you'd tell me."

Eric concentrated on the outline standing in front of him. Blaine appeared fuzzy, but his shape was distinct. His voice sounded nearer, clearer too. Maybe he'd live after all.

"You don't remember anything?"

"No." Eric growled.

Blaine stood over him and bent down close meeting him eye to eye. "Well, someone knocked you around pretty good. You've got quite a bump on your forehead."

Eric lifted a hand to press into the area where his initial pain came from. "Shit." He jerked his hand down then inspected his damp fingertips covered in blood. He scraped the tips down the side of his jeans to brush away the wetness. "Feels like someone took an anvil to my head. My ears won't quit ringing, and I can't see worth a damn."

"I'm betting you've got concussion." Blaine stood upright to fumble inside his pocket to remove his cell phone. "I'm calling an ambulance."

Eric extended his arm out in protest. "Don't. I'll be fine."

"No you won't. You need a doctor." Blaine rotated toward the bed. He stared at the motionless body for a long moment before he turned back to Eric, his expression grim. "Nothing here is fine. Even if you don't want help, he needs it."

Eric followed his friend's gaze and almost heaved. He was at Finn's. The beginnings of how he happened to be in this room and his gruesome discovery deluged his memory. He'd found Finn dead.

The sight of his lifeless body created a rush of regret and sadness. At that moment, Eric understood a bit of those feelings would follow him forever. He couldn't honestly say he'd liked Finn. Or respected him. But they'd lived through an experience along with three others, most people could never understand. While the bond wouldn't be broken in death, the end of his life, of Drake's life, sealed Raging Impulse's shattered fate forever. These men's presence in the world would definitely be missed.

"I don't mean to be an ass, but it doesn't matter if we call for anyone now or later. He's beyond help."

"The police need to be notified. Besides, reporting a murder is the law." Blaine glanced back to where Finn lay, then eyed Eric. "Was he like that when you got here?"

Eric groaned as he nodded and gave a sour grimace from the head jar.

"Did you get a good look at anything? As in who might have done this to him?"

Eric inhaled a painful gasp. "I knocked and no one answered. Tried the door. Found it unlocked, so I walked in. Discovered him, then everything from there goes blank."

Eric strained his memory and stared across the room. He gazed through the window and out into the night. A sinister aura dangled heavily over the atmosphere. In the back of his mind he remembered something, but he couldn't shake any of those recollections loose. Maybe things were better this way. Possibly he'd blocked everything because of the horridness, or it could be this damn headache causing his memory loss.

God, his head hurt.

Blaine nodded. "The door was open when I got here, too. The scene was kinda creepy to tell you the truth. I figured you and Finn left for a pint or something and forgot to close up. I was about to leave. Had my phone out to call you, then a moan came from inside. I followed the sound. I found you laying here bleeding and him"—he shot another glance to the bed—"like that."

Eric refused to view Finn's dead body again. "Bastard."

"You think Dugan did this, don't you?"

"Not personally. I'm guessing the son of a bitch hired someone and is paying 'em with our money to kill us off."

"He might want to get a refund. The shooter's missed his target as much as he's hit, thank God."

"He still managed to kill two of us." Eric rested against the wall and stared through the open window. Something was wrong. The window. It'd been closed when he initially entered into the room. The drapes were drawn too. Someone had spread the curtains apart. He gaped at the hangings as they slightly lifted from a wisp of a breeze flowing inside.

He squeezed his eyes shut. Surreal images lapsed within his head as if he was screening a mental slideshow. Darkness plagued his memories, scents of blood, smoke, and death sprang to life in his mind. The crack of a gun, fiery metal, and the searing pain became real.

His eyes flew open. "I've been shot," he said in a hoarse whisper.

Blain was looking down. His gaze snapped up to Eric. "What?"

"I've been shot."

"Where?" Blaine's tone sounded almost disbelieving.

"In my arm." Eric dipped his head to his left side. "I think it's only a flesh wound."

Blaine gave a humorous laugh. "I'm not sure if I'm relieved or more worried. I'm certain of one thing. You're fucked up. We need to get you some medical help, right away. And we really want the police here now." He turned and punched in the numbers.

Eric preferred not to think about any of it. The realization he had a bullet lodged inside of him and worse, someone had tried to kill him, was more than he could psychologically deal with. He wanted out of this place. He wanted to forget this night ever happened.

Eric gave him a frustrated scowl. "I dropped my phone when the bullet went in me."

Blaine pointed toward the room's entrance. "I picked it up and put it on the dresser. Didn't realize it was yours."

"We'll get it on the way out." Eric held out his uninjured arm. "Help me up. I need to leave."

Blaine stared at him as if he'd lost his mind. "What you need is a doctor."

"I'm fine." He glanced at the open window again.

"We should go. Now." Sharp needles prickled down his spine. He took the chills as a sign of warning. He'd ignored his gut earlier and he ended up shot and bashed in the head. He wouldn't make the mistake of not listening to his instincts again. "This place is giving me jitters. Like we're being watched."

Blaine didn't move. "And how do you plan on getting home?"

"The same as I got here."

"You came on foot, Eric. You're in no shape to walk back."

"You drove your car, didn't you?"

"I'm not putting you inside my vehicle with the amount of blood you're leaking," Blaine told him indignantly. "Besides, you're only speculating as to what's wrong with you. Your injuries maybe a lot worse than you believe, and I refuse to have you bleed out and die en route to somewhere. I've already called in the police and the EMT's. At least let them inspect those gashes." He paused to survey Eric. "Let's do the right thing and keep our asses out of trouble."

"Under the circumstances, I think we're in deep shit no matter what we do."

"I hear voices coming from the front. I'm betting the authorities and the ambulance have arrived. I'm going to get them."

"I wish we could avoid all of this. But we have no choice, I guess. There's no way to turn back the clock."

Blaine bent forward and inspected him again, then stood upright. "Nope. Right now we need to focus on your arm. It needs tended to and someone should put a Band-aid on that gigantic bump." He took a step in the direction of the doorway. "Sit tight while I lead them inside."

"Tell 'em to hurry." He gave a small nod toward the body. "No offense to the dead, but I'm not comfortable staying in the same room with a bloodied corpse, even if I did know him. Besides, the smell is getting to me."

"Yeah, the stink is bothering me too. Be right back with some help."

Eric glimpsed down at the hole in his skin. Blood oozed like crazy though it wasn't as traumatic as he'd thought it'd be. He didn't understand much about bullet wounds, but he figured this must be a clean shot.

Blaine led the authorities inside. Medical personnel and police swarmed the area. An EMT attended to Eric's head and worked on his arm, while homicide questioned him and Blaine. The detectives definitely believed a pattern was forming. The members of Raging Impulse were quickly dying out, and the cops warned them to pay attention to their surroundings and be extra careful. The medics rolled in a stretcher and stopped in front of him, but Eric waved them away. "I'm fine."

"You should go to the hospital and get checked out," Blaine reasoned.

"The EMT's looked me over," he argued and pointed at his bump. "This is probably a concussion and the bullet hole is most likely a flesh wound, just as I said." He held out his good arm. "Get me up."

Blaine stepped to where Eric sat and grasped the offered forearm. Balancing between the wall and Blaine, he hoisted to his feet. Blood rushed from his head, and his world faded in a hurry. He fell forward, conscious enough to catch a nightstand before he toppled onto the floor.

"Are you sure you don't wanna rethink this decision?"

Eric forced his eyes shut, opened them, and blinked. "I'm fine. Just give me a minute." He took several deep breaths to make the fog clear. "You're gonna have to help me, at least until I get my balance."

"I'm helping you right over to that stretcher. You're headin' to the hospital." Blaine put a shoulder under Eric's undamaged arm to heave him the rest of the way to his feet. He remained immobile until Eric became stable.

"Ready?"

Realizing he was in no position to argue, Eric gave a slight nod. Blaine assisted him to the gurney and lowered him down onto the slender padded mattress. Eric groaned as he laid back. A female EMT picked up his legs and placed them on the top, then covered him to the neck with a light sheet, while the male busied himself sticking an IV into his hand.

"Better?"

"No," Eric groused. "Be sure you get my cell phone."

Blaine stayed beside him, snatching Eric's phone from the dresser as they left the room. They gradually made their way through the house, the emergency techs carefully maneuvering him to the front door which remained open. Dull beams from the outer lights swathed the faded tiles. A path that led to freedom. Eric's heart did a slight hop from the relief to be leaving. Outside, the EMT's stopped to readjust his IV.

"Hey, I just thought of something," Blaine looked at Eric and frowned. "Where is Richard?"

"Don't know, don't care."

"Isn't it funny he's nowhere around? He's never very far away from Finn. This whole situation is odd."

"Goes beyond odd. It's fucking bizarre."

Once they'd furthered themselves from the scene, Eric motioned he needed to stop. The rocking from the movement made him nauseous. They halted in front of the dark house near a low, zigzag fence. One attendant put something into his saline drip to curb the nausea while the second medic climbed inside the ambulance to radio the hospital.

Flat on his back, Eric stared into the sky. The evening was unusually clear. There seemed to be thousands of stars above. Tonight he considered them lucky. He had the urge to thank each and every one of them that he was alive. This night could have turned out so different. The darkness closed around them and was far from quiet. Distant traffic buzzed from an unseen freeway, blending with the nocturnal creatures as they boisterously made their presence known.

Blaine, who remained beside him, finally spoke. "This is insane. First, Drake's dead. Dugan comes up missing, Mitchell is hurt, and now Finn's gone. I won't mention your misfortune."

"Appreciate that."

Eric's gaze skated around the walkway to Blaine, who'd moved to the curb. A blast of cold air slashed across them. The breeze drove a heap of litter and scattered it over the deserted road. He shivered and wished he'd brought a jacket.

He tugged the sheet closer to his neck. "Did you get a good look at the person lying on the bed? Are you sure that was Finn?"

Blaine gave a wry smile. "I hate to admit this, but I'm a bit squeamish when inspecting dead people. I've never seen one shot in the head before. I didn't want to get too close."

"I hear you."

"So to answer your question, no, I didn't get a decent look. You think there's a chance the body might not be his?"

Eric lifted his right shoulder. "I suppose anything's possible. But if it's not him, where is he and who's lying dead in his bed?"

"Dunno. There are a lot of questions with no answers."

"Yeah, and more questions keep coming in. I've got a feeling we're not going to find those answers anytime soon."

****

Damn. He hated when his plans went astray. He should have waited to get rid of Finn later. Yeah, he'd have loved to send him off in a grand exit with hundreds around to witness his demise like Drake. But trying that feat twice would be too risky. The fact Eric nearly caught him made him want to hit something and smash it into pieces. After several deep breaths he calmed, remembering the importance of remaining cool. His strategies and his success depended on his being in control. But Eric's appearance after he'd executed Finn threw him way off. Forced to adlib, and react on his feet after he'd just killed someone else...hell, there was no time to think outside the box. That left him unprepared. His shot at Eric? He couldn't operate accurately under such pressure.

Then Blaine showed up. Who could've known

tonight would be a fucking' Raging Impulse reunion? It was best for him to disappear with so much going on. So he had climbed out the window. He held in a laugh as he crouched by the opening and listened to Eric and Blaine try to decide what they should do. The hilarity of the situation was almost worth tonight's risk.

Did Eric recognize him? Would he identify him to the police? He was unable to hang around to hear them question him. Eric seemed groggy. Hopefully the big knot on his head made him doubt reality. Still, it'd be best for him to lay low for a while. Wait and see.

From across the road, he lurked in the shadows and viewed the two men at the scene. He needed to leave. The police would soon be scanning the neighborhood and he couldn't afford discovery. He rolled the bike silently down the street and glanced back at them as he mounted the motorcycle and hit the gas.

****

Eric looked out into the darkness. From a distance he could make out a single taillight fading into the night. His stomach tightened as he fought the urge to jump off the stretcher and follow the crimson light. He sucked in a long breath and wished this damn dizziness would go away. Even lying down, his head continued to spin. The tech appeared from behind, and after administering some more drugs into the IV, he manipulated the rollers across the bumpy concrete, moving toward the waiting ambulance.

Blaine slanted a quick side glance at Eric and veered in the direction of his vehicle. "I'm going to stop by the house before I meet you at the hospital."

"Wait."

A fleeting vision of the weapon pointed at him

elapsed through his mind. So vivid, the cold barrel of the gun pressed against his temple seemed all too real. He shuddered and drove the disturbing image from his head.

"Don't go to our house. The killer might realize he didn't finish the job with me and be waiting there. You may be in danger too."

"I'm sure I am." Blaine shot Eric a hard look. "We're all targets, aren't we?"

Eric took a hand out from underneath the sheet and rammed his fingers through his hair, then stuffed his arm back under the covers. "I suppose you're right." He nodded to the emergency vehicle. "Um, would you mind riding with me?"

Blaine glanced at his car parked by the curb and shook his head. "Not at all."

A moment passed and the EMT's picked up the stretcher and thrust him inside the back of the ambulance. Eric groaned from the shift, his entire body throbbed, but his rolling stomach had settled. Blaine climbed in behind him and sat down. The medical personnel followed and continued to monitor Eric's vitals as the driver spoke into the radio from up front. The paramedic asked Eric if he was still in pain. He nodded. The woman hooked something else into his IV and told him he'd feel better soon.

"Bet you weren't planning a ride like this."

Blaine grinned. "Stephanie and I agreed to continue our date after the meeting. She's at a friend's who lives down from us waiting for me to call her." He inspected Eric's cell he still held between his hands. "I suppose I'll have to tell her the rest of the night's off."

"Fuck that."

Blaine gazed at him.

"Once I get to wherever, you phone her and arrange to meet somewhere."

"I'm not gonna leave you."

"Look, all you're going to do is wait while they run tests and stuff. You might as well go out and end the night on a happy note. God knows we need some joy. You should get yours while you can."

Blaine peered down at him. "What do you mean while I can?"

Grogginess overtook him. Whatever the lady put in the saline drip was making him drowsy. His eyes drooped, but he forced them open. "You go see your girl tonight," he murmured. "'Cause I think we oughta leave."

"Leave?"

"Hmm. Get out of town. When I'm better. We should disappear. Hide somewhere until he's caught."

"Might not be a bad idea. As soon as the doctor gives you the okay, we'll take off for a few days. Hopefully the police will solve this in a hurry."

"Shouldn't be hard." Eric's eyes closed and he mumbled, "I remember now. I saw….Darla…"

Chapter 11

"Thanks for letting me stay here to wait for Blaine."

"You're always welcome," Darla said, almost mechanically.

Darla sat on the sofa with her hands folded in her lap. Her head swung back and forth, her gaze followed Stephanie pacing the floor, her friend's mouth moved twice as fast as she walked.

"I'd be crazy to drive all the way to my place," Stephanie was saying, "and have Blaine come over to my part of town when Finn lives close to yours and Blaine's neighborhood. This makes more sense for us to meet here."

"Your idea to wait here for Blaine is much better, Darla replied.

"I'm so excited we're going to continue our evening," Stephanie rambled. "At first, I was a little disappointed. Especially when he told me we needed to cut our date short for this meeting. We were having such a great time. Then he suggested we get together after. I felt so relieved." She flashed Darla a quick, bright smile. "And you're going to meet him."

Darla had to admit she experienced a bit of the green-eyed monster over Stephanie's joy. Not that she resented her. She only wished she had something to celebrate in the romantic department so they could share in this fun together. Yet, the idea wasn't feasible as long as she was in rejection recovery. Still, she wanted to meet Blaine. Purely for Stephanie's sake. Her motives had nothing to do with the fact he was Eric's friend, song-writing partner—band mate. *Right.*

Stephanie glanced at the clock and frowned. "It's been over an hour though. Blaine said they wouldn't take long."

"He drove to Finn's house, didn't he?"

Stephanie nodded. "He was supposed to meet up with Eric. He walked, so maybe Blaine is giving him a ride home before we continue our date."

Darla flinched at the mention of Eric's name.

"Blaine also told me Eric would want to discuss their situation, whatever that is, after they're through with Finn. But Blaine promised he'd cut that short too. Apparently Eric wasn't ecstatic over us dating with the issues surrounding their band. So Blaine might have changed his mind and agreed to talk things over as a way of appeasing Eric. He's such a pleaser."

"Then that's probably why he's late. They're debating." Darla stopped. "I was also wondering about Blaine wanting to go out tonight with all the drama going on in his life."

"I did ask him if he was sure tonight was a good idea. He explained he just wanted a normal evening. To get away and not think of any of the tragedies. And he hoped to do that with me."

"He sounds like a sweet guy."

"Hmmm, yeah." Stephanie stopped wandering. She moved to the windows, wrapping her arms around her waist and stared outside. "I hope he's okay."

"Why wouldn't he be?"

"Blaine drove me past Finn's place while we were out. He lives in a rundown part of the subdivision." Stephanie rotated toward Darla. "I didn't realize the section existed. Everything in this region is nice, though I'd be afraid of driving through that area of town by myself. Blaine being there, even with Eric, might be a risk. The neighborhood is dark and icky. Who knows what happens at night."

"Probably nothing." Darla lifted her shoulders. "I've met most of my immediate neighbors. I'd think I would've been notified if we had any criminal activity around here. I've explored too. I know where you're referring to. The sector is older and in need of renovations, but I don't believe the block is dangerous."

Stephanie stared at Darla. "So why is he late? You don't think he's trying to get of rid of me, do you?"

"Now, what are you talking about?"

"Him saying he has to do something, but he's lying. He's using this as a way to blow me off."

Darla shot Stephanie an aggravated scowl. "He wouldn't ask you out in the first place unless he liked you. Think, Steph. If he wanted to end the date early, he could just say he had something else to do and skip the suggestion that you hook up later. Let things go there."

"I guess."

"You guess?" Darla stared at Stephanie. She couldn't understand why her friend was dissecting her evening with Blaine. She'd never been a worrier before, especially when it came to men. This guy must have really gotten to her.

"People don't always tell the truth, Darla. You should understand that from your own break-up experience."

"I get it. I don't believe he's lying to you, but for argument's sake let's say that's what he's doing. At least you'll know before things become too serious."

"Regardless, he'll break my heart if he dumps me."

"Look at the bright side. You won't be like me and waste years waiting for his lies to materialize." Darla smiled. "Everything is going to be fine. I'm sure Blaine will be here any minute now. In the meantime, let's change the subject to keep you from worrying."

"Good idea." Stephanie bobbed over to the sofa and sat down next to Darla. "We can talk about your trip. Kind of last minute if you asked me."

"Not so much. I've been considering going home since the breakup. I've thought about staying for the summer. To heal and regroup, you know? Plus, it's been a while since I've been to Texas and I'm homesick."

"When are you leaving?"

"I have some loose ends to tie up, although they shouldn't take long. This is the last week of school, but I don't need to be in class. I'll contact my teacher's assistants. They're qualified to administer finals, grade them, and then they can send me the results to post online from my parents' house."

Darla hadn't said anything about a trip to her friend because she didn't want it to appear that she was running away after being dumped. It almost seemed cowardly. The last straw came when Eric so carelessly blew her off on her morning walk. She'd gotten his message loud and clear. The kiss meant nothing to him and neither did she. He lost control because of his upsetting situation.

And he apologized for it. Then he backtracked, which totally confused her. Even though she'd considered spending the night with this man, she decided against it, for no other reason than her emotional welfare. His presence weakened her. The idea to get as far away from this man as possible and keep her head straight was a good one. But because of the rush, this trip wasn't exactly organized.

"After I take care of my work duties and some last-minute details I can go. I plan on leaving within a couple of days, possibly as early as tomorrow if everything falls in place. I figure I'll make the California-Arizona border in a few hours, catch a little sleep, and get into the western part of Texas before I'll need to stop to take a real break. I'll be at the southern tip after another day's drive, so I should arrive home by Tuesday."

"I know you're looking forward to visiting your family. I'm sure they're excited about seeing you too. How long has it been since you've gotten together?"

"Almost a year."

Stephanie opened her mouth to reply when her phone rang. She glanced at the caller ID and squealed, "Blaine." She jumped off the couch and half skipped, half ran to the other room. The call only took a few minutes. She dashed back to Darla and stopped, fingers fanned across her chest.

"He's at the hospital. Blaine. He asked me to meet him at emergency right now."

"Is he okay?"

"He sounds fine."

"Did he say why he's at the hospital or the reason he wants you there?"

Stephanie shook her head. "He promised he'd tell me after I get there." She dropped her arm and sat down next to Darla. "I want you to come with me."

"What? I can't—."

"I need you to take me," Stephanie interrupted. "I don't have my car. Plus, the stuff going on within their group makes me afraid they've had another disaster and it concerns Blaine, but he's not telling me. Please, Dar, I'd like you to be with me. For moral support."

"My going isn't a good idea."

"Just come until we find out what happened. If Blaine is okay, then you can leave."

Darla considered her friend's dilemma before she rose from the sofa. "Let me get my keys.

The drive to the hospital wasn't a long one. Blaine sent Stephanie a text telling her at which of the building's entrances he'd be. Darla parked near the approximate zone. They both exited the car and rushed inside. They found him at the appointed entry. Stephanie vaulted into his arms while Darla lagged behind. He squeezed Steph before he led them down a corridor through a small waiting room and into a tiny emergency area without any explanation.

Darla's stomach bottomed out. Eric lay slouched in a hospital bed hooked to an IV. A heart monitor and other tubes were attached to various parts of him. Faded streaks covered his jawline linking to a huge knot on his forehead. A rusty hue smeared his shirt as a dark, red stain streaked his arm. His skin was white. His shadowy eyes nearly sunk into his head. He appeared like a mere ghost of himself.

No one spoke. Darla and Stephanie divided a peek between Blaine and Eric waiting for an explanation, though neither grasped the need to share as to what had happened to Eric.

Blaine finally caught on and gave Stephanie a crooked smile. "Sorry 'bout bringing you out like this. I was gonna put us off for another time, but he insisted you and I finish our date. Although we may just go to the coffee shop. I don't want to leave him alone too long."

"Coffee is fine." Stephanie twisted to Eric. "And no, he doesn't need to be alone. What happened?"

"We ran into a little problem at Finn's."

"A little problem?" Darla piped in.

"Yeah. Paramedics looked him over, but we're still waiting for a physician to examine him for a final verdict." He glanced at his watch. "We've been in here for over an hour."

"This isn't right." Darla had remained inside the doorway. She did a half turn and stepped into the hall. "We need someone to check on him, pronto."

Eric required help. Though she was less than thrilled by his recent behavior, she would insist he get the proper care.

Blaine leaned forward and grabbed her forearm. He spoke to her in a low voice so only she could hear. "I don't disagree, but he's doing his best to be brave. I know he's in a ton of pain. It'd make him self-conscious if we don't allow this to play out his way. Let's give it a few more minutes."

She nodded at Blaine and took a step inside moving closer to Eric "Maybe we can ask for some ice for your head?"

His frosty blue stare caught her eye and stopped her in her tracks.

"I'm a lot better and I'm ready to leave," Eric told Blaine in an aggravated voice. "You promised we'd only stay for a while and it's long past that."

"Yeah, but you're not going anywhere until the doctor sees you," Blaine answered in the same annoyed tone.

Eric shuffled his legs and laid further back though he didn't reply.

Blaine eyed Stephanie. "Can we talk a minute?" He gestured to the doorway. "In the hall."

"Sure." She smiled at him before she shot Darla a worried glance. Then she pointed to the entrance. "We'll be right out here if you need us."

Darla kept an eye on them until they disappeared. Once gone, she anxiously returned to Eric. He'd managed to relax. He'd tilted his back and shut his eyes. His chest moved up and down in an even motion, though his body twitched ever so often. He fell asleep too quickly. The massive swelling could only mean something serious going on. Him injured frightened her more than she cared to admit.

She twirled a lock of hair while she continued to observe him. A wet cloth would be a big help in wiping away the dried blood and make him not appear so incapacitated. But she'd have to touch him and she wasn't sure she could handle that. Even bloodied and beaten up, the guy somehow managed to arouse a series of flutters deep down in the pit of her stomach.

The door opened. Blaine and Stephanie returned to the room, holding hands both wearing big smiles. Nervously they looked at Darla, then back at each other. Blaine gave Stephanie a slight nod.

"Darla. We need a huge favor," Stephanie rushed,

clutching Blaine's hand tight between both of hers.

Darla's brows dropped as her insides delivered a swift kick. Whatever they wanted wasn't going to be good. For her. And she was sure they'd persuade her into honoring their request. Stephanie glanced at Blaine.

His head bobbed again.

"Blaine wants me to take him to pick up his car so I need to borrow yours." She inhaled. "Eric shouldn't be alone and we"—she glanced at Blaine one more time—"were wondering if you could stay"—she returned to Darla—"and watch him until we get back?"

Darla gnawed on her bottom lip as her heart skipped a beat. Spending another instant with Eric Boyd, even battered and bruised, left her excited, but flustered. Though tempting she couldn't trust herself around him. The man was too unsettling and he'd figure out how much he rattled her.

"Why can't you and I go get the car and you drive back here? Hopefully by then the doctor will have visited and he can leave. Besides, he'll be uneasy if he wakes up and finds someone unfamiliar with him, and he doesn't need to be agitated."

"You're over thinking this."

Darla glared at her friend. Love did some strange stuff to people. Like turn their brains into spaghetti. "What if something worse happens while I'm with him? I won't have any means to handle the situation. I have no authority to make medical decisions about his health. At least Blaine can contact his family and get permission for emergency issues."

"I don't believe he's in that bad a shape," Blaine assured her. "He's drugged up, and been pretty much in and out of consciousness since I found him. He becomes dizzy easily. I think he'll be fine after some rest. I wouldn't suggest this if I didn't have to get my car. I'm not comfortable leaving it in Finn's neighborhood. And I'm not comfortable with the two of you driving in that part of town alone, after dark. We'll make the trip quick and I'll take over watching Eric as soon as I get back, Darla. I promise."

She didn't miss the concerned glance Blaine gave a slumbering Eric.

"He'll probably doze the whole time anyway."

"I'd rather pass on this responsibility. I'm betting he has a concussion. I read you're not supposed to sleep with head wounds, and there isn't anybody stopping him. The medical personnel seem scarce around here. Suppose something happens, and I can't find anyone to help. What if he doesn't wake up?"

"I don't need no damn sitter," Eric moaned from behind them. "You can all hit the road."

"You should be so lucky." Blaine grinned at Darla. "The drugs make him more agitated than normal."

Eric wrestled to level his body and extended his arm to Blaine. "As a matter of fact, let's all go. Take me home."

Blaine turned to Eric. "After the doctor visits and gives you the okay to leave. Until then, you're staying put." He gave Eric a warning glance. "You'll be safer here."

"Safer?" Darla questioned. "Is he in danger?"

Eric ignored Darla. "I could care less about my safety at the moment." His gaze speared into Blaine. "I'll go anywhere, hell, sit me at the curb. I don't wanna stay here."

"You don't have a say," Blaine argued. "You need to lie down and sleep. I'll come back soon and we'll be on our way." He twisted to Darla with a smile. "I hope you can overlook his bitchiness and not give him another knock on the other side of his head. Although, go ahead if he gets too bad."

Darla almost grinned. She liked Blaine. Stephanie may found her a good one this time.

Steph clutched together her hands, held them out in front of her, and gave her a meaningful look. "Please, do this, Dar." This short trip would take a lot longer than implied by the way her friend was acting. "I'll never ask you to do anything else for me again."

"Not true."

"Okay, well, I won't ask you to do anything else for me this week."

"It's Saturday, Steph. The end of the week. So your promise doesn't work either way."

"I can't stay here." Eric tried to get to his feet. He made it halfway, swayed, and fell back onto the narrow hospital bed. His weight drove it backward an inch as he landed with a loud grunt.

Darla waved an arm at him. "He can't even stand without help."

"Your concern is touching, but I wish you'd quit acting like I'm dying. I assure you I'm as healthy as I was last night and will be glad to prove it to you. Again."

Darla whipped around. A sardonic smile slowly crept across Eric's bloodied face. Her glare in return was hopefully sharp enough to cut through metal.

"Wait. Yeah, Darla." Blaine snapped his fingers and bounced a look between Darla and Eric. "Have you two met before?"

Eric ducked his head, but Darla nodded.

"They ran into each other at the party," Stephanie interjected with a giggle. "Darla spilled her drink on Eric, and he was accommodating. They've already become good friends. I see no harm in her staying with him. He's not well from his tumble. Darla's great at giving TLC. Besides, she ruined his shirt with her wine. She owes him."

Darla spun to Stephanie and glowered. She mouthed a thank you as Stephanie relieved her of her car keys.

Blaine took a step closer to Darla. "Your eyes are beautiful. Dark." He studied her for an extended moment and turned to Eric as a slow smile crawled across his face. "I'd even call them haunting. Wouldn't you, Eric?"

Eric didn't reply. Blaine chuckled as he glided to Stephanie. He took her hand and slanted his head to whisper something into her ear. Stephanie giggled again.

"Seeing as you two are old friends and all." Blaine grinned. "I'm gonna take it you can work out whatever conflict's going on between you. M'lady and I are heading over to get my vehicle." He nodded at Eric. "I'll check out our place before we go and bring you back some clean clothes." He guided Stephanie outside, each saying, "Thanks, Darla, and take care, Eric," as they disappeared into the hallway.

Hands on her hips Darla viewed the entire scene, as it played out, powerless to stop it. She stared at the closed door for several minutes before she pivoted to Eric, who'd propped himself up on a stack of pillows.

"I'm guessing this trip will take a while. They're probably going to continue their date."

"Of course they are. Blaine's nothing but a horny son of a bitch."

"What a nice thing to say. He's your good friend, isn't he?"

He flicked a sapphire gaze over her. "Call 'm as I see 'm, luv."

She eyed him up and down. "So what happened to you? Did you call 'm as you see 'm one too many times and someone beat the crap out of you?"

Eric actually laughed, then flinched. With a sluggish move, he maneuvered his hand to reach into his pants pocket and removed his cigarettes. He strained into a sitting position and stretched an arm to her, offering her a blood-smeared hand.

"I need a smoke. Get me outside. I'll tell you the whole sordid details."

Darla maintained eye contact as she walked around the bed and snatched the pack away from him. She held them above her head. Then she smiled.

Eric stared at her as if waiting for her to move. "Are you gonna stand there or are you going to take me out?"

"Let's get things straight, right now." Darla crossed her arms over her chest and gave him a stern glare. "You're hurt and as long as you're in this condition, we're playing by my rules. You can forget about puffing on anything. I'm not going to help you tar and nicotine up your lungs any more than they already are." She waved the package in front of him and shook her head. "No smoking on my watch, buddy."

126

Chapter 12

Eric stared longingly at the package woven through Darla's fingers. He transferred his gaze to her face, which he could see clearly now. His vision had finally returned, plus the meds from earlier were beginning to wear off.

"Fine," he snapped. "I won't smoke." He bowed his head and muttered, "Right now."

"You're pale. You need medical attention." She dropped her arm and spun toward the exit. "I want to go talk to the nurse and find out when the doctor is coming."

"Not necessary. I'm okay."

"You certainly don't look okay." Darla stopped and turned back to him. She clutched the cigarettes between her hands and examined the package as if debating whether to believe him.

"Well, I am." He leaned forward. With his good arm, he pressed against the mattress to sit straighter, but the whirling inside his head drove him back into the bed. "Soon as everything stops spinning, I'm going home."

"How do you plan on getting there?"

"I'll walk if I have to."

"By yourself?" Darla smiled. "Can I watch?"

Eric raked an annoyed look over her, before he

returned to her grinning face. "You've got a bit of an edge, don't you? I never would've believed you to be such a smartass." He released a sardonic chuckle. "The way you kissed me last night should've given me a clue you weren't as innocent as you like to give off, eh?"

"Interesting."

"What is?"

"You so intrigued about our kiss."

He casually lifted a shoulder. "I'm not intrigued."

"Except this is the second time you brought up the subject tonight. And you also referred to it on the beach earlier today." She gave him an inquisitive look. "I wonder why?"

Eric touched his pocket before he remembered his cigarettes were sandwiched in between her palms. Still, he wished he had one, along with the nerve to light up. He ignored her question and asked one of his own.

"Why did you kiss me back?"

Nervously, she combed her fingers through her thick waves as if to consider her next words. "Because, I—" She sighed. "I can't tell you. I don't have an answer."

"I think you do," he retorted in a soft voice.

"The night was crazy. You, the murder, and the storm was a bad one." Her mouth twisted. "Everything was—strange."

He stared at her, giving his head a modest shake. "Yep, the night was a wild one. Even in my world."

"You don't think all those occurrences aren't weird in mine? I doubt there are any set rules on how to behave in such a situation in anyone's universe."

"So you're telling me the reason you kissed me was because the oddness of the evening." His voice conveyed his doubt.

"I was flustered from everything. And seeing you on the beach just increased the tenseness." Her tone raised an octave. "Why else would I do something so crazy?"

Eric waited a moment. "Because of what's happening. Between us." He intentionally let the words drop like dead weight and then sat back to view her reaction.

Darla's jaw plummeted. The cigarettes she gripped glided through her fingers and fell to the floor. The package slid across the faded tiles coming to a stop after hitting a wall under a chair.

Even in his depleted position, he had to hold back a laugh. And despite the horrible events of the entire night, he liked her. If only for a few minutes. She was feisty. Prettier than he first thought. By her outer appearances, she was in good shape too. He admired the almost black cascade of curls flowing over her shoulders. He also enjoyed listening to her. She had a nice voice. He never gave much attention to the different accents in the states, but hers definitely had a cute southern twang.

"Don't pretend you don't feel it. We've a load of chemistry between us, luv."

More unspoken thoughts hung in the air.

She hacked a dry cough. "Okay. I've noticed."

"I'm sensing a 'but.'"

"But I don't know if I want to do anything about the situation. I just got out of a relationship. The romance didn't end well, at least from my standpoint. Getting close to someone else so soon after doesn't seem to be a smart idea."

"You like to put your cards on the table." He nodded. "I respect that. To be clear, I'm only talking about a good time. Nothing more."

Darla's eyebrows shot up. "What an enticing offer." She folded her arms across her middle. "You sure can tempt a woman."

"Sarcasm?"

"Oh, you got that." She paused. "I shouldn't be surprised a good time is all you want. Our romantic kiss should've given me a clue, eh?"

"What was wrong with the kiss?"

He'd never had any complaints about his kissing techniques before. On a normal plane, he enjoyed the process, although he found the act more of a necessity to get to the next physical level as opposed to anything romantic. Admittedly, his behavior toward her last night was unorthodox, though he didn't find the moment unpleasant.

"Nothing. For a woman who appreciates a lip lock that stems from zero. Frankly, I don't care for unfeeling kisses." She lifted an eyebrow and gave him a slight grin. "My turn to call 'm as I see 'm."

He stared at her. Damn. It happened again. He was doing fine holding his own and WHAM, she'd taken over, leaving him baffled on how to deal with this gutsy lady. And he certainly hadn't hidden his feelings very well. Still, he wouldn't go down without a fight.

"Fair enough. But you need to understand, I'm not the type of guy who plays games."

"So you told me."

"Glad you remembered. Let me be clearer. I don't believe in this whole love, happily-ever-after crap. An attraction exists between us. I acted on that. My thinking is, once you return from your trip we'll see things through and let them run their course. No reason to make any more of this than what it is."

"You attitude is such a cynical one." Darla unfolded her arms and gave her head a negative shake. "Someone sure did a number on you."

"No one did any kind of number. I've been all over the world and met a lot of people. I have found most of them are either alone, unhappy in their relationships, or they've had their heart stomped on by a person they thought would be with them forever." He pointed a forefinger in her direction. "You're a prime example of what can happen when you give blind trust to someone."

"Yes, but your outlook confuses me." Her expression mirrored her words. She held her arms out to her sides and lifted her shoulders. "What about all those beautiful love songs you write?"

"Easy. I write what the people want and I get paid. Well."

She dropped her arms and squatted, and then glided to her knees. "I'm totally disillusioned."

"Just being practical, luv."

"Good to know. I'd hoped your head injury was the cause of you spouting out this butt load of nonsense."

Even though he hurt, Eric laughed. Darla placed her hands on the floor and crawled under the chair. He raised his head from the bed to get a better view. A grin stretched across his face as he watched her squirm in further, her ass swaying back and forth like a flag in the breeze.

She retrieved his smokes, then she inched backward. "What happened to you anyway?"

"I was shot."

Darla rose and bumped her crown on the underside of the chair. "Shot?" She wriggled from under her hole. She sat on her knees and gaped at him. "In your head?"

"In my arm." He pointed to his forehead. "I'm not exactly sure what happened here."

"A bullet is lodged in you and you're telling me you're fine? Seriously, you need to let me go find a doctor."

"The wound is clean. They're gonna tell me to take two aspirin and call them in the morning. And I'm sure I'll be expected to answer a lot of questions, and I've already told the police everything I remember."

Darla studied him for a long moment before she bombarded him. "Who shot you? Where were you? Are you sure the slug is in you? Does it hurt?"

"I'm gonna have to answer a bunch of questions anyway, aren't I?" he mumbled, and then sighed, "No clue who did the shooting. I was at Finn O'Conner's place when the gunfire happened. The shooter got him too. The hole is in my upper arm. According to the paramedics, the pellet is still in me, and yeah, it hurts like hell."

"So this took place at your meeting? And Finn was also shot. Is he here too? Is anyone with him?"

"Not exactly." Eric hesitated. "He's dead."

"As in murdered?" Darla gulped and paused. "This is the second person within the band that's died within hours, and Mitchell Young was injured from an attack." Her brow furrowed. "Your former manager is missing? Someone is targeting Raging Impulse's members, aren't they?"

"Kind of seems so." Eric sighed again. "Though

we did get some good news. After the disaster at Finn's, Blaine received a call saying Mitchell's condition had improved."

"Was he able to tell them anything? Is this the same creep who pushed me last night?"

"The word we got was he'd gone out to walk his toy poodles. The blast exploded from behind, like Drake's. Though he was luckier. The bullet blew off his ear and a piece of his scalp, but didn't lodge inside his skull. And no, he can't identify the person who shot him."

"Aren't you afraid?" Before she gave him an opportunity to answer, she rattled on, "Wait. Your drummer raises little dogs. Isn't he the big buff guy with a shaved head? He has tattoos all over, right?"

"That's the guy." A sudden wave of dizziness swept through him. He eased back, closed his eyes, and clutched the bed's sides.

"Are you all right?"

"Yeah," he mumbled "Why?"

"You were already pale. But now the tiny amount of pigment that was left in your skin has disappeared."

"No worries, luv. Just need a quick nap." Thankfully, the wooziness had subsided and fatigue replaced the vertigo as he drifted off to sleep.

A loud rap jerked him awake. Eric slowly raised his head and blinked. Darla sat across from him, her fingers still wrapped around his smokes. She watched him with a concerned frown.

"How long have I been out?"

"Over an hour."

Blaine and Stephanie entered the room following the knock. Hands still connected, both wore sheepish grins. Blaine carried a small suitcase and set the bag down near the doorway.

He walked to where Eric lay. "You're looking a little better." He turned to Darla. "You must have a positive effect on him." He rotated back to Eric. "Has the doctor visited you yet?"

"No, and he still won't let me go find one," Darla put in.

Eric took a deep breath and expelled noisily.

"One should be here soon." Blaine cleared his throat and looked at Darla. "We were wondering if maybe you wouldn't mind giving Eric a ride home after the doctor comes, if he's released."

"Given the circumstances, Blaine and Eric are considering disappearing until the police catch this guy," Stephanie explained. "We'd like to spend what little time together we can before they go."

Another tap came from the outside, followed by a doctor entering the room. A nurse was close behind. He glanced up from a clipboard that he held, and studied the group, then instructed everyone leave.

Eric's three guests disappeared. The physician checked his knot, the bullet hole, and his eyes and pretty much made the same inquiries as the paramedics did earlier, and again with the nurses, when he was transported into the hospital.

The doctor confirmed he had a concussion. His gunshot appeared to be non-threatening and unless the circumstances changed, they'd leave the slug in his arm. He wrote a couple of prescriptions and suggested he stay the night, although the decision was up to Eric, then he left.

Darla peeked around the doorway.

"They talked you into it, huh?" Eric said.

She fully stepped into the room. "Stephanie is my best friend and she likes Blaine." She walked to the bed. "I'm glad you are thinking about leaving town."

"Seems a good idea, though I don't know if it's going to pan out. I hate the thought of running away from my problems."

"Of course you do, but in this situation I'm not sure you have a choice." Darla perched on the arm of the only chair in the room. "We spoke with the doctor. He wouldn't tell us much, although he did say he'd prefer you stay the night."

"Yeah, but it was only a suggestion." He threw the covers off. "One I'm rejecting."

"You're not in any condition to leave. Besides, someone tried to kill you. You'd be safer here than at your house."

"Don't matter. I'm going home."

"You're kidding. I don't know you well, but you must enjoy a good fight."

He chuckled. "Glad you're picking that up. It'll make our future relationship easier."

Darla rose from the chair. "I'm too tired to spar with you anymore. Let's go, if you insist on leaving." She bent and picked up the suitcase. "But at least call in the police and get you some protection."

Eric gave a scornful laugh. "Right. I'm not an American citizen. Although I may be famous, I was in a teen band. And we're not exactly appreciated by anyone over fifteen. I can't imagine them going to great lengths to protect Blaine and me. It's gonna be on us to take care of ourselves. Besides, Finn's and my turbulent history is well documented. That alone could put me on top of the suspect list, despite my situation."

"I'm guessing the law failed you at some point too? Or do you have other reasons for such a cynical attitude toward the police? In fact, with everything?"

"Everyone has failed me," he said in a bitter tone. "Except Blaine."

"Still, you need to do whatever you can to take precautions to keep safe."

"Your concern is noted, but don't worry about me. I'm aware of the consequences. Everything will come out when it's supposed to."

Darla studied him for a long time. "You know who did it, don't you? You know who shot you."

He opened his mouth to tell her no when a trace of memory zipped through his mind, a picture so rapid he couldn't grasp it.

Eric smiled at her. "I don't know anything, luv."

Chapter 13

Darla drove through the streets of the neighborhood, slowing at Eric's house. He struggled to sit up higher for a better view. Media vehicles from around the state surrounded his property. Not that he was surprised. Those bloodsuckers loved famous homicides.

"Shit," he mumbled and fell back into the seat. "Good news travels fast, I see. Fuckin' soul suckers."

"Death makes an interesting story." Darla glanced at him as she carefully maneuvered the road. "I'm shocked you didn't have any around after Drake's murder."

"We had a few try to talk to us. But this…" He shook his head in disgust.

"And you're popular again too."

"How's that?"

"The killings seem to have increased Raging Impulse's popularity. The radio's played your old songs all day. Downloads are going through the roof."

"Sad way to regain exposure."

"True," Darla agreed. "I doubt if that was the killer's intent. Do you want to try and get past this mess or is there a plan B?" She didn't wait for his answer, but continued to guide her SUV down the street bypassing the mob.

"Plan B."

"Which is?"

Eric had no clue to where she could take him. Perhaps a hotel? Not a bad idea, except he preferred not to spend any cash if he didn't have to, being he had little to spare. Plus, it'd be nice to be close to someone in case he needed help.

"Your place?"

Her head jerked in his direction, her eyes grew bigger than saucers. "You want to stay with me?"

Eric smiled.

"Oh never mind." She whipped the car into a nearby drive, flinging the gear into reverse, and backed onto the street. "But you'll behave yourself."

He gestured toward the group of news people. "Keep driving like that and they'll spot us. They're good at watching for things out of the ordinary."

"Sorry." She shifted into drive and gunned the gas. "It just occurred to me we may be in your shooter's driveway, and I wanted to get away as soon as possible."

"My shooter's drive? What are you talking about?"

"The guy who shot you. The person who's killing off your band lives in this neighborhood. Or so we believe. Stephanie thinks she saw the motorcycle rider the night he killed Drake when she and Blaine walked to the bar, although she didn't realize who he was at the time. He disappeared into a garage near here as they walked by. The door was closing so she didn't get a good look."

"Did she tell the police?"

Darla nodded as she sped past the vultures parked around his place. "The problem is, she doesn't remember in which part of the neighborhood she noticed him. She's so gaga over Blaine, she wasn't paying much attention to anything else. She's not a lot of help, but at least they're able to possibly centralize the guy's location."

This information was interesting. And disturbing. His suggestion to Blaine that they disappear had been half-hearted, along with the influence of whatever pain meds they'd given him. Now the idea not only made sense, but seemed necessary unless he remembered what he'd seen before his world went black. He'd overlooked something. He knew it. If he could recall the missing link, then this nightmare would be over.

Darla whipped her vehicle into her carport and turned off the ignition. "Stay put," she commanded. She grabbed the keys and jumped out to hurry around to his side.

She opened the door and waited for him as he inched to the edge of the seat. Although difficult, he tried to make his actions look easy. But even the smallest movement triggered a rush of pain to rip through his body, and it was too much to hide. Teeth planted firm into his bottom lip, Eric turned to place his feet on the concrete and grasp the car's rim. Slowly, he rose. Dizziness and queasiness overcame him. He swayed and stumbled forward before he caught a pole inside the carport.

Darla hurried to him and took his arm to drape it around her neck.

"Go ahead and put your weight on me," she said with a tiny tremble in her voice. "I'm stronger than I look."

That he had no doubt. He leaned into her, one arm

dangling across her shoulders, her hand clasped round his wrist. Her other arm slipped around his waist, fusing their bodies together. He dropped his chin to meet her gaze. She shivered. Even in his debilitated state, a white-hot fire coursed within him. He held on to her tight, drawing her closer in.

"Are you ready?" Her voice was barely above a whisper.

He gave a small nod. Darla guided him through her house and to her sofa. She sat him down then disappeared and returned moments later with his baggage.

"Would you like to get a shower? You can change into some clean clothes and maybe lay down. You'd be a lot more comfortable."

"That'd be great." The idea of getting out of his sticky clothing and soaking away his soreness sounded fantastic. He wouldn't mind going to bed, either. With her.

She indicated an opening to one side. "My guestroom has a walk-in shower. It's over here. Feel like you can go that far?"

"Not without help. I can't stand for a long time either. I'm fine while I'm still, but when I'm on my feet or if I move too much I get dizzy."

"And you were going to walk home."

He grinned at her. "Join me in the shower?"

She rolled her eyes and shot him an unimpressed look. "The master bath has a sunken tub. Do you think you'll be able to maneuver inside one of those?" Then without missing a beat, "By yourself?"

"Can you help me get there?"

"Of course. I'm a Texas girl. I can do lots of

things."

"Yeah, well, we Scottish men are pretty tough too."

"You must be." Darla picked up his bag. "I can't believe you didn't stay in the hospital for the night, although I'm not sure leaving was one of your better ideas."

Eric chuckled. "Obviously, you haven't read much of my press. My critics claim I've 'ad lots of bad ideas."

"I prefer to form my own opinions." She smiled. "I'll get the tub ready first, then come back for you. Do you need anything else?"

"I could use some pain relievers if you've got 'em. The crap they gave me has pretty well worn off, and I'm unable to get these prescriptions filled until tomorrow."

"If you'd stayed at the hospital, you'd gotten another dose of the good stuff."

"Maybe you'll give me a dose of your good stuff."

She put a hand on her hip "You're really going there? I can't believe you're even thinking in that direction after being shot. Not to mention the gigantic knot on your head."

"What can I say? I'm a guy." He made a gesture toward his lap. "Head injuries and bullet wounds have no effect on the entity between a man's legs."

"A mind of its own, I get it." She giggled. "I have ibuprofen. Let me start the water, and then I'll bring them to you."

She turned to leave.

"Darla?"

She skidded to a halt and looked over her shoulder.

"Thank you."

"I'll get things ready for you." And she disappeared.

He leaned back against the sofa cushions. He took the opportunity to inspect the room and get a better grip of what this woman was about. The home was smaller than his, but had an opened, airy atmosphere. Everything appeared spotless, each item in a proper place. The only indication of something amiss was a leather jacket folded neatly over the arm of the couch, near where he sat.

Shane's coat.

He swallowed, doing his best to ignore the implication, hoping nothing had happened between Shane and Darla other than she'd borrowed his coat. He didn't think so since his manager was the type to brag. Shane hadn't mentioned anything. Still, the sight of the jacket made him fume. He pushed the thought away and continued his study. Huge windows situated across the back, left uncovered, displayed the clear night sky. The ceilings were high, and vaulted with natural wood beams. A decorative fireplace positioned in the front of the area was the counter focus. The walls were bright, painted in cheerful colors, while the furniture and fixtures projected an eclectic flavor. The place combined a mixture of class, fun, and, elegance. Like the owner.

Darla reentered the room. "Tub is filling."

"This is a nice place."

She glided to him. "I only wish it were mine. I'm glad to be living by the sea though. I grew up on the Gulf of Mexico. I missed being close to the water."

She helped him get to his feet, slipping his arm over her shoulder. He inclined into her, using her as his personal crutch. He did his best to ignore the wooziness, throbbing, or the bleeding through the bandage of his bullet wound. It oozed down his forearm and dripped from his fingertips.

"What, do you rent?"

"No. Friends of my boss, the Sundays, own the place. I'm house sitting indefinitely while they travel the planet. I couldn't afford this area any other way."

Together they took a step. She guided him through her bedroom and on into the bathroom. She released him as soon as they crossed the threshold. He leaned against the pedestal sink while she hurried to the bathtub to twist the streaming faucets off.

Steam drifted above the water. Or at least he thought water was in the bath. He couldn't be sure what was inside because a mass of bubbles hovered on the top, covering everything. Eric stared harder. Did they sparkle? Suds floated everywhere. Over the side, skimming onto the mat, soaking the floor.

Darla beamed and gestured toward the tub. "Bath's ready."

He bent forward to sniff. "What hell is in there and what's that smell?" He gave his head a slight shake. "My hair may be long, I might wear an earring, but there's nothing feminine about me. I don't do pink crap or sudsy baths. Alone anyway."

"I did not put in any pink crap or bubbles." Darla's expression morphed into exasperation. "I sprinkled a little lavender aromatherapy to help you relax enough to sleep, which you'll need to get well."

He frowned. "You and I obviously don't have the same idea as to what a little is. It doesn't matter how much stink you put in, I doubt it's going to make me better." He gave her a side glance, "but I appreciate the efforts."

"I can tell."

"I do. Although, if you're serious about helping me, then come take off my shirt."

She stood across the room and studied him close as if to determine whether he was joking or sincere. He didn't move, but waited until she finally understood he did indeed mean for her to help him undress. She hesitantly walked to him. They faced each other, standing toe to toe like rivals.

With unsteady fingers, she grasped the hem of his shirt and gradually lifted it to his neck. The backs of her warm hands grazed his skin weaving tiny, electric jolts into each nerve ending. His mouth dried.

Maybe her undressing him wasn't such a good idea, but it was too late to stop the process. In more ways than one.

She maneuvered the wounded arm, carefully peeling the fabric away from the dried blood. Once the material dislodged, she lifted the shirt over his head, then slid it down his good arm, allowing it to drop onto the floor.

Careful as she was, the extra movements forced him to clutch onto her shoulder and keep a tight hold of the sink to stay upright. He continued to grip both after everything stopped spinning, but only long enough to kick off his shoes.

Timidly, she stepped away after he released his grasp and rushed to the bathroom door. "I'll get your medication."

"What about my pants?"

She turned around and stared at him. He actually

heard her gulp. He held in a laugh at her obvious effort not to gawk at his near nakedness on her way back to him. She returned to stand in front of him, silently gaping at the top button of his jeans.

Licking her lips, she placed her trembling fingers on either side of his fly. The featherlike pressure of her barely there stroke produced a rippling stir deep in his gut. The sensations continued to grow.

She slowly unsnapped the metal fasteners away from their worn outlets, one by one. Eric's heart thudded harder against his chest as inadvertent caresses drove him close to the edge, to the point of ignoring his pain and doing the impossible. She stopped and stared at the opening where an obvious bulge made his desires known.

He brushed her mouth with his. "I'll take it from here, luv. Even in my decrepit state, I'm not sure I'll be behavin' if I let you go any further."

Darla dropped her hands and spun to hurry away.

"Don't forget the ibuprofen. And bring the whole bottle. I need a bunch."

She came to an abrupt stop, then did a slow rotation and pointed a forefinger. "You'll get the appropriated dosage amount as directed on the instructions. Nothing more."

Eric turned his back, shoved his jeans and underwear down his legs, exposing his backside to her. Darla gasped and rushed out of the bathroom. He chuckled. If he didn't feel like shit, he'd be having an awful lot of fun. He held on to the sink and strained to step out of his pants and boxers. The effort was agonizing, but he managed. Thankfully, the room was small and he made it into the tub, although he struggled when sitting, almost blacking out twice.

The water lapped over his body, the heat soothed his skin. He had to admit, the stuff Darla added did relax him. He closed his eyes and drifted in and out of an uncomfortable doze, unable to erase the memory of Finn's dead body or the stony chunk of steel slamming against his temple. And he'd seen stuff while under the medications at the hospital. But now his reality was questionable. The person holding the gun was nothing more than a fuzzy image.

He fully awakened when Darla reentered, carrying a bottle of water and the ibuprofen. She walked to the bathtub. Their fingers touched as she gave him the medicine.

"How are you?"

He popped the pills into his mouth, then tipped the water bottle up, draining over half in one gulp. He hadn't realized he was thirsty. "I'm fine," he lied, before he finished off the drink.

"I'll let you rest." She started to leave.

"No, wait." Eric lifted a hand from the tub to reach out to her. "Stay," he whispered. "Please. I don't want to be alone right now."

He had no idea what possessed him to make such a request, nor did she ask him why. She simply sat down on the floor next to him.

He sunk lower into the water, leaving only his head and one arm exposed to rest on the edge. Darla grasped for his hand to hold in hers, their fingers interlocked. Mixed sensations of comfort and intimacy welled in his chest. The act alone frightened him. The urge to repel her gesture was overwhelming. Yet he didn't let go.

Instead, he squeezed her hand and closed his eyes.

The fears he faced drifted through his mind. He'd lost friends, he was broke, and a killer was after him. But what scared him the most, what terrified him more than anything was this woman, this unaverage teacher from Texas.

Chapter 14

Darla sat on top of the bedcovers, leaning against a mound of pillows. She contemplated the sunrays that peeked through the blinds, etching shadows of vertical strips across the hardwood. A slight movement stirred beside her and prompted her attention to return to what she'd done most of the night.

Stare at Eric sleeping.

She released a deep sigh and swallowed an ocean of moisture that seemed to form in her mouth every time she looked at him. He lay on his stomach, the sheet twisted around his waist. His bare back was exposed, one leg stuck out from under the covers, his face buried into the pillow, while the rest of his head remained concealed by a muss of hair.

She lingered, taking in his broad shoulders as her gaze flowed downward to inspect the taut contours of his back. Again. Like she hadn't already mentally imprinted his upper torso into her memory forever.

He had a rough night. She should be worried over his health, but she couldn't help thinking about him in an entirely different way. Instead of concern, her thoughts persisted toward erotic daydreams, twisting her emotions into a vortex of heated hunger. Restless with need, she burned in certain areas, making her want for him too hard to ignore. Last night, even in his banged up state, he was clear. He wanted her. But just for sex. Could she? She'd wrestled with this question since they'd met. Would she be able to give her body to a man realizing once the physical part was finished, things were over? Given the way she ached for him, would it matter? For the umpteenth time, she mentally shoved these disrupting desires away.

She bent to inspect the cavity penetrating his outer arm. The redness around the exterior area concerned her though his forehead appeared better and his color had returned to normal. Curious, she racked a hand across the shaggy fringe and brushed away the strands from his ear, fighting the urge to plunge her fingers into the softness of his hair. Until he told her, she'd never noticed his piercing before. Now she found the tiny diamond twinkling from his lobe. She licked her lips. His delicious lobe.

He half-opened a blue eye and peeked up from the fluffiness of his pillow.

She withdrew her hand. "You're awake."

"You were rocking the bed. I figured you were about to get me up." He stretched his long body releasing a loud yawn. "Again."

"No. I think you're out of the woods."

"I was never in the woods."

"I beg to differ. The bump on your forehead was bigger than a baseball. The doctors believe you have a concussion, although they weren't much on information as to how to treat one. So I checked online, and you did show several symptoms. My following the directions, waking you every two hours, plus adding ice helped bring the swelling down quite a bit. Although you need to keep an eye on the area for a few days."

"Thank you for your Internet expertise, Nurse Darla."

"Now you're being an ass." She put her hand to his forehead to comb his bangs through her fingers. "The knot is down about half the size from last night. The icepack did the trick." She let his hair drop and leaned over to get a better view of his bullet wound. "This is angry, though. The inflammation worries me." She lightly laid a palm over the hole. "And the place is warm."

He flinched with a hiss.

She removed her hand. "Does it hurt?"

"Hell, yeah, it hurts. 'Specially when you mash on it."

"Quit being a baby, I barely touched you. I suppose I'll get the same foul response I've been getting all night if I suggest you make another trip to the doctor."

"You suppose correct."

She stretched across him to retrieve a tube of ointment from the nightstand. "Let me put some more of this antibiotic cream on."

"What's the point? The stuff isn't doing any good. The place keeps getting worse. You've smeared enough greasy shit on me. I should never need an oil change."

"This is the only medication I have. I don't know what else to do until we get your prescriptions filled." She cleaned off the blood with a wet wipe, then unscrewed the lid, and pressed the end of the aluminum cylinder to expel the cream. She put a fair amount on the tips of her fingers before she dabbed the medicine over the wound.

"What? The Internet doesn't give additional instructions on how to treat a gunshot?"

"As a matter of fact, there are some directions." She sat back as she twisted the cap onto the medication. After she laid the tube down, she plucked a tissue from the box sitting by the bed to wipe the excess from her skin. "It says for you to go back to the doctor."

"Funny." He flipped over. "What I really need is a smoke. Except you have my only pack, so that's not gonna happen either, I guess."

"Your lungs will appreciate me someday." She put the tissue down, then waved a palm over him. "This is the problem. Every time I smear ointment on you, you turn over and rub everything off on the sheets. That's why the salve isn't working."

He sighed loud, spun around, and raised his brows. "Happy?"

"No matter if you're lying on your back or front, every time you move, you wipe the stuff away." She leaned in to re-smooth the balm over the gash. "I know we left the hole uncovered to allow some air to get through, but let's cover it for the day and see what happens." Without waiting for him to reply, she rolled from the bed, going into her bathroom for the required materials. Then she walked back into the room to settle next to him again to dress the wound. "What's with this tattoo?"

He glanced over his shoulder at the etching of a lightning bolt striking into a heart with wings covering his back. "Like it?"

"I think it's interesting." She shifted to get a little closer to tape down the gauze. "Definitely expresses your views on matters of the heart. I mean, there's no better way to say love sucks than inking the sentiments onto your body." Darla pressed down on the final strip of medical tape, and then sat back to view her work.

Eric looked at her. "You're not much of a morning person, are you?"

"I didn't sleep a lot last night."

"Nobody made you stay awake."

After she helped him out of the tub he'd been close to passing out, complaining of a severe headache. To add to his problem, the warm water washed away the clot over his wound, inciting a stream of blood to flow down his arm. She put him into her bed, cleaned him, and compressed the gunshot until the bleeding stopped.

He was in such crucial need, she barely noticed his nakedness when she assisted him from the bathtub and dried him off. The discomfort she'd experienced earlier from undressing him disappeared as she slid a pair of boxers over his legs to cover his lower body.

He claimed he couldn't make it to her guestroom. He had such a difficult time walking into her bedroom, he convinced her he was in awful shape, hence her decision, however bad, to stay with him and keep an eye on him throughout the night.

Eric grinned. "You should have crawled under the covers with me, laid your head on my shoulder, and slept against me."

Uneasy, she twisted a ringlet. His condition had definitely improved. He appeared to be in fine form today.

"I've some sure fire ways to make you tired if you would've had any trouble nodding off."

"You can't do anything. You're hurt, remember?"

"I'm much better this morning, thanks to your tender lovin' care." He put his good arm around her and drew her closer to him. "Let me return the favor. I'll relax you enough to where you'll sleep through tomorrow. Only fair I get to wake you up every two hours same as you did me, but not for icepacks or cream."

"I don't think this is a good idea. You may re-aggravate your injuries." She attempted to shove him back, but he resisted.

"It takes more than a lump on the head or a bullet to stop me." He swiped his lips across hers. "Plus, I need to prove to you I can kiss you to your satisfaction."

She gently pushed him away. This time he moved. "I have no idea what you're thinking."

He rolled onto his side and shot her a wary gaze.

"Okay, I do have an idea," Darla suppressed a smile. "Or more like I felt what was on your, ahm, mind when you were close to me."

Eric laughed as he glanced down at the obvious bulge between his legs showing from under the sheet. "I'm sure you did."

Darla gave him a light tap on the head. "Focus." She frowned at him and laid her hands in her lap. "Let's be clear here. I realize in your circles, certain things are done in a more casual manner. You have a freer attitude than I'm used to."

Eric chuckled and repeated, "Certain things in a casual manner. You're talkin' 'bout sex, right?"

"You know what I mean."

"Then come out and say the word, luv. Fuckin'."

Darla stared at him. "First off, I'm not that crude. And second, why do I need to say anything when you know very well what I'm talking about?"

"First off, you may not be crude, but I get the

impression you might enjoy things a little down and dirty every once in a while."

Darla's gasp triggered Eric's grin to widen.

"And second, you and I both see where this is going. So don't act all proper. Let things take a natural course."

"You think whatever you want about me. My point is we live in entirely different universes. Natural or not, this isn't going to happen."

"Sometimes universes collide. The explosion can be earth shattering."

"Not this one."

Eric rolled to his back with a laugh. "We'll see."

"You have such an ego. I mean, do you think you can just look at me with those deep blue eyes, flash your cute little dimples, and believe you'll mold me in your hands like putty?"

"Putty?" He propped onto his elbow. "No, I don't want any clay, but you? Yeah, I want you in my hands." His mouth curved as his eyes shined wickedly.

Her heart bumped in double time. How was she supposed to react to this? This was too much. Him, in her bed, all muscled and bare-chested, being naughty, charming, and sexy rolled into one. Not to mention his obvious erection.

She held up a hand. "Okay, stop. No more talking about—sex. Not happening."

"Whatever you say, luv." Eric lay back again. He angled his head in her direction, his mischievous, know-it-all grin intact. "You like my eyes and dimples?"

"I'm not...yes, I mean no."

He rolled to her, rising until his face was even with

hers. "So which is it?"

Darla forced herself to turn away. He traced a finger under her jawline until he found her chin and gently returned her to him. He tilted her face even with his and rubbed his lips against hers, then paused before he kissed her with amazing tenderness. He pulled back, gazing into her eyes, asking a silent question.

"You're not playing fair," she murmured.

"No. I usually don't." He chuckled quietly. "Did I meet your approval this time?"

Darla understood this flirtation was because he wanted sex, yet somewhere deep inside she wished he was serious. She needed this. So she hurled away her doubts, the fears and, accepted the reality; she was his entertainment for a short while. Without caution, she slid her arms carefully under his, letting her hands meet across his lower back. She drew him closer to hold him more secure against her, then buried her head into his good side.

"Oh, yeah, I approve."

He eased in a few more inches and smoothed the wild curls away from her face. His eyes were dark, pupils dilated to show his desires mirrored hers. He dipped his head as their mouths hungrily merged.

She let out a little sigh. He lost it. And she lost it. The heat from his body singed her skin, his hands slid beneath her shirt, finding her breasts. His touch, his kisses, and oh god, his tongue had her gasping for air, almost helpless and unaware the tiny moans filling the room stemmed from her.

Somewhere in the swirls of passion, she realized. This was the moment. The second they'd been leading up to since they'd met. In this instant, nothing else mattered. What existed between them was propelled by some unknown entity. The attraction was much stronger, more powerful than either of them imagined. Their bodies, souls were meant to come together, if only for this one moment, this one time.

He broke the kiss and slightly rose above her. He urged her T-shirt up and slid his hand down the front of her sweatpants and under her panties. She caught a breath. The soft pressure of his thumb circling, stroking, and sliding between her thighs drove her to relinquish control. He understood exactly what to do and he did it very well. If anything described a feeling as too good, this would qualify.

A small tidal wave surged through her, the promise of bigger explosions on the way. Her need for him expanded beyond the plane of wanting more. Pure carnality detonated within her. She opened her legs wider, to invite him in. She wanted all of him.

He crawled over her, sank down on top of her, and growled in her ear, "We need to get these clothes off."

He kissed her lips softly before he shoved her pants and underwear down at the same time, and tore off his boxers. The mere sight of him naked, made her hotter, the craving for him to be inside her amplified. He elevated over her, then lowered to cover her body with his and settled between her legs, his lips once more finding hers.

She froze, then put a hand on his chest to stop him.

He sucked in and stopped. "What?"

"You need to get off me," she hissed.

"Why? What'd I do?"

"It's not you," she whispered. "I think I heard the front door open. Someone's here."

In a fluid motion, Eric rolled away from her. As Darla crawled out of bed, she yanked her shirt down, located her sweats, and slipped them over her hips.

"Stephanie sometimes stops by for coffee in the mornings," she said in a low voice as she headed toward the door.

"Get rid of her."

Darla walked into the next room and stopped her in her tracks. Her jaw dropped to the ground. Impossible. If she wasn't seeing this with her own eyes, she wouldn't believe it.

Finally she found her voice. "Um, Mr. and Mrs. Sunday?"

The owners of her house stood inside her living area. Mr. Sunday was at the bay windows, his back to her, while Mrs. Sunday was inspecting the new paint job on the walls with a sour expression. Both whipped around. The woman raked a scrutinized gaze over her, but Mr. Sunday grinned.

"Darla."

She fleetingly met their eyes, but quickly dipped her chin to hide the blush coating her skin. She maybe should've re-adjusted her T-shirt better, except she hadn't expected her uninvited visitors to be the proprietors of her home.

"Did we wake you?"

Darla raised her head, taken aback by the casual question. "Um, yes, I mean no, um," She peeked at her bedroom door. "What are you doing here? I wasn't expecting…"

"It's obvious you weren't anticipating company, dear," Mrs. Sunday replied in a haughty tone.

Her husband glanced at his wife. "Under normal

circumstances, we'd have called so you could make other arrangements for a place to stay, but we spoke with your boss, and he told us you were on your way to Texas. Did your plans change?"

"No, I had to postpone the trip. I'll probably leave in the morning."

"What are these brown stains on the floor?" Mrs. Sunday looked down then transferred her attention to the furniture. "Whatever it is, it's spread over the sofa too."

"Maids day off?" She gave a lame chuckle and did a quick scan at the stains.

She didn't notice Eric was bleeding last night until she'd got him into bed, and she especially hadn't realized he'd dripped on the hardwood or ruined the couch. "I'll get it cleaned."

Mrs. Sunday pointed to the fabric. "I don't believe that's going to come out."

Darla was ready to explode, unsure how to handle the situation. Yes, they were the owners. But they needed to get out of here, pronto.

"I suppose we could find another place to stay for the night." Mrs. Sunday suggested in a vague tone. "You'll be leaving tomorrow then?"

"I can be ready tonight if necessary."

Mrs. Sunday gave a nod as her inspection transferred from the ruined fabric to Shane's coat across the arm of the chair. Darla seriously needed to return his jacket.

"Tomorrow will be fine." Mr. Sunday hardly tore his eyes away from her. Even though she had on sweat pants, she was acutely mindful her underwear was in the other room. The lines in Mr. Sunday's forehead deepened and he finally looked in a different direction. "What's with all of the traffic in the neighborhood?"

"Oh, we've had some trouble in the area."

"Trouble?" they both exclaimed, alarmed.

Darla opened her mouth to explain the situation, but halted. The couple simultaneously flinched and spun round to stare in the direction of the bedroom. Darla became still as a statue. Her heart rate plummeted; her mind prodded her to look. She slowly turned to her room.

Eric stood in the doorway. He leaned against the frame his arms folded with an angry expression over his face. "Everything okay, luv?"

Chapter 15

Mr. Sunday stuttered an awkward apology and his wife looked appalled as they hurried toward the door. The couple exited without a glimpse behind. They didn't mention when they'd be back or if they planned on returning later. Darla watched them leave through narrowed eyes. Once her unwelcome company disappeared, she stomped to the front door, and gave it an extra shove, then twisted the lock with added force.

She whipped around to Eric. "What the hell do you think you're doing? I don't need you coming in here announcing your presence—" She stopped to process her thought.

"I didn't announce anything. I hardly spoke a word."

"You were standing in the bedroom door half naked." With a thumb pointed to her chest, she stated, "This was my problem, and I can take care of myself."

"Your problem?"

"I'm being very clear, here."

"That old guy was practically slobbering all over himself. The perv kept staring at you, looking at your tits through that thin shirt, and the woman behaved like a first class snob."

"They own this house and are friends of my boss. They also contribute large donations to the university where I work. Do you realize the position you put me in?"

He gave a disbelieving snort.

Darla glowered at him with tightened lips.

Eric hacked a soft cough. "If they were as highbrow as they projected, then they should be more considerate of personal space. You're allowed a private life. What goes on during your time is no one's business. If the boss doesn't like it, well fuck him."

"Some people don't take to that kind of attitude. The Sundays clearly got the wrong idea about how I live. They may tell my supervisor they'd prefer someone else living here. I could lose my home and this might cause problems between me and my boss."

"Sorry if my conduct gets you in trouble. Bottom line, I didn't enjoy the way those assholes treated you. That's why I made my"—he gestured over his lack of attire—"appearance."

Darla's scowl deepened as she studied him. He wasn't happy with how they acted toward her.

This admission pleased her. And he was correct. Owners or not, those people were pretentious and warped. Their shocked expression over the sight of Eric emerging from her bedroom followed by their race to the door prompted a hint of a smile. Her grin slowly spread across her face before she burst into uncontrollable giggles.

The corner of Eric's eyes crinkled as he joined in her laughter.

"Did you see them?" She couldn't contain her amusement.

"They hurried out of here fast. Wheeew." Eric made a flying motion with his hand. "I'm surprised they didn't leave skid marks on the floor to go with the blood stains."

They shared a smiling stare. Their amusement instantly died.

"Might be another reason I made my entrance." Eric's voice was low and rough. He stepped to her. "I didn't appreciate the interruption."

Darla's heart gave a decisive thump as her mouth watered. The morning light shined onto the arch of his muscular shoulders. His chest was adorned with a dark strip of hair that trailed across the middle and stretched over his pecs. The red-hot vision made her forget everything except what stood in front of her.

He lowered his head, demanding her full attention. "Now where were we?"

His lips hovered over hers. A slight warmness from his breath tickled her skin. He slid an arm around her waist to draw her into him. She inhaled to savor his scent, an unmistakable reminder of his maleness. She tilted back to look into his indigo eyes. They revealed hunger, sparking her yearnings to surge. Neither spoke. No words were needed. He wanted her as much as she wanted him. Without thinking, she boldly pressed her mouth into his.

At first, he tensed, but his shock only lasted for a millisecond. He glided a hand around the back of her neck, his fingers intertwined into her curls to angle her head slightly. He deepened the pressure with his lips to take charge. Sexual currents sparked a tide of fiery intenseness scorching her inside and out.

Their kiss didn't last long. The click of the lock forced them to jump apart. For the second time that morning, they had unwelcome guests. Stephanie and

Blaine entered the house. Whatever they were discussing discontinued the instant they walked inside. Their surprised gazes bounced from Darla to Eric.

"Oh, you're here." Blaine grinned.

Eric directed his eyes upward and mumbled, "Is there anyone who doesn't have a key to this place?"

Blaine's smile widened. "Are we interrupting?"

"Not anymore." Eric adjusted his boxers.

Blaine drifted closer to inspect Eric's head. "Your bump looks better, but your disposition hasn't improved much." He gave Eric a quick once-over. "Nice outfit."

Eric fixed an annoyed glance on his friend and turned away.

Stephanie pointed a forefinger toward the street. "Whose car was flying out of your drive as we were coming in?"

"Homeowners." Darla smoothed her hair. "They got word I was leaving town and dropped in to check out their home."

"They just stopped by?" Stephanie rolled her eyes.

Darla nodded. "They didn't call first, so their visit was a *pleasant* surprise."

"It's like a revolving door around here today," Eric chimed.

"Well, you might want to stay inside, regardless," Stephanie told him. "We drove past your house. Reporters are everywhere."

"Yeah, we found the same thing last night, which is why I'm here."

Blaine sniggered. "I bet that's the reason."

Eric frowned at him and ignored his jab. "I assumed the gathering at our place is because of Finn's death, unless someone else we know died and we've yet to be informed."

"As far as I know, we're all accounted for. Our discovery of Finn's body is all over the news. I hear the police are looking for his brother to bring in for questioning," Blaine warned. "He seems to have vanished, which is interesting."

"Good. When they find him they can lock him up for being a bloodsucking leech."

"The detectives called me this morning," Blaine told Eric. "They are satisfied with us leaving town and suggested we do it immediately. They believe we're in some deep shit."

"I'm not feeling the idea anymore."

"What? Drake's dead. Mitchell is recovering with round the clock protection guarding his hospital room. We found Finn's body. Someone shot you and conked you on the head hard enough to knock you out and fuck up your memory. A crazy nutcase has it in for our group. We need to disappear."

"All the more reason to stay and figure things out before we go anywhere. Besides, we have a solid notion of who is behind all of this."

"There's a rumor going around he's been sighted. Here. In the area."

"Good. We should smoke him out."

"Yeah." Blaine grimaced. "Let's hang here and be sitting ducks for a murdering maniac."

"How do you know he won't follow us?"

"I don't. But the police said our best bet is to vanish until they can catch the guy."

"And what if that doesn't happen." Eric's voice rose. "People get away with shit all the time. How long are we supposed to hide? They expect us to run and put our lives on hold indefinitely."

"Protecting ourselves only makes sense. Someone might want me dead and the thought of dying doesn't thrill me much. If you view me as a coward, then so be it, but I'm scared."

The two had closed in on each other and stood nose to nose. Darla's intuition told her the men were tighter than brothers. This was one of those sibling type disagreements. She doubted the altercation would come to blows. Still, someone needed to intervene so they'd cool down to discuss their options in a more reasonable manner.

"Coffee." She squeaked the interruption. "Who needs coffee? I do. I'm going to go make some." She didn't wait for any replies and hurried off toward the kitchen.

"I'll help you." Stephanie gave the guys a worried glance before she followed.

Darla retrieved the carafe and shifted to the sink to hold it under the faucet. She stared out the window, listening to the men quarrel from the other room while she filled the pot with water.

They'd lowered their voices. She was unable to make out what they said.

Stephanie spoke in a quiet tone. "We had no idea Eric was here and we certainly didn't mean to interrupt." She hesitated. "He seems to have improved nicely. Has he let you in on anything?"

Darla's mouth leveled into a straight line. "Not much." She poured the water into the coffeemaker. "Eric claims to be an aboveboard kind of guy. Although I'm getting the vibe he's a lot more complex than he lets on." She placed a dry filter into the coffeemaker's basket. "This is only a feeling, though I'm guessing he has a handle on who put a bullet in him and the rest of the band, or at least he knows who's behind it, but he's not talking."

"They're both staying tightlipped about the whole thing. Blaine hasn't mentioned a word to me either. I even asked. He ignored me and changed the subject."

"The only point that makes sense is what we first assumed. Their missing manager is involved."

"I think so." Stephanie cleared her throat. "Blaine plans to disappear for a while. He believes Eric should too."

"A given, considering their ongoing argument." Darla scooped grounds into the filter, then stopped. She turned to Stephanie with a frown. A slew of mental warning bells clanged loud in her head. "Did Blaine tell you where he is going?"

"I don't think it's been decided." There was a long pause. "I'm considering taking a trip myself."

Darla gave her a doubtful glance.

"To my sister's. Remember, she lives in Great Falls, Montana."

"I do remember. She runs a lodge, right?" Darla finished filling the machine with coffee before she flipped the switch. She rotated back to her friend, leaned a hip against the bar, her arms resting across her middle.

"Yeah, um." Stephanie took a breath before she rushed on. "Since you're going to Texas, there's no reason for me to hang around here. I've got plenty of vacation time saved at work."

"Plus, you've wanted to go visit her for a while." Darla returned to the cabinet to take down four cups.

She placed them on the center island. "Didn't you tell me she lives in a lonely, desolate area?" She pointedly regarded her friend. "A good place to lie low if one needed to."

Stephanie averted Darla's obvious glare.

"The plans are made. You're taking Blaine with you."

She gave an uneasy nod.

"And Eric? He's already been shot. He needs to disappear too if he agrees."

"Yeah, Eric. Ahm. We were thinking he could go with you," she suggested hopefully.

"You want me to take him with me. To Port Isabel. To stay at my family's house." She stared at Stephanie. "Are you crazy?"

Darla definitely didn't like this idea. Yeah, she had difficulties concentrating this morning. Her mind wouldn't quit contemplating what would've happened between them if there hadn't been interruptions. But she'd deal with that. Taking him to Texas, spending the next few weeks in his constant company would be a major risk for her—a risk of her losing her heart, if it wasn't too late already.

"What's the problem, Dar? By the looks of things, you two are getting along well." Stephanie's eyes widened. "I mean very well. Besides, Blaine is the greatest guy I've met in a long time. I don't want to stop seeing him, plus we get a chance to help them."

Darla raised her brows.

"To keep them alive." Stephanie's expression turned anxious. "I would die if anything happened to him."

"What if we can't? What happens if we take them

and the killer gets them anyway? Stephanie, you always do this. You don't think. When you meet a guy, you throw yourself into the relationship headfirst without giving consequences a second thought. You're right. Someone is trying to murder them. Someone who possibly assassinated two people, maybe a third if the drummer doesn't live. If this person wants them dead, they won't hesitate to get rid of whoever gets in their way. We'll be putting ourselves and our families in danger. Your sister has a husband with two little kids. Did you think about that?"

The conversation between them stopped. The quiet hush amplified the coffeemaker's hiss as the aroma of caffeine filled the small kitchen. Low vibrations from the voices in the other room echoed in the background. Darla hurried to the counter to reach for the pot. She removed it, walked to where she'd laid out the dishes, and poured out the liquid.

"Another thing. You're asking me to travel sixteen hundred miles with a guy that has a bullet in his arm and a head injury. He's okay now, but what if he takes a turn for the worse?" She replaced the carafe, picked up two of the cups, and nodded for Stephanie to carry the others. "He's stubborn anyway, and when it comes to getting medical attention, the guy's bullheadedness goes beyond senseless. I don't want to get into this situation any deeper than I already am."

"Might be a moot point, Dar. He hasn't consented to going anywhere. This is only an option in case he agrees."

The women walked into the other room. Eric was also returning to the room now dressed in jeans and a button-down shirt.

"We're doing what the police suggested and leaving town. We just need to call them and let them know where we'll be, in case they have to contact us. This seems like the only savable solution." Blaine leaned closer to Stephanie and lowered his voice. "Did you talk to her?"

She bit her lip with a nod. "Did you talk to him?"

"He did," Eric answered. "And I'm now inclined to agree that leaving the area might not be a bad plan. I also think the idea of us going in different directions is a sound one. If someone is after us, they'll travel a long way to find us both." He eyed Darla as he took the mug from her. "I realize it's a big imposition and possibly a dangerous one, but can I go to Texas with you?"

****

Darla had some errands to run before she left for her trip, plus she agreed to pick up Eric's prescription medications. Still unsure if allowing Eric to accompany her to Texas was a good decision, she was glad for the opportunity to get away and think about why she consented to go along with this crazy idea.

For Stephanie, the choice was evident. She'd obviously fallen hard for Blaine and would do whatever it took to keep him safe.

Darla's circumstances were different. Did she care about Eric enough to endanger her life if the killer followed them? The answer was a clear yes. Her family was a different story. She wouldn't put them in harm's way. Fortunately Eric didn't want to gamble with their lives either, and told her he'd find other accommodations once they reached her hometown.

This solved most of her problems. The long drive remained an issue. They'd be alone the entire time. Her physical wellbeing was one thing, but was she prepared to jeopardize her heart too? This guy had her on an emotional ledge and she feared she was about to take a deep plunge. She dreaded the emotive fallout once they parted ways.

She sighed and glanced at the dash's digital clock as she drove into her carport. She'd planned to be back much sooner and on the road, except a traffic jam kept her on the freeway longer than she'd anticipated. Now she was late. Darkness had already fallen. Perhaps it would be better to wait to leave tomorrow, then she reconsidered. She didn't want a repeat with the Sundays in case they happened to make another appearance.

She found Eric asleep on the sofa. She'd covered the blood on the couch earlier with a blanket and arranged for some furniture cleaners to come pick it up later in the week. Eric offered to pay to have the stain removed or to buy her a new one if that wasn't possible. She walked past him and onto the hall closet. From there, she dragged her luggage out.

Eric groaned, slowly raising his head. "You're back."

She tried to avoid staring at him, all cute and groggy from sleep. She swallowed and clutched the suitcase handle tight, using it as a restraint not to charge over and attack him. Mussed hair, his jawline covered with a dark shadow from missing a shave, he managed successfully to appear both roguish and sexy at the same time.

"There was a huge pileup on the 101. I sat on the road for an hour." She pulled her bags into the middle of the room. "Did you succeed in getting past the press and inside and out of your house with your stuff?"

A hint of a smile played on his lips as he sat up. He waved to a stack by the glass door. "We're experts at sneaking by the paparazzi."

She eyed his two small suitcases sitting next to three guitar cases. She turned back to him with raised eyebrows.

"Priorities, luv."

"You managed to get five items out without the tabloids noticing you? You are experts."

Eric's grin developed into a full smile. "You'll be finding out soon enough."

Darla shook her head and ignored the jolt between her thighs. "Save it." She picked up her bags. "I'm going to go pack. I've left my SUV open. Can you move and load your stuff in the back?"

"I should be able to."

"Good. Keep the lights off in the carport. I've made sure the interior car lights are out too. Since the house sits on top of a slope, we can be spotted from anywhere in the neighborhood. I don't want anyone, meaning any reporters, to catch us." She paused. "Be sure you don't press any of your stuff against my hanging clothes. I just picked them up from the dry cleaners and would rather not have them wrinkled."

He gave her a small salute as he stood. "Aye. M' finger pads won't graze a stitch of your fine garments, luv," he replied, exaggerating his brogue.

She ignored his smart ass comment and continued, "A cooler is behind the driver's seat filled with sandwiches and drinks, if you're hungry. I plan on eating once we get on the road."

"I'm not ready for food. I'll eat when you do."

Darla hurried, packed her things, then rolled her

suitcases out to her car and placed them beside Eric's. She'd put the third seat down earlier, so there was plenty of room. Even though he appeared better, he would need to sleep. She threw a spare blanket and pillow in the middle section. Now all that was left for her to load was Eric.

She strolled back inside. Through the windows she observed him on the deck having a smoke. She opened the door and stepped out, wondering where he'd gotten the nicotine but didn't ask.

She pointed to the cigarette. "You're aware you can't do that in my car, right?"

Eric angled away to exhale. "Yes. I believe you've made your opinion clear about my bad habit."

"It is a filthy addiction, although I realize a hard one to do without. Are you going to be all right? Not smoking for a long time?"

"Does it matter?"

"You should quit."

"Heard it before." He flicked a cool gaze at her. "Maybe Raging Impulse was only a teen band, but I did all the rock and roll clichés. I won't go into the gory details, although there was a short stint where I got hooked on pills. I even went to rehab a couple of times before I was able to kick 'em. When I quit doing drugs, I stopped drinking. I eat healthy. I exercise to keep in shape. So I have one harmful weakness."

Darla did her best to digest this confession and not appear surprised. Up to now, he'd been flippant or vague about who he was. His almost allowing her into such a dark place in his past showed he was coming to trust her.

He gave her a side glance. "I bet if we dove into

your personal habits, we'll find you possess a couple of bad ones too."

"I enjoy ice cream. A lot."

"See?"

"Too much ice cream may only hurt me. It doesn't pollute my surroundings or damage anyone else from second hand effects." Darla paused and frowned at him. "Wait a minute. You said you don't drink, but you had one at the party."

"Diet soda, luv." He tossed the butt over the side of the deck, turned to her, and smiled. "I do have one other vice." He grasped her arm and tugged her to him, bringing her snug against his chest. "I'm more than willing to let you help me with this one." He nuzzled her hair aside, lightly trailed kisses down her neck.

Swells waved in the pit of her stomach. She took a long, deep breath and dragged her body away from him, about to remind him they needed to get on the road. But the burning fire in his eyes persuaded her to remain quiet.

He drew her back to him. After a slight hesitation, he pressed his mouth against hers. One arm curled around her middle, while his other hand sifted through her curls. He hugged her closer into him, fitting the notch of her thighs into the thickened hardness of his erection. A spur of thrills roused and burst between her legs where she grew warmer.

A growl vibrated in his throat. His body bore into hers, directing her with his weight and drove her into a chaise lounge behind them without breaking their kiss. He lengthened his arm toward the bottom to trigger the chair to fall back flat and maneuvered over her.

Darla reluctantly pulled away. "We need to go

inside and do this."

"It's dark. No one can see us."

A vaguely familiar crack whizzed over their heads.

"Shit," Eric yelped.

Instinctively, they rolled off the lounge, clutching one another as they crashed to the boarded surface. Darla landed on top of Eric, who grunted loud as they hit the ground.

He struggled to catch his breath. "Are you okay?"

"I'm fine. You?"

"No new injuries, but the old ones hurt like hell."

Darla peeked. "What's going on?"

He cupped his hand around the crown of her head to haul her into him. "Keep down." He covered her with his arms. Darla clung to him, her face buried into his shoulder. Another deep, piercing pop rang out from the night followed by a chink, like metal hitting glass.

Darla jerked. "Someone is shooting at us."

Eric tightened his hold around her, his voice sounding a little more than a rumble. "Texas girl knows the sound of a gun."

"Damn straight I do." She struggled to escape his grip, but even with a bad arm he kept her from moving. "Who's firing at us?"

"Not so loud." He put his lips to her ear. "I can't get a good look at who's doing the shooting."

"We need some guns too."

"Hold on. Don't go crazy." He raised his head to do a quick survey. "I don't hear anything now."

Darla stayed motionless as she strained to listen. "They might be moving for a different angle on us."

"The car is unlocked. I'd say keep low and get inside. Then make a break for the SUV."

"What if they see us? There could be more than one."

"I'd rather take a chance and try to survive this, as opposed to us staying put and getting my ass shot off."

She didn't respond but rolled off Eric. She crouched down to crawl into the house with him close behind. Holding hands, they made their way through the darkened rooms and onto the carport. The doors to the vehicle stood open.

They separated. Darla squinted to gauge out into the night. With the exception of the faint roar of the ocean and the rumble of a motorcycle, the neighborhood sat quiet. Eric's steps were light as he walked around to the back to quietly latch the SUV's rear hatch as he and Darla shut the side doors with ease.

"I left the keys inside," Darla whispered

Eric reached for her hand. "You're not going anywhere by yourself."

****

He hid his bike and returned to the SUV to view the chaos he'd caused. Standing in the darkness, he watched them disappear into the house. He peeked around the carport's edge and inside the loaded vehicle. They only thought they were escaping him. What a surprise he had in store for them. He chuckled softly. It didn't take a rocket scientist to figure out their plans. Just took a little attention to detail. Eric and Blaine were turning tail, leaving town with their new girlfriends. Cowards. But this wasn't news.

He forced a diversion, and if he hadn't hit a pot hole and messed up his motorcycle, it'd have been an exciting one. No matter. The distraction gave him the time to set up what he needed. They'd be meeting again in the near future.

He'd done a lot of work to achieve his goals and had some fun too. Like randomly shooting while Eric was in the throes of making his same old moves.

He did have a single regret. If he had arrived a few minutes earlier when Eric stood alone outside, he would have taken him out with a solitary shot. Then only one more issue to resolve.

Yet, he was disappointed Eric behaved so carelessly. Where was the challenge in that? Perhaps the girl had his thoughts in a cloud, or it could be the gash on the head making him think unclearly. No matter. He couldn't wait until the entire band was gone and that would be soon. Very soon.

****

Darla and Eric hurried in, grabbed the keys, ran back outside, and climbed into their seats. She inserted the key, turned the ignition, threw the automobile in reverse, and backed out. In the street, she put the gear in drive, then hit the gas, screeching the tires hard enough to leave rubber ribbons in the asphalt.

Darla clutched the steering wheel. Her heart pounded like a loud drum in her ears. They didn't speak. Both carefully scoured the area as they exited the subdivision. Once on the highway, she stretched to adjust her mirror for a better rear view. "I don't believe anyone followed us, do you?"

"Doesn't look like it." Eric continued to search the night.

"Just a wild guess, but this is the same person who shot you before, right?"

"Probably. I hate to think I have multiple people trying to kill me, though I suppose it's a possibility."

He burrowed further into the leather seats, still cautiously scanning the neighborhood.

"I'm surprise the windows at your house didn't bust when the bullets hit 'em."

"They're bulletproof."

He turned to her with a surprised look.

"I researched the area after I moved in. A drug lord from South America lived in my home about twenty years ago. According to the story, he was paranoid about his safety, so he had shatterproof windows installed. Not that they did him any good. They found his head washed up on the beach, close to where you live. The authorities never discovered his body."

"I'm sorry."

"Huh?"

"I've put you in danger. Anyone connected to me isn't safe. Coming with you was a bad idea."

"I can take care of myself. Besides, where would you go? I mean, I know there are other people in your life. Like family members? They may be at risk too if you're around them or they could be in danger, regardless. You might want to warn them, if you haven't already."

"I haven't spoken to my family." Eric squirmed in his seat. "Everybody who's been hurt lives in the US, not in Scotland. Most of my relatives are either in Aberdeen or London. I'm not worried yet."

"You should call them."

"I will."

Darla's nerves calmed, and she relaxed her grip on the steering wheel. "How come none of you moved back to Scotland after the band broke up?"

"I can't speak for the others. For Blaine and me,

staying here seemed like a better opportunity. Besides my parents and I are not on the best of terms, right now."

Darla glanced sideways.

"They've never been happy with my decision to join Raging Impulse. They don't view music as a career choice but more of a hobby."

"You proved them wrong."

"Didn't matter. They're disappointed in me. My mum and dad aren't poor, although they aren't well off either. I earned a scholarship to the University of Aberdeen. They were excited because I'm the first to go to college in our immediate family."

"To study music?"

"Actually the degree is in architecture. I met Drake, joined the band, and promised my parents I'd finish school." He gave her a sad grin. "I was young and had only one goal in mind. In the end, I didn't keep my word. They're not pleased with me, so we don't talk much."

"How close were you to graduating?"

"Two semesters."

Her eyes widened. "Eric, complete your education. For no other reason than to honor the agreement. You can go to school online nowadays. Granted, parents should support their kids regardless if they approve of their choices, but find a way to make up with them. Life is too short not to be close to your family. You must get in touch with them. You need them with all of the havoc around you. Besides, I'm sure they're proud of your accomplishments now."

He stared out the window for a long time. "They'll be less happy when I tell them what's recently happened." He exhaled a huge sigh. "Our former manager embezzled most of our money and has disappeared with it. We're broke."

Darla hesitated, not sure how to respond to this confession. "I read your manager wasn't a very good guy and he didn't treat the group well. But that's low."

"I'm guessing he thinks it's a form of payback. He did make us famous. I'm sure after what we did to him, he views us as traitors."

"What happened?"

"Our last performance was crazy. We were on stage. Finn was always a pain in the ass, but that night he was hell-bent on pissing everybody off. He got into my spotlight one too many times. I reared back with a fist and knocked the shit out of him."

"You did? You don't seem like the violent type."

"I'm not. But that night he got to me. And plus, I've always been the outspoken one, the cynical member of the group. They held me at fault for starting everything, which is true. The one punch turned into an all-out brawl. Dugan and our security team rushed on stage to break us up. I had a bloody lip, so I ducked out and went into the dressing room to stop the bleeding. I discovered Dugan had left his computer on, and he was looking at some disturbing pictures online. Little boys, young men. We knew he was a bad guy, Darla, but this was sick stuff. I showed the rest of band, minus Finn. We decided to call in the authorities right then. Everything else is documented."

"So he holds a grudge."

Eric nodded. "A big one."

"Big enough to want to kill you guys?"

He turned away and stared out the window.

"Have you explained the money situation to your parents?"

"I've thought about telling them. But how do I do that? How do I say I was stupid, got involved with a perverted crook, lost everything, and now I don't have a pence? What will they think of me after they realize I worked my ass off for eight years, only to find out it was nothing but a waste of time?"

Darla nearly veered off the road from his admission. She clutched the wheel to steady the vehicle. His vulnerability startled her, even scared her a tiny bit. It took him down a notch. It made him seem equal to a regular person who made mistakes like everybody else.

"They are your family. They love you, no matter what. And turning the guy in was the right thing to do." Darla briefly dragged her eyes away from the highway to steal a glance at him. "Eric. You can always find a way to earn money. But you'll never recover lost time."

"We'll see."

"My older brother is a lawyer. He works for a prestigious firm in Austin. When we get to Texas, I'll call him, if you want. I don't know what he can do to help you personally, but he might give you some direction."

"You'd do that for me?"

"Why not?"

"That's really nice of you." He sat still for long time before he spoke again. "You family must be pleased about you getting your doctoral degree."

"They are. But I also believe they wish I'd hurry up and get out of school."

Eric fidgeted and released a soft groan.

"What's wrong?"

"I guess I've overdone it today."

"You think?"

"Yeah, I'm achy."

"I packed the ibuprofen." She opened the console between them and fetched the bottle. "Maybe you ought to take some. Your meds from the doctor are in my purse behind my seat. Would you rather have those?"

He took the container from her, popped the tab, and shook out two pills. "No, this will work for now. I'm gonna get a drink. You want one?" Eric extended an arm behind her then jerked his hand away. His gaze snapped to the backseat. "Stop the car."

"Is something wrong?"

"Pull over and stop the car."

"Why?"

"Because there's a body back there."

Chapter 16

Both feet on the brake, Darla jammed the pedal to the floor. A right jerk of the steering wheel had the SUV skidding onto the shoulder for twenty yards before she slid to a bumpy stop well off the highway. She flung the gear into park. Doors flew open as they bolted from the vehicle. Darla ran around to Eric and clutched his arm with both hands. Together they rushed to the front, standing in the headlights glow, and stared at the automobile.

"This is so not our night," she panted.

"More like not our weekend."

"Who's in my car?" Her voice turned shaky.

"How the hell do I know?"

Eric had his fill of dead people. The discovery of a second one within twenty-four hours left him a little more than unnerved. He didn't want to fall apart in front of Darla. Thus far, he'd done his best to keep everything together, but he was on the verge of losing his mind.

"You're sure a body is in the backseat?"

Eric glared at her, frustrated. "I've found plenty of 'em lately. I think I'd recognize a dead person when I see one."

"Just this one." Darla let go of him and edged closer to the driver's side. "Or are you holding out and you've discovered more?"

He pointed to the corpse. "This guy and Finn."

"I didn't realize you were the one who found Finn, but you haven't exactly told me what happened last night."

He looked down and stared at his shoes. Under the circumstances, he should tell her something since she was deep in the middle of his mess.

"I guess you're right. You're in danger because of me. You need to understand the shit you've gotten yourself into." He proceeded to give her the abbreviated version of the previous evening, ending with him shot and knocked out. She listened, nodding in certain places until he finished.

"How horrible." She opened the car door and stood on tiptoe to peer inside. "I'd block the whole episode if I were you." She took a step closer, reached in, and turned the light switch to the left. The interior flooded with a dim glow.

"What are you doing?"

"I'm going to find out who this is."

Her calmness surprised Eric. As if she viewed dead people every day. Darla leaned halfway into the vehicle while he nervously moved behind her to peek over her shoulder. A torso lay stretched across the backseat, the head covered with a blanket. A limp arm rested on the cooler. Long legs coiled in the floorboard shaped in an awkward position. Though the night was cool, Eric broke into an icy sweat. Darla crawled into the driver seat, perched on her knees, and faced the rear. She bent forward to reach for the middle area.

Eric stepped away. "You're touching him?"

"No. I'm going to remove the blanket. We can't

identify him if the face is hidden." Grasping the cover between her forefinger and thumb, she gave it a light tug.

Nothing happened. The binding had wedged around the skull and refused to budge.

"I need the head lifted so I can unwind the blanket and get it off him." Darla glanced over her shoulder. "I don't suppose you'd want to raise him?"

"Don't suppose." He stared at the body. His hand shot out to grab the hem of her shirt and pull at her. "Wait a minute. He's breathing."

Darla dropped the cover and whipped around. "He's what?"

"Breathing."

She turned and lifted her chin and gazed at the sleeping "corpse." "Yeah, he is." She looked back at Eric. "He can't be dead if he can breathe."

"No shit."

"Well, it's good he's alive." She climbed out of the seat, but kept her focus trained on their uninvited guest. "How do you suppose he got there?"

"Dunno. The car was open while we packed, plus we loaded in the dark. Everything was chaotic the last few minutes before we left. I find it super odd someone gets into your vehicle, goes to sleep, and doesn't wake up after all the noise we've made. Something's not right."

"Seriously."

Eric nodded his head and snapped his fingers. "Ah, now I remember what was wrong."

Darla squinted, as a confused expression spread across her face.

"No smell. When I found Finn, he stunk up the

room. No death scent with this guy."

"See. You're not as experienced at finding bodies as you thought."

"Surprisingly that doesn't bother me much."

"Lots of weird stuff going on tonight, huh? Like those bullets flying over us earlier. I know we've already discussed this, but who's shooting at us? You must have some idea as to who's trying to kill you."

"We need to get moving. We ought to wake this guy up, and drop him off someplace, or maybe call the police to come get him." He thrusts his hands into his pockets and gazed down the lonely highway. A sliver of tingles trickled down his spine.

"What about your missing manager? Could the shooter possibly be him?"

Eric stepped in front of her and leaned forward to look inside the vehicle. "I wonder who this is." He glanced over his shoulder. "I'm betting it's someone from the neighborhood."

"Fine. Keep changing the subject. But this discussion isn't over."

"Never thought it was, luv," he murmured.

They gazed at the unwanted passenger. The person appeared to be male, with a long body and a broad chest.

She closed in behind Eric to get a better view. "I guess it's okay to lift his head and uncover him now. You want to do the honors or should I?"

"Be my guest." He pulled out his cell, thinking phoning the authorities would be the best route.

Darla inched her way toward the backseat. "So finding dead bodies really freaks you out, huh?"

A corner of his mouth lifted. "I don't know what

gave you that idea, luv."

Darla turned to him and laughed. He did too, for the first time in a long while. Their eyes met. For a brief moment everything in the world was right.

Darla broke the stare to gaze down the highway and frowned. "That car is coming toward us kinda fast, isn't it?"

He swirled in the direction of the road. "Yeah. Is it heading—?"

Out of nowhere the vehicle was upon them, barreling in their path. Eric seized Darla and flung her down. He dropped next to her, releasing a loud oomph when he hit. He landed on the ground the same moment the car swerved at them, missing them by mere inches. He held her in a tight embrace. They rolled farther away. Chunks of rocks and gravel bit into his skin. They slid coming to a standstill into the lowest point of the crevice, Eric lying on top. He lifted his head to view the taillights of the would-be assassin vanishing into the dark.

Darla was buried under his weight shoved at him and screeched a muffled, "Damn, I wish people would quit trying to kill us."

The second he rolled off her, she sprung to her feet. Eric eyed her to make sure she was okay. "Are you hurt?"

She didn't answer, but broke into a run. She appeared to be chasing the car. He perched onto an elbow with a low groan. His body ached from yet another tumble. Pushing up to sit, he leaned over, spat out a wad of dirt he'd picked up when he'd sank to the ground. He needed to learn to keep his mouth shut whenever he was diving away from would-be assassins.

James fucking Bond, he was not.

Curious, he surveyed Darla's darkened outline as she raced down the road. "Where the hell are you going?"

She skidded to a halt and spun around. "I'm trying to get the license plate number for the police."

"By running after them on foot?" He chuckled. "They're drivin' about eighty miles an hour, luv. I don't think you can go that fast." With his good arm, he maneuvered to his feet, picked up his cell phone and motioned at her. "We need to get out of here. Whoever that is may turn around to come back for another try. We're a target as long as we're not moving."

Darla jogged to where he waited. "You think that was on purpose?"

Eric gave her an impatient look.

"Oh. Yeah, maybe. I thought possibly we were dealing with a drunk driver. Did you notice the way the car weaved up and down the road?"

"I suppose the person might be sloshed or high," he conceded. "I don't want to take any chances, though."

"You're right. We can't keep letting our guard down. Sooner or later someone may get lucky." She leaned closer to him. "Are you all right?"

He pulled his lip between his teeth with a nod.

Darla looked up at him. "No, you're not."

"The crash to the ground got me a little rattled." A gooey wetness seeped from his upper arm. He ignored the blood and touched her elbow. "Come on." He walked her to the SUV.

She gestured at the still sleeping guy as they approached the car. "What about him? Are we going to wake him?"

"Fuck it." He broke into a trot, hurried to the driver's side, and climbed inside. "We'll deal with him later."

"I love the eloquent way you put things.

"Just get in."

Darla didn't question the driving exchange and jogged to the passenger seat. "We're going to have to do something with him soon."

"I was about to call the police when we were attacked by the NASCAR wannabe."

"Maybe this guy is here for a reason, and that car swiping at us was a form of divine intervention to keep you from doing that."

"I doubt there was anything celestial about it." Eric turned the ignition. He hit the gas as she shut the door. "You sure I can't smoke in here? I could use a cigarette."

"I'm almost tempted to let you. Or more like join you."

They drove in silence for a stretch. She slightly rose to peek over the steering wheel. "You can slow down now." Darla relaxed into her seat. "I'm all about making up for lost time, but you've been cruising at nearly ninety for the last fifteen miles."

"Closer to a hundred." He let his foot off the accelerator and reduced his white-knuckled grip on the wheel. "Not a great idea for the police to catch us right now."

She threw a glance at the backseat. "No, it isn't. I'm sure there's a hefty fine for going that much over the speed limit."

"Plus, I'm not allowed to operate a motor vehicle because of an incident in my past. Blaine does all the driving."

"Good to know." Darla propped an elbow on the window's edge and twirled a strand of hair through her fingers. "Now we're back on the road again, we're probably out of danger. Any idea of what we should do?" She made a motion with her head toward their unwanted passenger. "About him?"

"Don't know yet. Let's find out who he is first. Can you stretch far enough to get the cover off?"

"No. Remember, he's managed to wrap the blanket around his head. I'd have to climb in the back with him to remove it, and I'd rather not. But we need to do something with him before we get to my parents. We can't drive into their driveway with some stranger in the backseat. They're not even expecting you."

"You didn't tell them I was coming? I know I'm not staying at their home, but isn't visiting unannounced against the rules of southern hospitality, or have I watched too many movies?"

"If they knew we were making this trip together, my mother would have already had an astrologist check to see if our signs were a match. And if they did, our wedding would be planned."

Eric's mouth instantly dried up as he slightly jerked the vehicle the moment the word "wedding" was mentioned. "Why don't you tell them the truth?"

"Sure. I'll explain you're someone I've just barely met, you and I've been close to ahm—" She raised her brows. "You know, and I'm helping you run away from a killer. Yeah, that'll go over real well, especially with my dad."

"Right. That's a terrible idea. Okay then. We'll figure out a reason for my appearance later."

Darla gave a loud yawn.

"You're tired?"

"Very. I slept some after you left with Blaine. Not long, because we needed to get ready to leave. Part of me thinks we should have waited to start this trip in the morning after a good night's rest. But since the Sundays probably want to throw me out and some maniac is trolling around my house trying to shoot us, going now was a better choice. Or it was before the evil death car tried to take us out."

The edge of his mouth turned up. "If we'd stayed at your place, you wouldn't be sleeping tonight anyway."

"Seriously?" She gazed at him with a hint of a smile. "You don't ever stop, do you?"

"Nope." He chuckled. "I'll give you a break because you did stay up to nurse me last night. I'm fine driving for now. Why don't you lay the seat down for a couple hours sleep?"

"I wouldn't mind a nap. I think I'll leave the seat up, though. Strange guy in the backseat is too disturbing. I don't want to be too close while I'm asleep." She wiggled further and closed her eyes. "Be sure you obey all the laws."

"I plan to, luv."

For the next three hours, Eric drove as Darla dozed quietly. After everything he'd put her through, he was glad she could rest.

The night was dark and the traffic was light. Fortunately, there were no more surprises in store for them. Up until this point, he'd functioned on adrenaline. Now the ache in his arm worsened and he couldn't relax. The ibuprofen bottle had disappeared when they'd fled out of the SUV. He was sure it lay in a ditch somewhere and his meds from the doctor were still in Darla's bag in the backseat with the stowaway. If he were going to finish this trip in one piece, he would need something to kill the pain.

Darla stirred beside him. "Where are we?"

"We're closing in on Yuma. Okay to stop at a gas station? I dropped the ibuprofen when we bailed. My arm hurts like hell and I want to get some more. And would you mind getting the medications you picked up earlier?"

"Sure. Do you want me to check your arm?"

"Later. I just need to get something to ease the soreness so I can finish the drive without coming undone."

Eric drove into the streets of Yuma, guided the SUV into a station, and stopped by the gas pumps. "We're fine on fuel, but we should top off." He opened the door, then put a leg out. "When I get back, we'll get this guy up and find a way to get rid of him."

"Maybe I should go inside for you. You don't want to get recognized."

Eric grinned. "I didn't shave for a reason. It's a part of my disguise." He stepped out of the vehicle and tugged a baseball cap out of his back pocket, then fitted it onto his head.

She crawled over the seat to lean through the opened door and held out the sack of medicine. "That's the best you've got?"

"It works." He put the gas nozzle into the hole and pressed the buttons before he hooked the lever to automatically fill the pump. Then he snatched the bag from her. "Thanks, luv. Back in a few."

"Um, Eric. Are you sure you don't want me to look

at your arm?" She gestured to his sleeve. "You have a huge bloody spot."

He glanced at the gory mess spread over his shirt then shrugged. "I'll get my jacket to cover up."

Eric pulled the bill of the cap further down on his head and slid the meds into his pocket. He walked to the rear of the vehicle for his coat and hurried into the store. Inside he cruised the aisles until he found what he was searching for.

After he paid for his purchases and the gas, he took his bag, and left the building. Out the door he did a swift glance over the grounds. The sight at the SUV stopped him short. He looked again.

"Shane?" he almost yelled. "Shit." Although unsure of the scene playing before him, the situation needed immediate attention. He ignored his pain and took off into a full run. "What the hell are you doing?"

Darla shot him an irritated glare. "He's about to puke."

"Is he—?" Eric pointed at Shane.

"Our passenger." She wrestled to keep Shane on his feet. "And the reason he's been sleeping so well through all the ruckus is because he's dead drunk."

Eric leaned in closer. Shane belched a foul burp. "Shit." He leaped back, waving his hand in front of his scrunched face. "He's fucked up."

"I know." Her tone sounded annoyed. "He's not going to throw up in my car. Vomit stink is worse than if he'd been the overripe corpse like we first believed."

"Listen, we should do something with him fast. We don't need to draw attention to ourselves." He took over the struggle with Shane, clutched his shoulder, and guided him toward the men's room.

Thirty minutes later Shane lay in the backseat, snoring peacefully. Darla and Eric were buckled in and ready to go with Darla set to drive again. Eric wiggled out of his jacket and removed his hat. He then turned and reached behind him and lifted the cooler lid. He retrieved two cold drinks, handing one to her.

"Are you hungry?"

She put the drink between her thighs and opened the tab. "No. A soda will be fine. I need the caffeine to keep me awake. I had a good nap and I should be okay." She raised the can and took a dainty sip. "This is for insurance."

Eric stuck his hand into the sack and retrieved several bottles of pain relievers.

Shane released a loud snort.

Darla turned the ignition. "It's odd that he ended up in the backseat, isn't it?"

Eric unscrewed the cap, shook out the pills and popped them into his mouth. "Not so unusual."

She stared at him like he'd grown two heads. "You don't find it strange that your manager passes out in my car while we're trying to escape a killer?"

Eric picked up his drink. "He keeps hanging around you, haven't you noticed?" He slid a glance in her direction as he placed his soda into a cup holder.

Her lips lifted a smidgen. She drove away from the station, maneuvering the car onto the highway, and pressed on the accelerator. "He seems like a nice guy."

Eric's fists clenched. Nice guy? "You think so," he retorted, keeping his tone cool and low.

"Maybe I mean intelligent rather than nice."

His chest constricted. "So the idea of him liking you doesn't repel you?"

"Repel me—what?" Her voice elevated to high then altered into squeaky. "Do you think I like Shane?"

"No, I…" How did this conversation turn on him so quickly? He'd made an observation. She didn't sound as if she was opposed to Shane's interest, even though he was. And he didn't seem to matter. His brain stirred into a mass of confusion. "I don't see why you're riled," he blurted. "You said he was a nice guy, no, wait, a smart guy. And you're a smart lady, so." The corners of his lips curved up into a sardonic smile. "I'm not understanding the problem."

Her glare at him was so deathly that he needn't be worried about a killer coming after him. Her stare was enough to do him in.

"Or am I?"

"I can't believe after all we've been through these past few days that you'd think my interest lies somewhere else," she hissed. "You totally infuriate me on so many levels, do you realize that, Eric Boyd?"

Okay, he'd messed up. Big time. He didn't understand his reaction. These sensations she brought on were unfamiliar—like he could be falling for her. Eric's stomach did a huge back flip as he shoved the thought out of his head. The mere idea scared the hell out of him, and he needed to find the nearest escape route. "Infuriation can go both ways, luv. Even so, this isn't a forever deal. You're free to be with whoever you want." He leaned into the seat and crossed his arms over his chest.

"I get it. Obviously you seem to think me with Shane is a good idea and—you know what—don't talk to me. Just stop before this goes any further."

"Darla, I'm just—"

"You're talking." She shot out a palm. "I don't care about anything you say. Seriously, if you speak another word, I might throw you out of this car and run over you with it. And unlike the guy who tried to take us out a while ago, I won't miss."

Chapter 17

"Got any coffee?" Shane moaned from the backseat.

Darla refused to answer. She didn't even flinch. Her eyes stayed glued to the road, fists clutched the steering wheel. So it begins. The moment she'd been looking forward to all night. Amid the snores, hiccups, burps, and other bodily noises men frequently expelled during their sleep time, she'd concluded she disliked them both. She wasn't sure why she was mad at Shane, except she was.

Therefore, she no longer wished to travel in either of their company. For proof of her newfound decision, she'd resolved once the two were awake, she'd inform them they'd need to find another mode of transportation. Neither would be finishing this trip with her.

Shane managed to rise, then fell back against the seat. He covered his face with his hands. "My head feels like it's about to explode."

Eric stirred and opened his eyes. He blinked at the morning sun. "Where are we?" He stared out the window, shielding his view with a hand.

Darla remained quiet. She gripped the wheel firmer and stomped on the gas. The SUV lurched as the automatic gears shifted, pitching the men forward, provoking grunts from each before she let her foot up. Like she'd be sorry for either of them.

This trip was supposed to be a nice and easy visit with her parents. Her vehicle wasn't the new meeting place for a has-been teen idol and his drunken manager. She couldn't fathom this guy's intentions. Or her own. She was ready to give herself to Eric, to feel something for him. And he was so callous. He indicated she should be interested in his friend instead. If this was Eric's way to detach from her after she'd helped him escape from his possible perilous predicament, then he could handle his own fights from now on. Bloodied or not.

Eric leaned across the middle, moving close to her ear. He spoke in a low, soft voice, "Still mad at me, luv?"

She stubbornly forced her eyes to stay ahead. She refused to take his bait and disregarded his charm.

Shane shifted forward and wedged his head between them. "What'd you do to get the silent treatment?"

"Apparently—" Eric groaned as he sat back into his seat. "I broke a rule."

"One?" she inquired.

"Good. You are speaking to me."

She gave a loud huff and stuck her tongue between her teeth and lightly bit down to make sure she wouldn't talk to either of them.

"Most women will usually tell you off when you've done something they don't like," Shane snickered. "Several times. You're in some deep shit if she's not talking to you, man. How's the arm, by the way? Heard about you getting shot."

"Oozing. Now about Darla. Maybe you can help

me. You're more experienced in dealing with—" He stole a quick glance in her direction. "Smart women. I evidently don't understand the intelligent type. I hang with girls who are out for a good time. They're uninhibited, not so uptight."

Darla shot him a cutting glare and hissed through her teeth. Did she hear right? Eric sought advice from Shane. About her? In front of her? This whole smart thing certainly had his boxers twisted into a gigantic knot. Could she help she actually used her brain? And she wasn't uptight. If she were speaking to either of them, she'd unload a huge piece of her mind on them.

"Right. I don't know her well, but my impression of Darla is she a lot more refined than the kind of woman you hang with. Intelligences like hers require finesse and I'm guessing she can be a little high maintenance," Shane explained. "I'm not an expert on academic sorts, although I've dated a couple. I was married to one of those party types, if you recall. She was into the club scene and had no problem doing crazy stuff." He snickered. "As a matter of fact, she used to be famous for hitting places without underwear and flashing the crowd."

"I remember."

"Part of the reason we're not married anymore."

Both men laughed.

"Wait a minute." Darla jerked the SUV to the edge of the road and braked hard. The car skidded to a halt, throwing them into the sides of the vehicle. "Just wait." She rotated and pointed a finger at Eric, then Shane. "Stop. Stop talking. You two are not doing—the thing." She spun back to the front.

Eric looked at her. "What thing?"

"The guy thing."

"We're not doing anything guyish," Shane defended.

"We're only passing time until you calm down."

She held up a hand. "Enough of that. Do not discuss me like I'm not here and don't—wait." She checked Shane through the rearview mirror. "Your wife goes to places without underwear—and shows people. That's disgusting."

"Ex-wife," Shane corrected. "And what'd I do to piss you off?"

"You stowed away in my car, dead drunk, scaring the bejeezus out of us. At first we thought you were—"

Eric stretched across the seat, touched her thigh, and gave his head a slight shake.

"Someone else," she finished. She couldn't believe those two. This conversation made her more determined to carry out her plan. She wouldn't feel guilty, either. "I'm dumping you off at the next town. Both of you. Then you can talk guy stuff all you want, about whoever you want while you figure out how to get wherever you're going." She should derive some level of comfort from making her intentions clear, yet somehow she didn't think she'd be able to carry out her threat. Still, she maintained her bravado. "You're both lucky I'm not throwing you out now." She glanced at Shane. "And I am not high maintenance."

"You kind of are." Shane looked from the front to the back window. "You can't drop us off here. We're in the middle of nowhere."

"Exactly."

Eric leaned closer to her and lowered his voice. "May I remind you of the bullet in my arm and possibly a killer on my tail, plus he's got a hangover from hell?"

"That's my problem?" She directed the car onto the highway and punched the gas. "You two deserve each other."

"You're intense when you get angry," Eric said. "You just say whatever mean thing that pops into your head, don't you?"

"Ooohhh, you wouldn't believe how much I'm not saying."

Several minutes ticked by, no one spoke. Finally Shane broke the silence. "Where are we going anyway?"

"Texas," Darla clipped.

"And we're heading that way, why?"

"As you are aware, a murderer is after Blaine and me. We believe it best to disappear until he's caught. And we're traveling in different directions to hopefully throw him off."

"Understood." Shane stretched his arms overhead, linked his fingers, and rested his hands on top of his head. "Would you consider not dumping us here? I'm sure you probably have a right to be pissed—"

"Probably?" she interrupted, still not in a merciful mood.

"Okay. Eric did something crappy to you, no surprise there, but in my defense, I'm here because I got some great news and I had to go out and celebrate alone."

Eric curved around the seat to get a better view of Shane. "What kind of good news?"

"Word is out. You and Blaine are behind "Eyes and Lies." No backlash, man, the song is off the charts. More radio stations have requested a copy and the downloads are going wild."

Eric pounded the dashboard. "Yes. Finally some respect." He leaned back and laughed. "You're the man, Shane."

"The music is all yours. I just got it out there. I plan to make a harder push when I return to Scotland. You guys seriously need to start thinking about returning to the UK for a mini-tour. I'm sure I can find some funds for something small, especially now."

"We'll talk as soon as we get back to California." Eric waited a beat. "By the way, how did you end up in the backseat?"

"That's a good question." Shane remained quiet for a minute. "Yesterday morning—yesterday? Right? After the news, I searched for you and Blaine, but neither of you answered your phones, so I had a celebratory drink alone. Though I may have had more than one. Then I tried to find you. I remembered Darla and figured you might be at her place. The next thing I recall is me waking up here a few minutes ago."

"I've had a night or two like that." Eric chuckled. "Woke up in some bed and—"

Darla's gaze snapped in his direction.

"I'm not supposed to be talking, am I?"

Her eyes narrowed.

"Okay, but one thing. If you're letting him stay, would you reconsider not dropping me off either?"

She pounded on the accelerator.

"You press that pedal much more, you're gonna stick your foot right through the floorboard and onto the road." She pressed harder. "It's your floor, though."

"Can we at least get some coffee before you throw us out?" Shane let his arms fall to his sides. "And I need to use the bathroom."

Eric bent toward her again. "I know you're not my biggest fan at the moment, but I'd like a cup too. A smoke would be great, also."

She glowered at him.

"Would it help if we said we were sorry?"

It'd help a little. Though she wasn't sure she was ready to forgive just yet, her anger did melt a tad.

"We really are sorry. I guessed it wouldn't be a good idea to piss you off, and believe me, it never was my intent to do so." Eric looked at Shane. "Nor was it his aim to upset you either. We do appreciate what you're doing for us."

Darla didn't speak but glanced at him long enough to see how the morning light molded a darkened outline across his face, the shadows intensified under his eyes. He gazed at her through sunken sockets, his skin beneath his unshaven cheeks appeared thin and tight.

Her expression transformed from anger to concern. Throughout the night, she'd been so mad at him she'd barely taken notice of how restless he'd been. He drank several bottles of water, downing them in quick gulps, and he'd gotten into the pain relievers and prescription meds numerous times.

"I'll drive and you can rest a little?" Eric popped his pill bottle open. "After Shane gets some coffee in him, his hangover will be better. He'll take a shift too. Give you more time to sleep. We'll get you home quicker if we don't need to stop overnight. You'll be rid of us faster."

As they approached the Texas border, she agreed to keep them with her, although wordlessly, and turned into the first convenience store she came upon. They needed gas and lots of coffee. Her stomach growled. And maybe some food. She hadn't taken advantage of the sandwiches she'd packed last night. Now she wanted breakfast.

Eric would benefit from a little nourishment and Shane certainly needed sustenance. Neither spoke a word when she stopped at a pump. Both crawled out of the SUV creaking from their respective ailments. Eric put on his jacket to cover his blood-stained shirt. A few light spots were on her seats, although she chose to keep quiet. They strolled across the parking lot, leaving her to fill the tank.

Both toted large paper cups when they returned. Eric puffed on a cigarette, carrying a bag. They walked directly to her.

"Coffee and breakfast." Eric extinguished his smoke, and handed her the sack, then took over the gas pumping duties. "Peace offering."

Shane held out a cup to her. She accepted both without speaking, ready for some food, and a little nap. She set her meal inside the car, ambled to the rear for a toothbrush, and trotted into the store. When she returned, she found the men seated in the front. Eric was on the driver's side, insisting he was okay to drive, though Darla had her doubts. Shane relaxed in the passenger seat.

Darla climbed into the back and buckled up. After a sip of coffee, she opened her bag and found muffins. With the paper quickly peeled away, she took a large bite and released a satisfied hum.

"Why aren't either of you eating? You both need food."

Eric turned the key and put the vehicle into gear

then drove the car out of the station and onto the highway. He plowed into his coat pocket and took out another smaller bag, tossing it into Shane's lap.

Shane lifted the sack high enough for her to get a good look. "We brought you a girly breakfast."

"As a thank-you for not leaving us in the middle of nowhere," Eric interjected.

"We got—" Shane put a hand inside the bag to pull out a stick of jerky and held the rod up. "—a manly breakfast for us."

"Meat and coffee. By the time we get through Texas, you two will be high fiving and smacking each other on the ass."

Darla slept, although not soundly because of the goings on in the front. The guys carried on a lively conversation with bursts of intermittent laughter. They certainly were good friends. She was surprised how close they were. They almost had a bromance between them.

She finally gave up on a nap and sat upright. They drove across the Texas border, then merged onto interstate ten, rolling past bare plains and mesquite mixed grasslands. Clock reset to Central Standard Time, Eric found a desolate rest area and stopped when the digital readout in the dash displayed straight up noon. He announced he was hungry. He poured out another mix of painkillers before he'd exited the SUV.

Darla removed the sandwiches, then handed them to Shane. After, she brought out chips and fruit to give to Eric. She picked up three drinks and carried them to where the guys were waiting. They set their meal on a concrete picnic table and spread the food.

Shane opened the plastic baggie and wiggled out

the sandwich. He glanced at Eric. "How is your gunshot wound?"

"Better."

"You sure? Looks like you're bleeding pretty heavy."

Darla raised her legs to spin on her butt, then she put her feet down, and jumped up to inspect his injury. A loud gasp escaped from her throat. The entire side of his shirt was covered in darkened rust, his upper arm smeared with blood.

"You're a mess. I should have insisted you let me take better care of this."

Eric glanced at the stain. "A little blood will spread a long way. It's not so bad."

"This is bad. When we're finished here, I'll clean and redress the wound." She returned to her seat. "And you'll change."

He looked up at her.

"Shirts. Blood on my leather seats? Not happening."

"I'll change."

"Lucky for you, whoever shot you has a sorry aim." Shane snapped the top of his soda. "Have you and Blaine come up with anyone who wants the group dead?"

"He says he doesn't know."

Darla gave Eric a scowl, which he returned with a playful grin. She ignored his flirtation. He could be as cute as he wanted. No more falling for him.

"I heard that Dugan had been spotted..." Eric shot Shane a sharp glare and shook his head. "Maybe some deranged fan?"

"Don't know. But since you brought it up." Eric

took a swig of his drink and wiped his mouth with a paper towel. "We do have a fan that's a little off. He has made a series of threats against us over the years. He's been quiet for a while, though. I'd totally forgotten about him. He used to turn up at our performances to heckle us. He drew a gun on Finn in an elevator once. The police arrested him and hauled him away. That's the last time he's bothered us."

"Must have happened before I met you." Shane bit into an apple. "What was his problem with you?"

"He claimed we took women's attention off him. Made it hard for him to get dates. Understand most of our fans were young, and he was older than we were. That should tell you what kind of mind he had."

"Do you know where he lives?"

"I don't remember. I'm even having trouble recalling his last name, although his first was Cy. I want to say he lived in the northeastern part of the country, around the New England area, but he followed us everywhere, so I might be wrong. We had a restraining order against him. It might've run out by now. I need to check."

"Not a bad idea under the circumstances."

A quiet Darla finished her lunch, picked up her trash, and walked to the rear of the vehicle to get the supplies for Eric. She took the provisions back to the table.

"Take off the shirt," she demanded.

"You're not gonna help me, luv?"

Darla gave him an irritated glare. He chuckled as he unbuttoned the front.

"This is a lot worse than before," she told him as she dabbed at the large amount of blood. "When we get to my parents, I advise you to find a doctor."

His non-response gave her a clear perception of what he thought of her advice. Darla re-bandaged his wound while Shane gathered up the food and rest of the trash. Once redressed, Eric put on a clean shirt and grabbed a quick smoke. Shane declared his head was clear enough to take over the driving duties.

"Do you think you can drop me off at the next good-size town with an airport?" Shane stole a glimpse at Darla who sat in the passenger seat. "No offense, but I don't want to go any further into Texas. I need to get back to California so I won't miss my flight to Scotland tomorrow."

"That shouldn't be a problem. A lot depends on the traffic, but we should be in San Antonio in about five hours."

"Damn. Texas is a big state."

"Yeah. Most people don't realize you can't drive through it in a short amount of time."

"It's hotter than hell here, too."

Darla enjoyed sitting in the warm spring wind as the burning midday sun beat down upon them. California weather was nice, but she missed the Texas heat. This was wonderful to her.

Eric stirred in the backseat. "Never been to Texas before, Shane?"

"No." Shane prodded in his pocket, pulled out his cell, and tossed the device to Eric. "Can you go online and make me some flight reservations back to Cali?" He started the SUV, directing the automobile onto the highway. "So Eric, we haven't had an opportunity to talk, but what are you going to do now? Any luck on finding an attorney to help you get your money back?"

"I was researching my options before I became target practice, then we had this impromptu escape, so I haven't had a lot of time to do a proper investigation. Darla's got a brother who's a lawyer. She thinks he might be able to help."

Darla glanced at Eric. "So what's with this song you guys keep talking about?"

"Blaine and I formed our own group. We're performing the kind of music we've always wanted to play, and Shane's got us moving in the UK."

"Are the radio stations here playing anything by you?"

"If you listen to stuff like Raging Impulse, then probably not. Our sound is harder, edgier. You wouldn't know Impulse members are involved. We decided to keep our connection quiet for obvious reasons. Up until now, the move has been a smart one."

"What's your band's name?"

"Spiraling UP."

"Hey, I have heard a song by you. You guys are good."

"There are a couple of smaller stations in the area that've been playing the tune," Shane said. "And their music does well because it's not like the kiddie crap they use to play."

Darla frowned at Shane and shook her head.

"Sorry. What I meant is your sound is more adult."

Eric laughed. "You can call it kiddie music, hell, most of it was crap. I can say that because I wrote a lot of those tunes. The songs from that era weren't our choice. Our manager and record label determined what we played. That's why I like working as an independent so much better."

"I happened to enjoy Raging Impulse's music," Darla interrupted.

"Females do."

Shane grinned. "The tight pants you guys wore didn't hurt you in the woman department either."

"Yeah, it did bring in the ladies." Eric lay down and closed his eyes. "That's the only good thing I have to say about being in a boy band."

Darla checked on Eric often. His complexion slowly paled until he'd turned white as snow. His lips looked almost bloodless. He didn't wake up when they'd dropped Shane off at the airport. At dinnertime, she forced him to get up, though he had a difficult time staying awake, and he barely touched any food.

After the meal, she redressed his wound. The bleeding had lessoned, but the redness spread. The injury troubled her, although voicing her concern once again fell on deaf ears. He popped more meds, smoked another cigarette, and returned to the backseat. After he settled, he immediately was asleep.

Darla drove the final leg of the drive, allowing the high beams to guide her down the familiar roads to her home. Her gazed remained glued to the bug splatted windshield. The last miles were the longest part of the journey. She wheeled into her family's driveway, threw the vehicle into park, and bounced out of the car. Her parents and younger brother waited in the front yard. Everyone hurried to meet her as Darla ran to them throwing her arms around all of them.

Amid the enthusiasm an alarmed voice came from behind. "Um, Darla. We've got a problem."

Darla turned. She clapped a hand over her mouth to hold in a scream. Her brother knelt next to Eric, who lay limp, passed out face down in the graveled driveway.

****

He tossed Finn's credit card on the seat next to the takeout bag as he sailed away from the drive thru. His mouth watered from the overflowing aroma of a double meat and large fry filling the car's inside.

He'd wanted to hold off. Eat his meal at Finn's place. But it'd been a while since he'd had any decent junk food, and he couldn't wait another minute for his dinner. Starved, he seized the burger from the sack, ripped the paper away, and took a huge bite. He released an enormous sigh as he savored the flavor, not understanding how Finn lived on crackers, cheese, drinking only whiskey or soda.

Actually, Finn wasn't living at all. He chuckled. Finn was dead. For safety measures, he drove back and forth down the block before he pulled into Finn's garage. He exited the car he'd borrowed, deeming his motorcycle too messed up to ride now. And he stayed away from the house he'd used for the time being, just in case. So he planned to help himself to Finn's stuff for the next few hours.

He entered through a side door. He'd come and gone since Eric discovered Finn's body, but avoided the room where the slaying occurred. Even though he murdered the guy, he couldn't stomach going into that bedroom. While he did retain some sort of conscience, he was fine occupying the rest of the place and used it freely.

Once the police and news vans left and the coroner's office carted Finn away, everyone disappeared. The house remained quiet. Nobody cared much about a murder these days. Up until now, no one asked him for additional ID nor did they question whether he was Finn O'Conner, though his death blared throughout every media outlet. This evening, he managed to come and go at ease enjoying Finn's car, home, and a slew of credit cards left on the dresser. People's indifference disgusted him.

He sat down on a sofa, picked up the remote, and flipped on the TV while he continued to eat his dinner. He marveled over his circumstances. Good as things were, he couldn't take many chances or become cocky. A tropical island without extradition was waiting for him. Time to get rid of Eric and Blaine. And after, he planned to disappear. Forever.

Chapter 18

A muffled noise hauled Eric out of a deep sleep. Stretched out in a strange but comfortable bed, he fought to keep his eyes open, blinking rapidly until he became fully awake. He struggled to sit. Once up, he straightened to catch a better view of the room hoping for a hint of where he was, and wondered how the hell he got here.

The bed faced large double windows that covered one wall. The unclosed blinds allowed the springtime's brightness to gleam inside and formulate a ladder pattern across the floor. The sun's position had him guessing the time to be somewhere around mid-morning. Located next to the windows were two shallow closets with folded mirrored doors. The remaining space exhibited various awards. Several posters of muscle cars and a couple of swimsuit models Eric remembered were popular a few years back also were tacked on the walls with red pushpins. The faint whiff of maleness lingered throughout. The assortment of odds and ends scattered at random made him think he was trapped in a teenage boy's sanctuary.

"You're awake," came a deep voice from the doorway.

Eric jerked. His attention shifted in the direction of a commanding presence who'd stepped into the room.

The man was thin, tall, his skin tanned and leathery. Eric didn't possess the knack of guessing ages, but this guy appeared to be in his early sixties. His hair was dark, streaked with strips of white. He wore it long, parted down the middle, and tied into a ponytail. It hung midway down his back. Kind of like a throw-back hippy.

"How's the arm?" Familiar dark eyes scrutinized Eric.

The two men sized each other up. The bloke may look similar to pictures Eric had seen of peace-loving, flower children of the sixties though his gut instincts nudged him, saying this person was anything but mellow. This was not someone to mess with.

"Hey, you're up."

Eric jumped again. He swung his gaze to the doorway. Darla strolled into the room. Engrossed with his surroundings and this stranger, seeing her surprised him, but only for a moment.

Her sudden appearance triggered a rush of familiar memories. Someone shot him. He'd traveled with her to avoid a killer, who might be after him and Blaine. They'd recently arrived in Texas on their way to Darla's family. Events up throughout the day were mostly clear, although last night's dinner seemed vague and after that, everything was fuzzy.

He looked at her. "How long have I been asleep?" He fought the sudden longing for a cigarette, knowing better than to ask.

"Almost two days. You look a hundred times healthier now that you're rested and had your arm attended to properly." Darla shuffled to his bed and bent forward to inspect underneath the bandage around his bicep. She murmured so only he could hear, "Told you to get some help." She taped the gauze back in place, stood up, and smiled at him. "Healing nicely."

Eric fell against the headboard. "You took me to another doctor?"

"Not exactly." Darla left his bedside to go to stand by the man who observed Eric a little too closely for his liking. "Daddy fixed you up."

"Daddy?"

She beamed at the lanky gentlemen next to her and gestured with a hand. "This is my dad, Lee Hennessy."

Lee Hennessy nodded.

Intimidation shot through Eric. He made a point to shy away from parents, fathers in particular, although in retrospect he couldn't avoid Darla's because he was a guest in his home. Still, he hadn't expected Darla's dad to be, well, such a hard ass. A scary one, at that.

"Thank you for helping me." Eric stared back at him. "I'm not sure what you did, but I feel a lot better. I suppose I was in worse shape than I realized."

"Yes, you were." Lee nodded. "The bullet in your arm had developed an infection. The wound itself wasn't life threatening, the slug didn't hit anything major. Went straight into the muscle, which is what the doctor told you, according to Darla. But when lodged into the skin, it took a small chunk of material from your shirt and that caused the problem." He stepped to the dresser to pick up a tray. "The only thing alarming me was the possibility of blood poisoning. A red line from the area hit will trace back to the heart if toxins invaded your body. I checked. You didn't show any signs. You shouldn't, but we'll watch it for a couple of days to make sure." He rotated to Eric and held up the partial pellet with long tweezers. "I kept this for evidence in case the police need it. Flat point. Lodged directly into your flesh."

Eric's stomach lurched at the sight of the object meant to take his life. Lee dropped the bullet into the tray, a soft clink of metal hitting metal dinged. He circled away to return the dish and tweezers.

"Because you were already passed out, I was able to extract the shell without much trouble. I stuck you with a shot of penicillin. We've kept the area doctored with Betadine in regular intervals too. That, sleep, along with Darla's momma's treatment should heal you quick. You'll be well soon, although expect some pain in the arm for the rest of your life. Gunshot injuries never completely go away." He turned to Eric and with a stern expression stared at him directly in the eye. "Next time you start having any swelling of that magnitude, you get your ass to a hospital immediately, understand?"

Eric swallowed hard and glanced at Darla for guidance, who instead gave him a wicked grin.

"Yes, sir. Are you a doctor, sir?"

"Nope. I'm retired. I fish."

Darla smiled at her father fondly. "Daddy was a medic in the military. After he did his tours, he worked as a paramedic on the island until he decided to give up work for relaxation a few years ago. He's very familiar about this kind of stuff, so you're well taken care of."

Eric ran a hand over his chin, surprised to discover several days' growth across his face. "How did you get the antibiotics?"

"Don't concern yourself." The corners of Lee's lips lifted slightly. "Just say I know people who know some other people. Let it go at that."

"*Maravilloso*. At last, you're awake." A small, curvy Mexican lady flowed into the room, straight to his bed. She grasped his whiskered jawline in the cup of her palm. "What beautiful eyes," she said in heavily accented Spanish. "It is good they're open." She released his chin then extended her hand to him gracefully. "I'm Darla's momma, Nohemi."

Eric stared at her. The woman was beautiful. She appeared much younger than Darla's father and definitely projected a more welcoming air he didn't get from her dad.

"It's pronounced Naomi in English, although I'm not sure if that helps you," Darla interjected.

Eric clasped her fingers lightly before he released them. Darla strolled to her mother's side, standing nearly four inches taller. Both possessed the same wild, dark curls. Darla had her father's eyes, although she retained her own style of beauty. He couldn't see she favored either of her parents much.

"I haven't properly introduced you, yet. Momma, Daddy, this is Eric Boyd."

Eric only managed a nod, overwhelmed by all the sudden attention and togetherness. It'd been years since he'd experienced any kind of caring or warmth like this. The recollections of his own home flooded his mind and almost choked him from the realization of how much he missed his family.

"You're hungry, *mi hijo*. You've been asleep for a long time. I make food this morning. I'll bring you some now. Then we get to know you."

"Momma, let him heal completely before you start delving into his personal life."

Darla's mother spoke to her in Spanish. Darla laughed before she answered, to Eric's amazement, in fluent Spanish also.

"I'll let you two be alone for a few minutes." Lee followed his wife out the door. He glowered at Eric. "Then you and I will be having an extended discussion."

"Daddy." Darla shook her head. Her gaze affectionately trailed her parents as they left the room. She looked at Eric. "Excuse my father. Sometimes he can be a little unnerving."

"A little?" Eric glanced toward the spot the man recently vacated. "He scares the shit out of me. I'm almost thinking I would've preferred to stay in California and deal with a killer than, what did he say…having an extended discussion with him?"

She laughed and sat down on the edge of his bed. "Is it a wonder when I was in school no boy ever took me out on a date more than once?"

"I can understand their reasons for not wanting to meet him."

Darla giggled. "My advice is just reply 'yes sir' to whatever he says to you."

"Thanks for the warning." Eric glanced at the patch on his arm. "This bandage feels weird." He made a face. "Like something's sticky underneath."

"Dad's not the only one with his own brand of treatments. Momma has her beliefs also. Her choices lean toward Native American folk medicine." She pointed to his covering. "There's a spider web wrapped around your arm, under the bandages."

"A what?" His voice cracked as his eyes skimmed the dressing again. The thought of a gummy web attached to his skin was disgusting.

"A spider web. The Native Americans used webs from arachnids for over two thousand years to fight infections, stop bleeding, and repair wounds. She'll swear it's what's healing you over what my dad's done or the doctor's treatments."

"She didn't leave any spiders in there, did she?" Eric frowned as he shuddered. He swore something crawled underneath, and fought the urge to rip the thing off, but stopped short, preferring not to offend anyone.

"No." Darla giggled. "That would be silly."

"Right. Spiders in webs are silly. Your parents are some fascinating people."

"You mean fascinating by the obvious cultural differences, or the obvious age difference, or their offbeat way of handling certain situations?" Darla smiled. "They're a diverse pair, but their story is an interesting, beautiful one." She relaxed on the bed and continued without any prompting. "Momma is Daddy's second wife. He married young, had a son, and joined the armed forces all about the same time. Once enlisted, he chose to make the Army his career, but the woman became fed up with him gone so much and divorced him while overseas. She took their child and disappeared. Dad was devastated. Right after he received his Dear John letter, he was wounded and required to give up the military. When he returned to the states, he was unable to find his ex-wife or his son.

"Unsure what to do with his life and sad about how things turned out, he moved here to Port Isabel to recover. His grandparents lived in the area when he was younger, and he had good memories from his time growing up. He got a job for the sheriff's department as a deputy. After a couple of years, he joined South Padre EMS operations, where he worked up until he retired last year. During the early times, he'd make frequent trips to Matamoros in Mexico, when entering the Mexican border towns was safer. He met my mother there. She tended bar at a cantina, serving drinks, and reading palms. At first, he was reluctant to let her read his, but after a few meetings, she convinced him. She claims when she did, she'd found her soul mate. They married six weeks later. They both say the marriage is the best thing they've ever done, aside from having us kids."

"Wonderful story, luv." He grinned. "Doubt if it'll change my perspective, though."

"Why would I expect it to? But true love does happen, whether you believe in the phenomenon or not."

"If you say so. Hey, do you think you can sneak me in a smoke? I need one, bad." His hopeful expression was met with a pair of disapproving eyes. He released a reluctant sigh. "Stupid question, I guess."

"I guess." She rose from the bed and gave him a half smile. "Be forewarned. When Momma says she wants to know you better, it means she wants to read your palm."

Eric's lips tightened, but he didn't raise any objections. Her family had taken him in and taken care of him, made him well while also keeping him safe. He couldn't say no if Darla's mum wanted to inspect his hand and spout out a bunch of mumbo jumbo about his future or love life.

He glanced at a baseball bat in one corner. A ball and glove lay on the floor and a hat with the letters PI sewn in the middle, hung over the bat's knob. "Whose bedroom is this and how did I get in here?"

"This room belongs to my younger brother, Adrian. As I'm sure you noticed from the spread photographs everywhere, he resembles Momma." She waved a hand at the pictures throughout displaying a handsome Hispanic-looking teen in various stages of school. "He was here when we arrived the other night. He helped carry you inside after you fainted in the driveway." Darla proceeded to give him an update on the events that occurred up until he'd awakened. "You'll meet him at some point." She placed her hands on her hips and glanced around the room. "But it'll be later. He moved out a couple of years ago. He lives and works in Harlingen, plus he has a busy social life."

"He's big in martial arts, huh?" He nodded to the numerous trophies won in tai kwan do or other karate-type competitions.

"He participated in lots of contests when he was in school."

"What kind of awards are in your room?"

"Mine are boxed up in the attic," she explained. "My old bedroom is now the guestroom."

"I'd like to see it anyway." A corner of his lip rose as he teased, "Give me a tour later?"

She opened her mouth to reply, but her mother interrupted. "I made breakfast." She breezed into the room carrying a tray of food. "You eat now. Then you rest. Later you'll get out of bed."

Darla's father shadowed her inside. "You ladies excuse us." He gave Eric a meaningful squint. "The two of us are going to have a quick heart-to-heart, while Mr. Boyd enjoys his meal."

****

Late that evening, Darla lay in her bed, doing her best to concentrate on her book. A light tap came at her bedroom door. She looked up from her reading and stared at the closed entrance for several seconds before she whispered a soft, "Come in."

Eric poked his head inside. "Got a second?"

"Sure." She put her paperback aside, dragging the sheet farther up over her as he entered.

"You're looking healthier each time I see you."

"I'm feeling much better."

Hands thrusts into his pockets, he wandered about until he stopped at the dresser to scan the ornamented surface, though he didn't speak.

"Is everything okay?"

He spun around and smiled ruefully. "I need to say a few things."

Darla shoved her hair away from her face and bobbed her head. He appeared uncomfortable, as if trying to find the right words. Fear welled in her chest and tightened inside. She webbed a curl through her fingers.

He cleared his throat before he spoke. A corner of his mouth slanted upward. "Had that chat with your dad. He insisted I give him the details on what's been happening and how I came to have a bullet lodged in my upper arm. Since you'd kept the specifics to a minimum, I had to come clean. To say the least, after I revealed everything, he wasn't thrilled I involved you."

"Dads can be a little overprotective."

"That's why I try to avoid fathers." He chuckled. "Yours is a bit of a hard ass, yet he seems like a pretty good guy. I explained to him about our money situation too."

This news surprised Darla, though she did her best not to let it show. Or her satisfaction Eric was comfortable enough with her father to tell him of this major life setback.

"I don't believe there's any way we're gonna come out of this without everything collapsing first." He gave Darla a weary grin. "But your dad thinks he can help me. He's contacted your brother. The older one, the lawyer you were telling me about."

"Barry. My brother's name is Barry."

"Right. Barry."

"We met for the first time five years ago when he and Dad found each other and reconnected. He's a decent man. He'll do whatever it takes to get this mess straightened out."

Eric nodded. "He plans on filing a bunch of papers—I don't remember what the legal terms are—against Dugan on the band's behalf. He's already got in touch with our record company and finished setting up an account to where they can deposit any new royalties. He's also connected with some private investigators he's gonna call. He says they're all good at what they do and one should be able to track the asshole down."

"Do you need to find Dugan before you can serve him with the documents?"

"It helps, but apparently it's not necessary we know where he's at."

"That's great." Darla smiled. "Recovering your missing funds would be a big step."

"Possibly. Barry needs the copies of my contracts I signed with Dugan as soon as possible, so he and several of his colleagues can study them and start the process."

"Fantastic. You must be excited. There's a chance you'll get your money back."

Eric lifted a shoulder. "I still think with Dugan disappearing, it'll be hard to recover. Your brother is anxious to start an investigation. The problem is, we signed those contracts. I'm trying to stay positive, but I don't wanna get my hopes up either." He roamed over to her dresser, picked up a knick-knack, and inspected the glass piece.

Then he returned the trinket and turned back to her. He seemed to be searching for words. "I wanted to thank you. For everything. For helping me. For taking care of me and being so good to me when I gave you no reason to do anything for me." He fidgeted. "I also want to apologize. For all the times I was an asshole. I don't mean to be. Some people just don't get my humor. And though it's not an excuse, I'm not used to dealing with a real lady. But you deserve the best, Darla, don't ever let anyone tell you, you don't." He turned his deep blue eyes to her. "Just wanted you to know."

With a slight grin, she bowed her head. "Thank you for the apology and you're welcome for the help." She raised her chin to meet his gaze. "You just require a bit of adjustment in attitude when it comes to dealing with women. While I appreciate the fact you're up front about your intentions, you need to remember every woman is a real lady, even if we don't always behave like one. You should treat them with respect."

"You're right," he agreed, but seemed uneasy. "I'd gotten spoiled from being in a band. Hardly anyone told me no. My mum would hit me upside the head if she knew about my behavior, because she taught me better.

I'd forgotten how to be nice for real until I met you."

"I'm sure your way of life was a big influence. I get that." She waited a beat before she spoke. "Don't be so hard on yourself. You helped me a lot, even if you didn't mean to."

"Any help from me to you was an accident, for sure." Eric released a short chuckle, and then turned serious. "I have one more thing to tell you." He paused. "I just got word from the detectives. They think they've caught the guy. The killer. He was lurking around Finn's place when they found him."

"Seriously? Who? Who is this crazy person? Your former manager?"

"Strange enough, the police have known about him for quite some time. A hired gun, like I believed in the beginning. And he carried the same kind of weapon that killed Finn and Drake. Plus, someone thinks they spotted him in the vicinity when Mitchell was shot. The detective claims he's lawyered up, so there's no confession yet or who is behind hiring him, although I'm betting on Dugan, especially since word on the street is, he's been spotted hanging around the same area."

"I heard Shane mention it on our trip here."

"Can't get anything past you." He grinned. "The Dugan sighting could just be a rumor. Still, the man from homicide seems certain the man they caught is our guy."

Darla's lifted her palms to her cheeks. "This is great news. Have you contacted Blaine?"

He nodded. "Yeah, he and Stephanie are having a good time. They're not returning to California for a while. The police don't need him, because he didn't witness anything. But they do want me to look at the suspect and possibly identify him. Maybe viewing him in person will jog a memory."

She dropped her hands to her lap. "You really can't place him?"

"No. I've been having bad dreams about that night, but I never see a clear face that I can remember. I wonder if I've blocked the image."

"That's possible. What happened to you and finding Finn dead must have been horrifying. How is Mitchell? Can he help?"

"Mitchell's not quite well enough, plus he doesn't remember any more than I do."

"Still, this is wonderful, and a relief that everything is over." Darla gazed at him with a smile. "This has been an adventure, hasn't it?"

"Yes. And I'm sorry to say our journey is ending soon."

"H-h-how soon?" she stuttered. "When do you leave?"

"In the morning. I'm healed enough to travel. I want to get this over with." He rubbed his forehead with his fingers. "I've arranged to meet with your brother in Austin tomorrow. After, we're going back to California to discuss Dugan with the authorities together. He says he'll go with me to talk to the cops about this murder suspect too as support, although it's not in his line of expertise. Then we can focus on the money situation."

"Sounds like things are beginning to fall into place for you. You get your freedom back and maybe even your money. How's that for a happy ending?"

"I hope. I'm afraid you're reaching for a silver

lining too soon."

"Don't be negative. The bad stuff won't last forever. Your luck is about to turn for the better. Actually, it already has now that the killer is in jail."

"That's exactly what your mother predicted when she read my palm earlier. She told me my life had taken a major turn and in a few weeks I'll be where I'm supposed to be." Eric laughed, but instantly his expression altered to dark. "I believe my world has improved because this lunatic killing my band mates was caught. I can relax for that reason, though it doesn't bring them back." He walked to the door, and then he spun around to face her. "So, I guess this is good bye."

Their eyes connected. Her heart jumped. Darla understood this was the moment. If anything was to ever happen between them, if she wanted to solidify their connection, physically, emotionally, the time for her to act was now. And she had to take the initiative.

The idea terrified her. He apologized, admitted his bad behavior. He wouldn't dare do anything to compromise his regret. If he did, he'd come off as a complete jerk. Therefore, it was up to her to let him know.

He touched the knob.

She took a solid breath, opened her mouth but the word "stay" stuck in her throat.

"Sleep well, luv."

Chapter 19

Eric leaned his head against Darla's bedroom door, resisting the urge to bang it into the frame. He only thought he'd known regret in the past. But having to leave her gave him a true understanding of disappointment. He did the right thing by telling her he was sorry for his boorish behavior, and he needed to make everything good between them before he left. He didn't want to leave her with a bunch of bad memories of their brief time together. Therefore, he chose to walk away.

Although he wasn't sure why he wanted her to remember him as a decent guy. Respectability closed off any possibility of him ever fulfilling his yearnings for her. He not only longed for her, hell, he craved her to the point of obsession. She'd been in his head from the moment they met and stayed with him since. Now he realized he'd never forget her. Not for the first time, he wondered if this is what love felt like, but hurried to shake away the notion. Eric Boyd didn't fall in love.

He stared at the door for a while longer before he took a deep breath and walked down the hallway and into his room. Once inside, he stood in the center, his mind muddled. The click of the air conditioner cycling on caught his attention. He moved to stand under the vent, bathing his body in the breezy cool airstream.

The chilliness helped, but the draft wasn't frigid enough to drop his internal thermometer. A cold shower might help to redirect his thoughts away from her, and his lingering physical needs, and the fact he passed on the opportunity to take care of them. Tomorrow he'd be gone. More than likely he'd never see her again. Besides, there were other things to think about other than dwelling on what didn't happen with her. Like what was next in his life.

Even with Spiraling UP's new hit, he was without resources. No money meant he and Blaine couldn't move forward with their music unless Shane managed to find some cash from somewhere else for this tour, and that wasn't a guarantee. Nor did he foresee them recouping their funds anytime soon, no matter how optimistic Barry seemed.

After he took care of business in California he had to determine what direction he should take. He'd tossed many ideas around in his head since he'd awakened this morning. Time spent with the Hennessys made him realize he wanted to visit his family and how he needed normalcy in his life. Maybe he'd take Darla's advice to finish college and earn his degree. If this new band didn't produce the way they expected, he may get a job as an architect. Yeah, he might have to work in a cubicle at first, but he hoped design would be satisfactory as an outlet for his creativity. He wouldn't totally quit music, though.

They could use this upsurge from their new song as a base. There were area club contacts he'd made early in his career and they'd let him play. He didn't even need Shane to pull any strings for that. Plus, he'd keep writing songs. No doubt his music would be about a dark-eyed southern teacher with wild curls.

The tinkle of his cell phone yanked him away from his daydreams. He almost groused at the idea of leaving it on all the time as he glanced at the caller ID. Darla's brother, his new attorney, was on the other end. With a heavy sigh he punched the on key. After a quick conversation, he pressed the off button, then gathered up his things to get ready for a shower.

He quietly slipped out of his room and tiptoed through the hall leading to the bathroom doing his best to resist looking at Darla's bedroom ahead. Instead of passing by her door like he should, he paused. On impulse, he put his hand on the knob, then let his fingers drop. He may never leave if he entered her room. The thought of intimacy with her had him searching for oxygen. His chest squeezed tight and he couldn't breathe. He needed air. Forgetting the shower, he quietly, continued down the hallway, past the living area and stepped outside into the humid darkness.

****

Darla stared into the blackened sky. The swaying of her father's boat normally sent her into a serene lull, though tonight the movement only reminded her of her unfulfilled needs. She should have stopped him and asked him to stay.

But it was too late. Eric was leaving and the sinking feeling in her gut told her he'd said goodbye for good. She sighed and again she wished she could be more like Stephanie, and not be so cautious in life and live in the now.

A slight thump from behind interrupted her melancholy moment. With a foot she whirled the pedestal seat around, surprised by the welcomed but unexpected intrusion. Eric pinned his eyes on her to hold her gaze. He didn't speak as he dropped a bundle of something onto the deck. Nervous flutters tickled her stomach as he glided across the boats surface to where she waited.

He reached her, clasped her hands into his, and urged her to her feet. His face hovered above hers. There was no need to question him about what he wanted. The fire in his blue eyes told her everything.

Without thinking, she lifted her chin with slightly parted lips. Fingers raked through her thick curls before he pressed into her, accepting her silent invitation with his mouth. A soft cry escaped from her throat, her arms instinctively slipped around him. The openmouthed kiss was hot, hungry. Their tongues interweaved heating her inside and out, her body screaming for more. She didn't feel any need to hold back. She wanted him. Against her, in her, she wanted him in every way.

He broke the kiss and asked in a hoarse whisper, "Is there someplace we can go?"

"Below. There's a bed downstairs."

He squeezed her before he released her, fingertips traced over her bare arms, then he laced his fingers with hers.

"Lead the way."

She steered him through an opening which led underneath into the boat's cuddy cabin. The only light was the moon's reflection shining past the uncovered window, haloing the bed that sat to one side of the room.

Inside, he directed her toward the bed and wrapped his arms around her, finding her lips with his. He gently guided her into the mattress, never breaking their connection, and then lowered his weight on top of her.

She slid her hands over his biceps, drifting across his shoulders, and clutched him behind the neck. She tugged him nearer, impatient to feel him against her. Not shying away from his desires, he silently understood her direction, and pressed his hardened penis between the softness of her legs, spurring her thighs to open and allow him even closer.

Eric let loose a ragged breath and moved away. "I've wanted you," he said in a rough growl, "wanted to fuck you since the moment we met."

"Ditto," she breathed.

He released a quiet laugh. "And you're the romantic?"

"Stop talking." She drew him tighter, putting her mouth back onto his.

A coarse groan quivered from his throat. He rose slightly to slide a hand between them, under her thin top to possessively cover her breast. Her nipple tightened as he stroked and shaped it into his palm. She basked in each caress sure she'd explode at any second. Fingertips skimmed down her back, past the waistband of her sweats to glide the length of her bottom, triggering her to elevate her legs, then squeeze and lock securely around him.

She tugged at his shirt. She wanted him naked. He desired the same from her and would have his way, raising enough to push her tank top over her head, after which he stripped her pants off. Once he had her undressed, his mouth hungrily closed over her nipple, his tongue sweeping around the tip to set off a series of internal upsurges.

A raw moan tore from her. She squirmed, arched

her back, and forgot about trying to get him undressed, fearful she may erupt at any second. Heat swelled throughout her body, soaring downward to pulsate between her legs. Hands scraped through his hair to clutch each side of his head. His hot, male scent bounded her. His closeness expanded a rush of absolute demand.

He stood up to struggle out of his clothes. Darla swept a gaze over his naked body and caught her breath. She'd waited for him, for this. Braced on one arm, he tugged her under him. His fingers skated into the middle of her thighs, finding her wet, warm, and ready for him. Light strokes propelled her to the verge of insanity, her body about to burst into flames. He took her hand to wrap around his solid penis, then put his hand over hers and together they guided him inside. She bit back a gasp as he lowered into her.

"Am I hurting you?"

She dug her nails into his shoulder. "I'm okay." Her voice was soft and breathless. "It's been a while."

"Like riding a bike, luv. Hang on. I won't let you fall off."

And then he kissed her as he gently edged deeper inside of her. Her hips instinctively rocked. The tightness gave way. Her release permitted the pleasure to balloon, riding against him while he hugged her mouth with his.

Eruptions flared. Small flashes grew into a mountain of staggering explosions. She broke the kiss, stiffened, and clung to him, holding on tight. Her mind went black as her body ignited until she expelled a loud exhale. She whispered his name before she fell limp. Only seconds later Eric wilted on top of her with the release of a satisfied sigh, neither moving for a long while.

Darla was the first to stir, though Eric remained still. He took slow, steady breaths. His body relaxed on top hers as if he'd fallen asleep.

"Give me another minute to recover and I'll get off." His warm breath brushed against her hair when he spoke. "I've been saving up for this." Gingerly, he raised his head with a small smile. "And yet, you managed to wear me out."

Darla blushed and grinned back. "Not yet."

Eric laughed and lazily rolled next to her, but made sure their bodies stayed in close contact. With an arm rested across her middle, he snuggled closer and kissed her on the side of the head. "You're full of surprises."

"So are you." She turned toward him and cupped his face with her palm. "I didn't expect to see you after we said our goodbyes."

"I'm kind of surprised myself." He moved his head enough to kiss the inside of her hand. "And so you're aware, this is a first for me."

"What is?"

"Doing it on a boat." He chuckled. "You really had this vessel rockin'," he teased.

Releasing a loud gasp, she shoved him away to work up into a sitting position. She looked down at her nakedness then snatched up a throw at the end of the bed for cover. "Excuse me." She spoke with a giggle. "I wasn't rocking alone. You were moving pretty good yourself."

"That's because you made me wait for you so long."

"So long?" she almost shrieked. "We've known

each other a week."

"Seven days is an eternity for me, luv."

"I'm sure. And for me, we've moved awful fast."

"It was meant to be." He sat up beside her and rubbed a hand over her bare back. "Plus, your mother's reading said I possess a strong sexual nature. From what just happened between us, I bet you do too. Can't fight it."

"My mother." Darla covered her mouth with a palm. "She knows." She turned to Eric with wide eyes. "She knows what we've done."

"How? She's inside and we're out here."

She gave him an irritated glare. "Did you not meet my mother?" Darla squeezed her lids shut and clutched the blanket closer.

He fell back into the pillows and dropped a forearm over his eyes. "God, your mum knows."

"What are you worried about, you're leaving in the morning."

He lifted his arm to peer at her from underneath the crook. "No, I'm not."

"You're not?"

"Barry called me after I left you. Something urgent came up. He postponed our meeting. He told me to stay put while he takes care of his business. I leave day after tomorrow."

A slow smile spread over her face. "So you're in trouble with me."

He raised his torso to move in closer and captured her lips with his. "Yep. If we're both in trouble—" He placed a hand on one shoulder to guide her back into the mattress. He parted her legs with a knee and maneuvered his body over hers. "I say we go for

234

broke."

****

Eric jerked awake from a deep sleep, covered in sweat as he shook away the same dream that'd haunted him since Finn's death. It took him a few minutes to remember his surroundings.

Soft skin, even breaths, legs entangled, bodies close. Naked. He was in bed with Darla.

His mind calmed, but the rest of him almost burst from a major high over the mind-blowing sex they'd shared. Sparks sizzled along each of his nerve endings. Her soft moaning of his name when she came echoed through his mind making him hot all over again. How could this not be exciting? The women he lusted for lay naked in his arms. She was amazing. This would be so easy to get used to. Lying with her, holding her after having incredible sex. Forget about everything else and be with her.

Wonderful yes, but they'd slept on her dad's boat and he sensed now wasn't a good time to linger. He wanted to dress and be in his room before Darla's folks were up. Her father told him he left for fishing early. Whether they were aware about last night or not, he didn't want to get caught here with their daughter, especially without any clothes on. Her dad probably owned weapons.

He shook her. She instantly flinched. "Huh."

"Close to sun up, luv. We'd better get inside b'fore your father comes out to go fishing."

She nodded and rolled out of bed. They silently dressed, and together they straightened the covers. Eric gathered his shower things, and hand and hand they walked inside until they reached her room. He brushed her lips with his. She sleepily stumbled into her bedroom and straight to her bed, falling into the messed blankets. With a final glance at the wild curls fanned across the pillow, he closed the door and whispered, "Thanks, luv."

Eric slept for another two hours, awaked by a heavenly scent of something cooking. His stomach rumbled. Hurriedly, he shucked into a pair of jeans, lugged a shirt over his head, and then followed the trail into the kitchen.

Darla stood in front of the stove, whipping the contents of a bowl with a wire whisk. She poured the mixture into a waiting skillet heating over a fire. A soft sizzle sprang from the pan.

She stepped to the refrigerator for a container and hurried back to the burners to add the concoction. He strolled inside, but stopped to give her a light peck on the cheek before he did anything else. He did his damnedest to ignore the sweet taste of her skin. Another first for him. He enjoyed domestication with her, yet he found the naturalness of it all disturbing.

"Where's your mum?" Eric scraped a chair across the floor to sit at a small breakfast nook in the corner of the room. Two cups and silverware were laid on placemats on either side. A steaming pot placed in the middle of the table seeped the welcoming aroma of caffeine. He reached for the coffee then filled both mugs. "Your dad's gone to fish, right?"

"Yes, and mom's at work." She carried a plate over and placed it in front of him.

"Your dad gave me a tour of his boat last night, but yours was a much better one." He stopped to grin at her. "A more intimate one. The bed is very comfortable, by the way."

She blushed and giggled. "The man wasn't kidding when he said he likes to fish, and he likes to do it in luxury."

She sat a covered clay pot next to him, then lifted the lid. "Corn tortillas. And," she motioned to a small bowl already on the table, "my mother's homemade salsa."

Eric took two tortillas and added a dollop of the spicy paste while she sat down across from him. "I like this," he pointed to the hot sauce with the spoon, "but I should be careful. I tried a sample when your mum was making the stuff. 'Bout burned up my tonsils."

"Salsa is an acquired taste."

He picked up his fork. "Let's see how your performance in the kitchen compares to your late night boat antics." He inspected the food getting another whiff of the delicious smell. "You realize you've raised that bar pretty high." The tip of his lip tilted upward. "Twice."

Darla giggled again. The pink tinge returned and covered her cheeks as she snapped a forefinger to her lips. "Shhh." She glanced around the room. "Somebody might hear you."

"Aren't we the only ones here?" He stabbed the fork at an egg and slid a bite into his mouth. "No worries, then." He pointed at the dish. "This taste great. What is it?"

"Omelet de huitlacoche."

He raised his eyebrows.

"Mushroom omelet."

"Why didn't you say mushroom omelet?"

"This is a Spanish recipe. It sounds prettier when

spoken in Spanish." She gave him an inquisitive look. "So what do you want to do today?"

He gave her a wicked grin. "You have to ask?"

Darla stopped in mid-bite, gripping her fork. "We can't do that here. I've already faked sleep to avoid my mother this morning."

"We can't?" He allowed a full minute to pass before he shook his head, "Darla, we did it last night." He leaned across the table to brush his lips against hers. "We've got the whole place to ourselves. All day."

Eric stood, grabbing her hand, and led her down the hallway and into his bedroom.

After they dressed, again, Darla offered to show him around Port Isabel and South Padre Island. The areas were small, but quaint. Tourism banners waved freely in the warm gulf breeze to promote the city's historic Lighthouse Square. As she drove him through, she pointed out a wealth of shopping and eating establishments off the waterfront. They spent the morning exploring the more interesting ones.

They crossed the Queen Isabella Memorial Causeway to the island. She relayed the story how a loaded barge struck one of the bridge's support beams causing a partial collapse back in 2001. The accident killed eight people, which devastated the community. Four of the dead were from Port Isabel.

At South Padre, they lunched at the restaurant her mother managed. She fussed over them the entire meal and made no mention of knowing what went on between them the night before, but Eric sensed she was aware.

They devoted the afternoon walking the streets, wandering in and out of the unique shops. Darla suggested taking advantage of the stables on the island and going for a horseback ride along the beach. The evening ended with the two of them enjoying a dinner outside with a sunset view on a gulf-front patio. When the outing was over, they climbed into her SUV and Darla drove them to her family home. The place sat dark and empty.

"Your parents are still working or fishing?" Eric removed his baseball cap, threw it down on the sofa, and, ran his fingers through his hair several times.

Darla flipped a light switch and shook her head. "They play a weekly game of Texas hold 'em with friends. It'll be a late night." She laughed. "Those two don't miss a chance to win a couple of hundred bucks, no matter who's visiting."

Eric shoved his hands in his pockets. His first instinct was to usher her back to the boat as he watched her turn on the lights on her way into the kitchen. The sound of ice clinking against glass echoed from the other room. Moments later she returned, carrying two drinks.

She handed him one before she sat down on the couch. "You can't be in Texas without some of my momma's sweet tea."

With a slight nod he accepted her offer, although he wasn't thirsty. Deliberations mulled in his mind as to what to do next. What he should say. He was leaving tomorrow, something they discussed throughout the day. She'd hinted about the two of them getting together when she came home to California in a couple of weeks.

"Are you tired? We could watch a movie or find a decent TV show."

He took a large gulp almost choking on the liquid. He struggled to swallow the mouthful of sugar. He coughed the too sweet drink down. "I think we need to talk." He sat the glass on a nearby table.

Darla stared at him long and hard. He watched her in return, doing his best to ignore the tight T-shirt and denim shorts that defined her lovely shape. "After everything is done in California, I'm planning to move on."

Darla didn't speak. The look on her face displayed pure betrayal. Her anxious expression almost made him want to change his mind. Choose the cowardly way out. Tell her he was joking. Let her discover his disappearance in her own time, like the old Eric would do. Except it was too late for second guessing.

"I wanted you to know what my plans were. I didn't want you to get the wrong idea about us. No surprises."

"I'm not surprised." She dropped her head. "Your viewpoints on relationships are very clear. You never misled me. Except I don't understand why you're leaving California. You're telling me you're going for good, right?"

"What I'm saying is even though we have a song doing well and Raging Impulse is enjoying some new popularity, I'm still broke. My only choice is to go home." He lowered his voice. "To Scotland."

"Are you ever coming back?"

He opened his mouth but waited, fighting for the right words before he replied, "Spiraling UP is moving well in the UK and that's where I need to be. I have no guarantee any success will happen here. There's no reason for me to return to the States."

A long pause stretched between them. She lifted her chin, her eyes mirrored questions running within her mind. "So I'm no reason, right? That's how you see me?"

"Darla. Don't go looking for double meanings in what I say."

Damn. Why didn't he think this through, word it in a different way? He realized she'd take everything he'd say personally.

She stubbornly raised her chin higher. "I'm not."

"I believe you are."

"You just said there's nothing to bring you back to the states. Except music. And yes, you've explained your views on romantic involvements, but I don't get them. I sensed a connection between us on every level, more than just chemistry, more than sex. I can't imagine you didn't get that too."

He put his hands on his hips, making sure his eyes wouldn't connect with hers. "I'm sorry, Darla. I am grateful for everything you've done. And you're right. I've enjoyed our time together."

"But it's not enough."

He shook his head and dropped his arms. "Let me tell you how men are. We settle when we're ready. And before we can get ready, we like everything in place or at least have an idea where we're going. I don't have either. No matter what I feel for you, this is not the right time for me."

She hesitated. "So you're saying you do have feelings for me?"

He didn't want to answer that question, wouldn't. If he did, the entire outcome of his life would alter and he'd already made up his mind. "Darla, I'm doing what

I need to do. I set plans for myself long before I met you. You're going to have to accept it."

"Of course. Ambitions can't change or expand, can they? Damn everyone else, let's only think about Eric." Arms crossed over her chest, she glared at him. "Why am I always attracted to such egotistical men? Do I have a big stamp on my forehead that says, *Please screw over?*"

"Stop saying stuff like that. I'm broke and I'm not sure what my financial outlook is. I can't offer you anything."

"I don't need you to take care of me. And I'm not about the money."

"I didn't say you needed me to take care of you, but if I'm with you, I'd want to. Couples should be able to give and take. We're not there by any means. The way things are at the moment my role in this relationship doesn't exist. You care for me. Period. And I am sort of about the money."

"Aren't you all? There's a lot of different ways we can be with each other besides financial."

His chin dropped. He gave his head a definite shake before he looked back up at her. "Do you realize how little we have in common? Darla, you teach college and you've earned two degrees. You're studying to get a PhD. I don't even have a real job. This whole situation doesn't work for me."

"Then just admit it. You used me like you use every other woman. Except with me, you stuck in some pretty words and I bought into the entire lie." She flew off the sofa, got in his face and yelled. "Money is not the only thing you severely lack in, Eric Boyd." Then she stormed out of the room.

The slamming of the back door told him he could expect a long night. A reminder. This is why he didn't get too deeply involved with women. Eric stared past his feet and onto the carpet. Fuck. He couldn't leave things this way. No matter what he did, he'd be dealing with complications with his conscience and he'd rather not. With a huge sigh, he traced her steps and followed her outdoors.

Darkness had settled. The backyard sat pitch black. He stepped inside and ran a hand along the wall until he located a switch plate and flipped the button. A faint glow lit the small path leading down to the dock. Surveying the surroundings, he didn't see anyone, although that meant nothing. She could be anywhere. She was more familiar with the area than he.

He patted his pocket, then removed his cigarettes. Taking a break for a quick smoke, he allowed his gaze to linger over the rippling gulf below. Her father's monstrous vessel slowly swayed in the twilight's heavy currents. Instincts told him that's where he'd find her. He tossed the cigarette butt into the water as he strolled down the wooden planks, over to the boat.

"Darla?" He called as he climbed up and down a ladder leading onboard. "Darla, are you here?"

No answer. Of course she wouldn't respond. She was pissed and rightfully so. Even if he'd made his intentions clear, he had to consider his actions of late didn't exactly match his words. Why wouldn't she get the wrong idea?

"I'm sorry." His voice rang loud into the night. He stepped carefully across the upper deck, running his hand alongside the railing, careful not to slide on the slippery surface. "Come on, Darla. Let's talk some more."

He stopped on the port side of the boat to stare into the darkened gulf. What should he do? Water lapped quietly against the vessel's hull as a light breeze shifted the watercraft easily back and forth, niffing the salty air with a fishy scent.

For a moment, Eric sensed complete peace. He started to turn and go down below, but an odd creak made him freeze. Out of the blue, spikes prickled across the back of his neck, making his hair stand on end.

Flashes of his nightmares raced through his mind. "Darla?"

"She's here. With me."

Chapter 20

Eric gradually inhaled as he slowly rotated. Dread seeped through his veins until he'd completely turned. In that moment his fears vanished. What he witnessed sent him into an uncontrollable rage, a fury that made him want to attack. Instead he swallowed his anger and forced his mind to stay cool.

Now wouldn't be the time to get stupid.

Darla's captor had her braced against him, facing her outward. An arm draped across her chest, a hand clutched her opposite shoulder. The other hand held a gun, aimed at her head. Eric ignored him and stared at her.

Horror swelled within him. A knot tightened in his chest and constricted, choking him, taking away every bit of his air. He may be suffering a heart attack. Her dark gaze speared back into him. The expression on her face said everything. This was his fault. Guilt stunned him as he eyed the weapon's short, stainless shaft rammed against his woman's temple. Odd reflections flashed through his mind. He'd done nothing but let her down since they'd met. Now he needed to be her hero. And he would. He'd save her. Or die trying.

Eric did his best to appear calm. He probed into his pocket. "So it's you."

"It's me."

"I remember everything now." Eric removed his package of smokes and used his thumb to flip the top open. "The night at Finn's was fuzzy for the longest. Seeing you with the gun paints a clear picture."

"I wondered why you didn't turn me in."

With his lips, Eric tugged a cigarette from the pack, flicked his lighter, and moved the flame to the tip. He leaned against the boat's rail and inhaled before he twisted away to blow out a slow stream of smoke. "I wasn't sure of anything. I've dreamed about the night over and over. Your face was never clear. I believe things would've stayed the same if you hadn't shown up here." He sucked in another drag and let go a puff of smoke.

"Couldn't take a chance."

Eric stared out into the darkness. "Why didn't you finish me off at Finn's? You had the gun pointed right at my head. All you had to do was pull the trigger."

"Because you weren't the target."

He contemplated his would-be killer. "How's that?"

"I never intended on killing you. Or Blaine. Not in the beginning, anyway."

"I don't understand. Raging Impulse members were dropping like f-bombs at a rock 'n' roll awards show. How could you not go after Blaine and me?"

He held the pistol up, away from Darla's head for one second before he placed the cylinder back onto her temple. "At the time, it wasn't financially beneficial to get rid of the two of you."

Eric gave Darla a quick glance. She hadn't moved. His stomach flip-flopped. Her eyes remained firmly planted on him, waiting for him to save her. He twisted to toss the cigarette butt over the side into the water.

"You could've walked away free, you know. The police have someone in custody they believe is the killer."

Darla stared at Eric. "If they truly think things through they'll figure out the guy they're holding isn't the murderer. I was already questioning how a professional hit man could miss so many times. Surely a good detective will come to think the same way."

"So what's the story, Shane?" Eric interrupted. "Why do you need to kill us?"

Shane scanned the darkness before he settled his eyes on Eric. His old friend's pupils had dilated. Dead. Like the man no longer possessed a soul. He licked his lips as his grip tightened over the handle of the gun.

"I only planned to kill Finn, and I'd decided to do it at the party for maximum exposure," he said though gritted teeth. "So I went and played guest. When Finn headed toward the bathroom, I slipped off and changed, then waited. I believed I'd shot him when he came from the lavvy." He stopped to take a rough breath. His voice trembled. "I liked Drake. He was always good to me."

"We all treated you well."

"Some were more decent than others, though decent didn't matter since I only dealt with you and Blaine."

"But that doesn't explain the reason you're killing us. Blaine and I always thought a lot of you. That's why we hired you to be our manager. Even without any experience we knew if anyone could help us take our music to the next level, you were the guy."

"That was the plan."

"I'm confused. What was the plan?"

"To get Raging Impulse back into the limelight. Then introduce Spiraling UP. The strategy was working too. God, the idea was so simple, so ingenious."

"Wait a minute." Eric gave his head a shake to clear it. "You mean to say you killed Drake and Finn, and tried to murder Mitchell as publicity for the band?"

Shane smiled. "Raging Impulse was deader than your friends. Now the band is all the rage again, pardon the pun. Sales are spanking. Perfect time to bring you and Blaine forward." He gazed at Eric and frowned. "Which I did. And look what's happened. Your song is on top."

"Oh my God. You've gone completely mad."

"You gotta be a little nuts to manage a rock band."

"Insane, yeah," Eric agreed. "But killin' people, friends to make money? That's nuthouse time."

"No argument from me, mate. But I need the cash. My ex and her lawyers are draining me in back child support. The more of you who die the bigger both groups become. I figure you and Blaine have enough recorded to keep me flush for a long time. That is if you're gone."

Eric clamped his mouth shut. Repugnance raged inside as disgust rolled through him from head to toe. He bit his repulsion back, taking a minute to digest these revelations and shove the idea that he was indirectly responsible for people's deaths aside. He had to move forward. He needed to think. To find a way to keep Shane talking, buy them some time. "So why did you shoot me if I wasn't the target?"

Shane's lips curved upward into a cutting smile. "I'm done playing twenty questions. It's time—you know. He put the gun to his temple to motion the release of the trigger then returned the barrel to Darla's head and shoved her toward the rail.

Eric visibly shuddered as his mind became completely blank. He had to think, to keep this conversation going until they might form a plan and get away. "Dugan? Are you responsible for his disappearance?"

Shane stopped and shook his head. "Nope. I wish I could tell you yes, but I can't. No clue to where that piece of human slime is."

"How were you able to leave the party on a motorcycle and return so quick?" Darla blurted.

"I can answer that," Eric interjected. "Shane is a runner. A gifted one. He even qualified for the Olympics a few years ago. He continues to train and runs marathons on a regular basis. He can get from one place to another in no time."

Darla slightly tilted her head. "Wouldn't it make sense to allow Eric and Blaine to help you by continuing to record?"

"No guarantee that'll happen if this frenzy fizzles over everybody's death. And this whole money situation with my ex is dragging me down. The best way to resolve that is if none of you were here anymore." After a hesitation Shane's gaze shifted to Eric. "You know how this is gonna go." His grip tightened around Darla as he forced her to the edge of the boat.

Eric's blood turned to ice and froze in his veins. Time ran out. Did he have any more stalling in him?

"Your problem is with me." He nodded at Darla. "You don't have a reason to hurt her."

"Well, well. You really like this one, don't you? Sorry, but she's heard everything." Shane's voice turned gritty, mean. He pressed the gun barrel into her cheek, forcing the upper half of her body to hang over the vessel's rim. "Now quit stalling. It's time to die."

"Easy, Shane, easy." Eric patted the air as he took a step toward them. "Think about this. Darla's right. The police will figure out the person they've got is the wrong guy. They'll know it's you and they'll find you. You'll sit in a cell for the rest of your life."

Shane spoke in almost a whisper. "Doesn't matter, Eric." His lips lifted into a malicious grin. "You'll be dead and I'll still get residuals. Criminals become wealthy from inside all the time. And you've already diagnosed me crazy. I can always be cured. Then I'll be rich and healed."

Darla released a soft chuckle. "Lot of good money will do you if you kill us in Texas. You can forget about rotting away in prison. The state is pro-death penalty, and we use it quite liberally."

Shane twitched. "You're assuming they'll catch me."

"This is Texas. We shoot now. Ask questions later. You may never make it to death row. Either way, you'll be just as dead as we are."

Panicked, his eyes shifted back and forth. With the gun he motioned at Eric. "Start the boat. Take us out into the middle of the gulf. No one will capture me out there."

Eric gazed at his manager, helpless. "I can't drive this thing."

"I can," Darla volunteered. She stared hard at Eric.

Shane stayed quiet, apparently to consider the situation. He tensed his hold on Darla, standing her upright, and pushed her to move. Together they stepped over the deck until they reach the second set of boat seats and stood behind them.

He gestured at Eric. "Come sit." Then he said to Darla, "When he's in the chair, I'll let you go. Your only job is to drive us out to the bay. Don't try anything or I'll shoot him now and worry about the cops later. Got it?"

Darla nodded. Her gaze remained on Eric.

Eric gulped. With difficulty, he forced his feet to walk over the damp floor and to the padded chair. He sat as directed. Shane guided the pistol away from Darla's head and turned it to Eric's as he released her. The metal against his temple felt exactly as he remembered. The same as he'd dreamt repeatedly. Darla advanced to the cockpit and reached across to open a deep compartment near the captain's seat.

"What are you doing, woman?" Shane drove the firearm further into Eric's head.

With a smile, she held something up between her thumb and forefinger though her other hand remained inside. "Key." She let it dangle from the ring. "Hey, Eric. Remember last night? You asked me what I'd won trophies in while in school."

Eric gave a slight nod.

She dropped the key and whipped a pistol from the slot. "Shooting competitions. Many." She raised the revolver and with both hands pointed the barrel at Shane's head. "And won." She held the weapon steady, staring Shane down, poised to shoot.

Eric's mouth fell open. "Um, Darla?"

"Not a smart move, lady." Shane's trill tone boomed as he drove his pistol closer into Eric's temple. A cranking popped in Eric's ear. His heartbeat raced. Shane had cocked back the gun's hammer. The night breeze blew gusts of warm air. Sweat beaded his forehead, his hair stuck to his skin.

Darla mimicked Shane by cocking the striker of

her pistol, only very slowly. "Do it. I'll splatter your brains a half second after you touch the trigger. Remember, I don't need to sneak up behind to hit my target. I can shoot a fly off the top of your ear." Her forefinger slightly stroked the trigger. She caught Eric's eye and hooked her chin. "Drop the gun or I'll drop you."

"Bitch."

A sudden blast of wind lifted from the water. The vessel swayed, throwing Shane off balance and the gun away from Eric. Eric clutched the seat with one hand and quickly pushed to his feet. He balled the other and threw a fist at a wobbly Shane, planting his knuckles into his nose. A sting traveled all the way up his arm, his hand soaked in moistness from splattering blood. Shane's head jerked. He staggered backward, catching the boat's edge. It took only seconds for him to regain his balance. Blood trickled spreading over his lips and chin.

He grinned, revealing blood-lined teeth. He raised his .38 and pointed it directly between Eric's eyes. Eric froze, flanked between the chair and the vessel's side.

A familiar hum whizzed past his ear. A thudded smack rang out. Shane collapsed.

Instinctively, Eric dived to the floor. His body bounced against the surface, he rolled across the boat's deck coming to a stop on his stomach. He opened his eyes, not grasping until then that he'd shut them, and lifted his head to look up at Darla. Her arms dropped to her sides.

She walked calmly to him. "Some people have to learn things the hard way, don't they?"

"Darla." Eric jumped up to bend over Shane. He looked at her, to Shane, and then back to her. "I didn't think you were going to shoot him."

"I didn't think you were going to punch him."

"Is he dead?"

She shook her head. "Killing him would be too easy. I was careful to only nick his shoulder. I want him to pay for what he's done." She leaned over to inspect the sprawled unconscious body before she swung a leg to kick his gun out of reach. "I think he hit his head on the base of the chair when he fell. He's knocked out. He's going to have a huge knot on his forehead after he wakes up." She straightened. "That's what I call poetic justice."

"I thought we were goners."

She held up a palm for a high-five. "Nice right hook for a guitar player."

Eric put his hand into hers, clutched it, and heaved her to him into a hug. "Great shootin' for a smart girl." He sighed into her hair and squeezed her tighter. "Great shootin', luv."

****

Darla stepped onto her parents' dock. A comfortable breeze blew off the waterway, driving gentle rollers to lazily lap against the pier. The evening sky spouted a display of vibrant pinks, oranges, and purples as the sun dipped behind the lower Laguna Madre Bay.

Eric, clean shaven, except he'd kept the mustache, sat relaxed in a lawn chair, an acoustic guitar balanced on his lap. He quietly strummed haunting notes that seemed to coincide with the slow moments of the setting sun. The wind blew his hair off his forehead, exposing the faint bruise serving a clear reminder that their far-off ordeal wasn't so distant. For the first time since she'd met him, he appeared to be at total peace.

Darla walked across the pier and stood behind him, gazing over his shoulder. He glanced up to give her a quick grin then looked away to concentrate on his music. She sat down in the lawn chair next to him. He stopped playing.

"Sounds pretty."

He grinned at her. "Pretty inspiration." He leaned in to kiss her on the cheek. The whiskers above his lip tickled her skin, in a good way.

"So what made you keep the 'stache?"

"I thought I'd try it out for a while. Something different." He outlined the rainbow of hair over his lips with both middle fingers. "What'd you think? Stay or go?"

She studied him with a smile. "I like it."

"Then I'll keep it." A corner of his mouth slanted upward as he set the guitar aside and stretched his legs out in front of him, crossing them at the ankles. "Are you tired? Last night was a long one."

"I'm okay. I'm just glad it's over. For real, this time."

Once the police arrived, they arrested a groggy Shane for two murders and two murder attempts before he was taken away in an ambulance. She and Eric were escorted to the station and were questioned for hours by the Texas investigators and the detectives in California via phone. They learned after surgery that Shane had confessed to the killings and remained in custody. As soon as he was well enough, he'd be returned to California for sentencing, and then to serve his time, which would probably be for the rest of his life.

Eric leaned over and took her hand. His fingers tightened around hers. He spoke in a voice no louder than a whisper. "What an adventure, huh?"

Darla was almost afraid to say anything else. She nodded with a sigh. "One I'll never forget."

He squeezed her hand again. "Thankfully, this is over and you can rest and actually enjoy your visit with your family."

"When are you planning to leave?"

He remained quiet for what seemed like forever.

Somewhere inside she held on to a small hope he would change his plans about going now with everything resolved. Realistically she knew different and she dreaded hearing another good bye.

He glanced at her, his expression flushed. He inhaled loudly. "I've already phoned for a car to come pick me up. A driver will be here in about an hour to take me to the airport. I'm scheduled to talk with the detectives in California first thing in the morning."

She squeezed her eyes shut, wishing she could stop her next question. "And then?"

"Back to the UK and back to work." He gazed toward the sunset and took another deep breath. "Blaine and I need to find us a new manager. I know it sounds callous, but we have to continue to move forward if we want to achieve our musical ambitions."

Darla nodded. One of her mother's favorite sayings was a person's actions showed where their hearts were.

And there it was. He still planned on leaving her and he wasn't coming back. Ever.

She wanted to be angry, but only sadness swept through her. Deep, desolate sadness.

Eric stood and picked up his guitar. "I should go inside and get my things. And I want to thank your parents for their hospitality."

Without another word, she rose from her chair and led him up the walkway.

An hour later she was outside again. An unfamiliar car had parked in the drive. Her dad helped Eric put his things into the trunk. After they finished, he gave her father a final handshake and jogged to where she waited.

He shoved his hands into his pockets and nervously glanced about before he aimed his gaze directly at her. He didn't need to speak nor did he need to say a word. He didn't have to.

The look in his eyes told her this would be their final goodbye. "I'm usually good with words, but right now I'm at a loss."

Darla choked and blinked away an onslaught of tears that seemed ready to attack her eyes. She merely shrugged and spun from him. His hand gripped her shoulder and circled her back to him. Arms around her, he crushed her body into his. For a few minutes neither stirred. Darla focused on committing the warmth of his skin, his male scent, and the power of his muscles against her to memory.

Eric gently pushed her back. He squeezed her shoulders tightly before he placed his lips against hers to softly kiss her.

He withdrew from her and shoved something into her hand, then spun around and walked to the waiting car without looking back.

Chapter 21

"I can't believe you're trying to talk me into this." Darla twisted an errant curl around her finger.

"Raging Impulse is playing only this one reunion concert. We'll never get this opportunity again."

"The advertisements are everywhere, Steph. I've read it a thousand times. They're participating in a benefit for drugs and alcohol recovery. They're dedicating the performance in honor of Drake Mahoney's memory. His family members are supposed to be in the audience. The press speculates the tribute will be amazing. Very moving."

"And we should attend because of our connections to the band." She held up two tickets. "Front row seats plus backstage passes. Extremely hard to get."

"Fine. Then you go."

"I am. You need to come with me."

"Give me one reason why I'd want to."

"First, because Blaine asked us to. Second, so we can celebrate. We haven't done anything to mark you getting your new job. We could make a whole evening out of it. I'm thinking dinner and a limo ride to and from the performance."

"Sounds wonderful, Steph. But I just don't have time. You know I'm leaving for South America next week to—"

"I'm aware." Stephanie rolled her eyes as she plopped down on the couch next to Darla. "You're going to South America with a group of archaeologists to assist in identifying the subtle differences in the tiers of stratigraphy. In layman's terms, how the layers of earth build up. Your presence will help them understand the variances between one deposit to the next, which allows them to grasp the way the past was buried. Icky, but I got it. What I don't get is you don't leave for another week. So seriously. Why won't you go with me?"

Darla tapped a yellow pad that sat on her lap with the end of a pen. She'd been excited to work on her list of needed supplies after she discovered she would be making the trip. Until now. The realization she could be close to Eric Boyd again ripped away the enthusiasm for her excursion and turned her stomach into mush.

"I'm pretty wrapped up in getting ready for this expedition. The position is too important for me to mess up. This opportunity could open a lot of doors for me if I do a good job. My focus is on my project. I wouldn't be any fun tonight because my mind will be somewhere else. We'll celebrate when I get back."

Stephanie's appearance this morning with an invitation to go to Eric and the Raging Impulse reunion performance caught her off guard. Already aware of the concert along with the fact the group was in town, her secret plans were to take a long drive up the California Pacific Coast Highway to view some scenery, explore the quaint shops, art colonies, and spend the night at a bed and breakfast. Yes, she'd be doing this adventure alone, which was sad, except she couldn't endure the idea of being in the same city as Eric Boyd. His memory and the time they shared resurrected too much pain.

Not that she revealed any of this information to Stephanie. They rarely spoke of Eric because she led her friend to believe the relationship had fizzled out while in Texas. She claimed their brief interlude to be a rebound thing for her and a fling for him. They'd said their goodbyes six weeks ago and she wouldn't go through that agony again.

Stephanie flipped the tickets at her. "You realize I had to pull some major strings to get these."

"Major strings, my ass. Blaine sent them to you."

"Actually, he phoned me to make sure I was coming." Stephanie smiled coyly. "He wants me to come backstage after the concert is over. Well, he wanted me to watch from the wings, but I want to sit in the audience and soak up the atmosphere."

"I think it's great you and Blaine managed to move your relationship to the next level despite all the turmoil."

"We make each other happy." Stephanie looked at the sizeable diamond on her left hand. "We're talking about getting married next summer."

"You two are definitely the definition of whirlwind."

"What's the point of dragging things out?" She shrugged. "When it's right, it's right. No use playing games. We're in love and want to be together."

"All fine for you, Steph. I'm glad everything worked out and I'm happy you found your soul mate. Eric and I are not anything mates. What I got out of this was the fiasco in Port Isabel ending with Shane McIntyre's arrest for killing Drake Mahoney and

Richard O'Conner and attempted murder for Mitchell and Eric."

Stephanie shook her head. "That whole mistaking Finn for Richard was a strange one."

"Yep. Finn cheated death twice." Shane had not only mistaken Drake for Finn, he also didn't realize the person lying in the bed was Finn's brother, Richard. Apparently, Finn had disappeared with a girlfriend for several days, and because autopsy results weren't completed, no one realized the misidentification until he returned.

"I don't think the whole Raging Impulse saga will ever go away."

"Me either. This is one of those things too far-fetched to believe. Yet it happened." Stephanie looked at Darla. "You get to be smack dab in the middle of it all."

"Don't remind me. The rag mags have forever labeled me as Eric Boyd's girlfriend. Whenever they rerun the story, which is a lot because of this performance I'm still referred to as his woman." She pressed down on the pen, drawing circles in the paper's margins. "I never was anything to him. We had one of his little good time affairs and then he was gone. And since he left? Nothing. Not a word."

"Eric is the real reason you don't want to go to the concert."

At first Darla didn't reply. She'd cut Stephanie off whenever she brought his name up in the past. But she couldn't pretend any longer. "I've no desire to see Eric again. If you want the truth, he disappointed me. Or maybe I disappointed myself."

Stephanie scooted closer to Darla and patted her on

the arm. "The seats are on Blaine's side of the stage. He'll never know you're in the audience. Plus, I made Blaine swear to not tell Eric you're coming with me. So you're covered in that area too."

"What about the backstage passes? Blaine's a nice guy, but I don't want to deal with any of that." She tossed the pen down. "I prefer not to see Eric in case he's with his latest one nighter."

"Wait for me outside. I won't be long. Come on, Dar. This is a once in a lifetime event."

"I'd rather listen to their band Spiraling UP. They've become huge practically overnight. With the exception of Finn, the lineup is the same too now Mitchell's recovered and joined them as their drummer. I like the music better. The sound is more adult."

"That's another reason we need to go. Spiraling UP just released their new record. Blaine's going to give us a signed copy. I can't wait to hear it."

"The music is good. Eric gave me a demo of their recordings right before he left."

"You didn't tell me he gave you anything."

"You returned from Montana with a ring the size of an asteroid from Blaine, Steph," Darla said. "A rough copy of songs hardly compares."

"I don't understand what the problem is. You've insisted all along you were never into Eric. He was only a rebound from the disaster with your ex. You barely speak of him. I'm getting he might be more. More than just a disappointment. Are you certain you don't have feelings for him?"

"Our time together ended with such a letdown. It almost seemed like I failed at something, although I'm not sure at what. Because of these stupid—emotions,

I'd rather not risk running into him."

"You won't." Stephanie sneaked a knowing glance in her direction. "Though, if you're telling me the truth and you aren't into him, meeting up with him again shouldn't be a problem."

****

Darla sat in the front row of the packed stadium, nervously waiting for the band to take the stage. She wished she'd been more honest with her best friend. If she had, she might be on her way to her bed and breakfast by now. Or not. Regardless of any confession, Stephanie would insist Darla come tonight, telling her she needed closure. This was true. She wanted a resolution to get over her sentiments for Eric Boyd. She'd watch him from obscurity and put the past to rest. Her decision to attend was a good thing. After tonight she could move on.

The overhead lights slowly reduced. The coliseum's beams dimmed lower and lower until they were in complete darkness. A wave of screams erupted from the crowd. Bright spotlights swung across the stage illumining a hazy mist rising from the platform's floor. Strums of music vibrated over the speakers, pulsating within her veins. A flashing Raging Impulse logo dropped from the ceiling and settled behind the drum kit. Screeches from the audience grew louder before they exploded as an invisible announcer introduced the band.

The stage lit up highlighting Raging Impulse. Eric began the show by playing a rip and broke into one of the group's biggest hits. Darla did her best to avert her eyes away from him except he was so near. She found his close proximity too tempting not to stare. In the beginning, she only allowed herself to take small peeks at him. Halfway through the first song, she'd locked her gaze onto Eric's side of the stage.

He never looked better. He'd kept his mustache, although he'd styled his hair different. He continued to wear it longer and the new cut worked for him. The well-fitting jeans and tight sleeveless shirt showed the efforts of his workouts. But his appearance didn't captivate her as much as his playing. Darla became mesmerized. He had a way of making the instrument a part of him. She sensed his passion. Sweat stained his shirt as he meticulously plucked away at the guitar strings and sang backup for Finn.

And after all the time of her mentally scolding him for his choices, tonight as she watched him, she got it. He projected a vibrant presence and he'd always stand out wherever he was. But up there, performing, he appeared truly in a place where neither she nor any women could ever compete. Darla's moment of realization was sobering and liberating. And a painful one. After the show's main performance, the group did two encores before they exited for good.

Stephanie's brows rose, asking a silent question. Darla shook her head.

"At least come backstage with me. You don't have to go in. According to Blaine, we should go behind the stage, follow a long hallway, and present the passes to the guards at the door. I will be allowed inside for a meet and greet."

"I'll just go back to the car."

Stephanie motioned at the ecstatic, rowdy crowd. "This is a total mob. We don't need to separate. Come with me and wait in the hall. I promise I won't try to persuade you to go any farther."

Darla didn't entirely trust Steph in that her friend wouldn't attempt to coax her to accompanying her into where the band assembled. Though if she were honest, she'd like to get one more glimpse of Eric before she walked away from him forever. Maybe she could get a peek through the door without him noticing her.

"All right," she agreed. "I'll go with you, but I refuse to go inside, so don't try to convince me."

The two women fought through the throngs of people trying to get to the platform. Stephanie was right. This was a mob. Backstage, a barricade was set up to keep the fans at bay. Guards stood at different intervals to make sure no one busted across although they stayed busy pushing those back who tried to infiltrate the stronghold.

Stephanie flashed a pass at a man in uniform. He moved to allow her inside. She spun to Darla and held up the second badge. "You're sure?"

Darla choked back a sudden rush of tears she didn't understand. "I can't."

Stephanie nodded but pressed the spare permit into her hand. "If you change your mind."

After Stephanie went inside, Darla shuffled to the far end of the line and found a small cubby to back into. She brushed at a rogue tear. The memories of the last moment she'd been with Eric became clear as if they'd just happened.

Before he left, he'd made no promises to keep in touch nor did she ask if he would. She didn't want to hear his answer, but she'd hoped…and held on to the hope of someday up until tonight. Now she understood. This life was too much a part of him. They would never happen.

The door to the room flung open bringing Darla back to the present. She stepped out of her refuge and quietly viewed the scads of people pouring outside. The crowd thinned as a number of large built bodyguards appeared from the band's chamber.

A ripple of panic swept across her. The guards were surrounding the band members. From the way the men had lined up, they were hustling Raging Impulse in the direction of the barricade, through a pair of gigantic swinging doors displaying a waiting limo outside. Each member would pass directly in front of Darla to get to the exit. She tried to shrink into her hideout. Fans shrieked and shouted their favorite's name, jumping up and down. The men obligingly turned with a smile to wave to them. Eric was last to make an appearance.

Darla strained to disappear into the mass of people, but their momentum to reach him drove her the other way and into the barrier. If he looked in her direction there was little chance he wouldn't notice her.

Eric grinned and held up a hand, pointing to the crowd inciting more deafening screams. Darla was close enough to tell his eyes weren't focused on any one person. The dread in the pit of her stomach rose to her throat as he approached. Her heart banged against her chest, twice its speed. Would he speak? What should she say to him if he did? His guards urged him forward, and then he passed her without even a glance her way. She released the breath she was unaware she held.

The instant he reached the double doors he stopped. Slowly he turned to face the crowd. Blue eyes immediately connected with hers, holding her gaze for the briefest moment before the guards steered him outside.

Darla stared at the closed doors.

"Are you ready to go?" Stephanie stood beside her. "I'm going to meet Blaine later, so if you're good let's get out of this mess."

****

Darla couldn't sleep. She got out of bed, threw on her jeans and a hoodie, deciding to go for a late night walk to clear her head. Outside, she found the salty breeze uplifting. She strolled down the beach, traveling as far as to the house where she'd attended the party weeks ago before she elected to reverse the other way and go home.

Wind whipped her curls in her face as the cool ocean rolled over her bare feet. The chilled night air raged off the water, pushing in a blanket of clouds over the darkened sky. A rumble boomed in the distance as glimmers of light flashed above, the smell of rain clung to the breeze. Goosebumps prickled over her skin. A mountain of nostalgia swept through her. The evening was too similar to the evening she met Eric.

At her deck, she mounted the steps. The walk didn't help her restlessness and she'd deal with another sleepless night. Maybe some ice cream would make her feel better.

She ambled across the planks to the back door. Hand on the handle, she was about to give the knob a twist, when she glanced at Eric's old house like she did every time she was outside. The lights were on. She stared at the lit home. The place had remained dark since they'd parted ways in Texas. Blaine was staying with Stephanie tonight. So, who was inside?

"Why didn't you come backstage?"

Darla flinched. She stayed immobile for a few moments, then forced herself to rotate around. The familiar steely indigo gaze pierced into her. Eric slowly rose from the chaise lounge at the edge of her deck. His eyes remained linked and held hers as he strolled across the boarded surface. He walked over to where she stood and stopped in front of her.

"How's the arm?"

"Better. It gives me trouble every once in a while like your dad said it would." He hesitated. "You ignored my question. How come you didn't come see me?"

She took a deep breath. She grabbed an errant curl and twisted the hair around her finger. "I had no reason to, did I?"

Eric's eyebrows shot up. He had the nerve to appear hurt. "We experienced quite an adventure a few weeks ago. I'd think that's reason enough."

Darla pushed away floods of emotion which she would need to deal with, although not now. "We did share something, a lot from my standpoint. But you've been quiet since. At least toward me. I've kind of gotten the impression you'd moved on. What did you say? You don't believe in this whole love and happily ever after crap. We had an attraction and you acted on it. Your way of thinking is we'd see things through and let them run their course. Pretty close to what happened, right?"

Eric laughed. "Ah, I love when my words come back and bite me in the ass."

"I bet." She chuckled too, though her laugh carried a sarcastic tone. "So why are you here?"

He shrugged and shoved his hands into his pockets. "I'm staying at my house for a few days. Wanted to say hello since you couldn't bother. Oh, and tell you congratulations. Stephanie told me you got a new job. Something about you assisting on an archeological dig?"

"The excavation is in South America. I'm taking a sabbatical from the college. I leave in a week."

"Good deal." He withdrew a hand, touched his shirt then as if he remembered something, he thrust it back into his jean pocket.

"You can smoke if you need to. There's no cause for me to care." She couldn't resist adding, "Anymore."

"Whether you do or don't—" He lifted a sleeve and turned to her to reveal a patch on his upper arm. "Trying to quit."

"I'm impressed."

"I listened to you." He released his shirt and looked out into the darkness. The wind was picking up and the growls in the distance were becoming louder, closer. After a few minutes of dead air, he turned back to her, "I took your advice about a lot of things."

"Which advice? I believe I gave you an enormous amount."

"You did cram quite a bit at me in a week." He chuckled. "Signed up online to finish my education. I'll graduate in three months and earn a bachelor's degree in architecture. Not as good as you but maybe someday."

"Still exciting. Especially since you guys are so busy. Now if this whole music thing doesn't work out, you've got a backup."

"That I do. I also took a short break. Went back to

Scotland. Had a good holiday with my family. Plan on going again for a longer one soon."

"I'm sure your parents are happy you reconciled with them."

"They are. And I am too. They were more understanding about the missing money than I thought they'd be." He grinned. "Granted, the news was out before I visited home so they had a chance to get used to the idea."

"My brother told me they haven't found him yet. Dugan."

"Every time we close in, the leads run out. We figure he's probably changed his identity by now." His mouth tensed into a straight line. "We believe we can kiss that money goodbye, but we're not giving up."

"You're doing well with your new band. The amount of income won't be as much as you once earned right now, though you'll recoup nicely in the long run."

"Yep." He smiled. "I can honestly say as far as my career is concerned, I exceeded my wildest dreams."

"I'm happy everything worked out for you."

"Almost."

Darla gave him a skeptical look. "What else do you want to achieve? A new number one record, song writing accolades, and respect from your peers. I'm sure cash will be rolling in soon."

"How long are you going to be gone?"

"What?"

"To South America. How long is your trip?"

"Three weeks, possibly four."

A cold blast propelled across the deck almost pushing her off balance. Eric put a hand out to steady her, but she quickly stepped away from him and crossed her arms.

"I told my parents about you. They want to meet you. I was hoping you could squeeze in a trip to Scotland sometime this fall."

"You told them...they want me to come—to Scotland?"

"Yeah. They're planning a holiday here, but that won't be till Christmas. They'd want to get together with you before then if possible. So, they'd like you to come stay for a time. They want to get to know you."

"I don't understand."

"I explained to them what you'd done for me. You saved my life in more ways than one. They're grateful for all of your help. They'd like to say thank you."

Although the confession touched her, she refused to revel in the happiness she experienced or to give him any ammunition to use against her due to her increasing vulnerable state.

She lifted a shoulder. "I didn't do anything but remind you of what's important. You got some of it right."

"I'm trying to get everything right," Eric said with a lazy grin. Then he looked away. "When my career fell into place, I realized nothing was in place. I also concluded my opinion 'bout relationships were wrong. I do want to be with one person." He paused and cleared his throat. "I want that person to be you."

"It took you six weeks to figure that out?"

"Okay, in some areas I'm a slower learner than others. After you, I couldn't return to my old way of life. I tried. Believe me I tried. I did everything to forget you, to go back to my carefree habits, but that style of living doesn't work for me anymore. Nothing jelled.

The fame, the money, those things weren't as important as I first believed. My life was incomplete. I fought to not come back to you every day since I left. Even had m' bags packed on more than one occasion."

"So why didn't you?"

He looked shamed. "I was too afraid. You deserve a man so much worthier than me, and I feared you'd recognize that while we were apart. Then I realized how we almost died and I became even more scared of being without you. I'm trying, Darla. I'm trying to be a better person, a better man, for you. Every song I write is about you, or I at least insert a connection to you somewhere in the lyrics." He slipped a hand into his pocket, removed something, and held it out to her. "A copy of the new Spiraling UP's disk. Read the back of the case."

She took the recording and grasped it between her hands as she silently read the cover.

For Darla. My song, my life.

She swallowed a gasp as she tried to keep the hand clutching the CD jacket from trembling. Her gaze returned to Eric.

"When I saw you tonight." He raked his fingers through his hair. "'Bout brought me to my knees. The bodyguards almost had to carry me to the car. I can't get you out of my thoughts, my dreams, or my head. I knew I had to take a chance and tell you. Even if you reject me." He turned to her and captured her gaze. "You know where this is heading, right?"

Darla smiled as she nodded. "But if you think you're going to get out of this easily you need to think again. I've been waiting. I need to hear the words."

Eric ducked his head and cleared his throat. "This

is a first for me."

"I get that. But that doesn't change a thing. You have to say it."

"I didn't figure you'd let me off the hook." He inhaled and stared directly into her eyes. "Okay, here goes. I now believe in the phenomenon of love. The reason I believe in love, is because I am in love—with you, Darla Hennessy. I want to be with you, forever."

"Not so hard, right?"

Eric chuckled. "You tell me." He gazed at her expectantly.

She took in a deep breath. "I'm in love with you too."

"I'm sensing a 'but' coming. I'm not prepared for a 'but.'"

"You left me six weeks ago and you made no attempt to contact me. I understand you needing to figure things out. With all the digital stuff available, how hard would it be to at least send me a message. Maybe even make me aware you were wrestling with something?"

"I'm sorry. I should've." He shook his head. "I'm still in the learning phases of this whole love thing. These feelings I've been dealing with confused me. I don't understand how to react to them."

"Not a good excuse. For all you know, I could've moved on."

"That was a chance, yeah. But I also kept tabs on you."

She raised her eyebrows.

"Blaine, through Stephanie. I knew there was no one else. Like I said, I fought every day not to come back to you. Yet if I'd found out if any guy so much as looked in your direction, I'd been at your front doorstep in a heartbeat."

"So you don't want this yet. Us. Time's still not right?"

"I wouldn't be here if I didn't want us. It took my heart a while to convince my head this is where I'm supposed to be. A verse in the first song I wrote about you says everything. Your haunting dark eyes brought something to me; your beautiful smile blew me away. Your love shined through making me love you until my dying day." He paused. "You're my inspiration for all my love songs, by the way."

Darla hitched another breath. "Pretty words, but you're good with romantic expressions and you're paid well to write them. How can I be sure you won't go again?"

"I've never lied to you. I was always clear on where I stood."

"Except you left some things out."

"For your own good." A corner of his lip rose. "I knew coming here I'd be in deep shit and I'd have a lot to make up for." The familiar wicked twinkle gleamed in his eye. "And believe me I can't wait to start doing just that."

Thunder boomed overhead followed by a pop of lightning. Tiny drops pelted their skin.

Darla observed the angry sky before she turned back to him. "I suppose you'd like to come inside now so you can begin your make-up process?"

Eric leaned over to swipe his lips across hers. "You so get me, luv."

A word about the author...

Debra was born in Waco, Texas, and is a lifetime Texan, living in different areas throughout her adult life. She enjoyed creating stories growing up, though the idea of becoming an author did not occur to her until 2004. Since then, she has worked on learning to write while pursuing her bachelor's degree, which she earned in 2011 in Business.

She now resides in her hometown of Waco and is an active member of the Central Texas Chapter of Romance Writers of America, where she is secretary of the group.

In her spare time she loves being with her son Stephen and his wife Astrid, and daughter Hannah and her fiancé Ryan. Besides writing she also enjoys traveling, shopping, a relaxing pedi, and a good plate of Mexican food.